C000002938

CONTENTS

Acknowledgements

The publishers would like to gratefully acknowledge permission to reproduce photographs as follows: Aerofilms, p. 42; Heather Angel/Biofotos, p. 152; Associated Press Ltd, p. 126 bottom middle; Austin Rover, p. 147; Automobile Association, p. 135 bottom, 136 top; Clive Barda, p. 5 middle; Barnaby's Picture Library, p. 32 top; S. Bayer, Crafts Council, p. 183 top; Andrew Besley, Barnaby's Picture Library, p. 65 top; J. Boos, Barnaby's Picture Library, p. 126 top; Boots the Chemist, p. 162; Alistair Bowtell Associates, p. 62; Tony Boxall, Barnaby's Picture Library, p. 153 top; BP Chemicals, p. 169, 174 top; British Airways, p. 108; British Alcan Aluminium plc, p. 165 bottom; Alan Butcher Associates, p. 172 bottom; Camera Press Ltd, p. 167 top, 181 top; J. Allan Cash, p. 34 top, 34 bottom, 66, 92, 121, 136 bottom, 150 bottom, 153 bottom, 156, 163, 165 top, 167 bottom; Bruce Coleman Ltd, p. 130 top; Ros Conway, Crafts Council, p. 183 bottom middle; Michael Cowen, Barnaby's Picture Library, p. 161; Peter Cronin, David Redfern, p. 106 top; Delta Cam, p. 27 bottom; Dollond & Aitchison, p. 173 bottom; D.P.R. Models, p. 64 top; Jim Duffy, 193–5; Ercol, p. 180; Fiat Auto (U.K.) Ltd, p. 98 bottom, 130 right; Formech p. 63; James Galt & Company Ltd, p. 122, 174 middle; Gecko, p. 30, 45, 54, 58, 59; Sally & Richard Greenhill, p. 4 right, 8, 23 26, 83, 90, 94, 103 left, 104, 105, 150 top, 150 middle, 154 top; Alan Hutchinson, Barnaby's Picture Library, p. 103 right; Hutchinson Library, p. 4 left, 5 top, 117; I.B.M., p. 27 top, 27 middle; I.C.I., p. 174 bottom; Jones + Brother, p. 32 top left; Knobs and Knockers, p. 166 top; R.P. Lawrence, Frank Lane Picture Agency, p. 5 bottom; Lego U.K. Ltd, p. 65 bottom; Lewis Rudy, Barnaby's Picture Library, p. 146; Milton Keynes Development Corporation, p. 154 bottom; D. Muscroft, Barnaby's Picture Library, p. 140; N.H.P.L., p. 4 top; Ordnance Survey, Crown Copyright, p. 42; Parker Knoll Furniture Limited, p. 93 right; M. Parsons, Crafts Council, p. 183 bottom; Philips, p. 32 top right, 32 bottom left; Project Office Furniture plc, p. 93 left; David Redfern, p. 106 top; Remploy, p. 93; RoSPA, p. 155; Alan R. Smith, Barnaby's Picture Library, p. 137; C.T.H. Smith, Barnaby's Picture Library, p. 134; Hugh Spencer, Frank Lane Picture Agency, p. 127; Sporting Pictures (UK) Ltd, p. 106 bottom, 126 top middle; TeleFocus, a British Telecom photo, p. 149; Ian Thomson, Barnaby's Picture Library, p. 114; Thorn Lighting, p. 101; G.H. Toft, p. 260, 61, 64, 68, 70, 82, 88, 89, 98, 115, 119, 123, 128, 130 left, 172 top, 191; Topham Picture Library, page 148, 165 middle, 166 bottom, 183 top middle; TRADA, p. 124, 179; Valor, p. 32 bottom right; Wimpey Group Services Limited, p. 181 bottom.

Many thanks to Jim Duffy and his pupils at Abraham Moss High School, Manchester for their contribution to Chapter 12.

PREPARING FOR YOUR EXAMINATION

After your GCSE or other course in CDT you will have to face an examination. It will be designed to show *what you can do* and *what you know*. This is important for you, and for other people such as employers and further education admissions tutors. They will want to know what you are capable of, so you should prepare for this examination as thoroughly as possible, so that you can perform to your full potential.

However, getting the best marks you are capable of is not as straightforward as it might seem. To get the best results you need:
1 sound preparation;
2 good examination technique.
The first thing to be clear of is exactly what the examiner will mark you on. There are five main examination boards offering GCSE examinations in CDT. Here is a breakdown of the structures of their CDT: Design and Realisation examinations in 1988. (Remember that these may change, so you should always look at the actual syllabus for the year of your examinations.) There are two other syllabuses, CDT: Design and Communication and CDT: Technology. This book will help you with all of them.

Coursework	50%
Open examination	
Design paper	} 30%
Written paper	20%
Coursework	50%
Design and	
realisation	20%
Written paper	30%
Coursework	40%
Design and	
realisation	30%
Written paper	30%
Coursework	50%
Design and	
appreciation	25%
Written paper	25%
Coursework	60%
Design	20%
Written paper	20%

How to prepare your coursework

Many different kinds of coursework can be submitted for GCSE; each examination board will have its own set of regulations which you must follow carefully. Here is an example from one of the examinations. The coursework would be given a mark for each of the headings:

1 Recognising the problem
2 Gathering information
3 Analysis (Making the problem clear)
4 Specification (Setting targets)
5 Generating (Thinking up) ideas
6 Developing the proposal (Detailed design)
7 Making
8 Evaluation (Testing the finished product).

You could present your work under headings **1–6** and **8** in a folio. Your teacher will mark the work and these marks will be checked by an examiner from the board. DO NOT LOSE YOUR WORK BEFORE IT HAS BEEN MARKED BY THIS EXAMINER.

REMEMBER *Your coursework will show what you can do, so make it the best you can offer.*

How to prepare for the examination paper

There are various types of paper: some expect you to design; some to make; some to write and draw about designing, making or the knowledge you need to practise designing and making. Clearly, you will need to prepare differently for each paper, but there are some general tips which will help:

1 Prepare and revise for the examinations over the whole of your course. Take every chance you get to *review* what you have learned both *to know* and *to do*. When you learn something new, compare it with what you already know. Constantly refresh your memory in this way.

2 About six weeks before the examination, begin to revise systematically. Find out about the examination structure and the type of questions asked. Look at past papers if you can. Sort out a list of topics to revise and plan a regular timetable. Stick to your timetable! As well as revising, practise answering examination questions, some just in outline and some in full. Time yourself. Do not try to outwit the examiner by attempting to predict what questions will come up . . . this hardly ever works. The night before, get everything ready, relax and get plenty of sleep.

3 In the examination, read the paper thoroughly before beginning to answer any questions. Get the instructions clear,

especially about how many questions you need to answer and how long to spend on each. Choose the questions you know most about. Plan them out in outline. Give the answer that has been asked for, not one you would have liked the examiner to ask! It will help if you understand the following words:

Annotate: to make notes to explain something;
Compare: to show how like each other some things are;
Contrast: to show how unlike each other some things are;
Criticise: to judge something;
Define: to describe accurately;
Explain: to make something clear so that someone else can understand it;
Illustrate: to make something clear with pictures;
List: a group of names or things written down one after the other;
Outline: to briefly describe the main ideas of something;
State: to say something clearly;
Summarise: to state the main points briefly.

Begin with the question that you know most about. If you get stuck, leave a space and go on to the next section. Return when you have finished. Write and draw clearly. Check at the end for spelling, accuracy and figures.

INTRODUCTION FOR TEACHERS

The importance of Craft, Design and Technology has been increasingly recognised in the last decade. At its best it is of obvious value in the general education of future members of a nation trying to revitalise its manufacturing base and evolve industrial and technological systems for continued economic development in the twenty-first century. From the school's point of view, it is a 'real world' area of activity which confronts pupils with concrete problems. This reality can be highly motivating and can help to draw together and reinforce the understanding fostered by more abstract and separate subjects. Apart from its intrinsic interest to pupils, its very activity is a powerful aid to learning. It can stimulate in pupils an understanding about themselves, their capabilities, and the role of designing and making in our society.

The onset of GCSE and Standard Grade in Scotland has made us focus very sharply on the nature and structure of Craft, Design and Technology. Its aims and assessment objectives have been specified unequivocally in the GCSE National Criteria and are reproduced below. Each of the CDT syllabuses offered by the five examining groups fits closely into this set of objectives. The nature of the syllabuses should give rise to learning which is active and experiential, and a large percentage of the GCSE marks will be earned by students for coursework.

CDT is an 'applied' area of study, and GCSE highlights its active, experiential nature: why then the need for a conventional class textbook? Clearly there is no need for a text which is packed with information and gives no stimulation to pupil activity. However, there is a real need for a class text which has the following characteristics. It should:

1 give pupils a coherent and balanced picture of designing which ranges from the 'why' to the 'how' to the 'consequences'; this picture should serve as a contextual backcloth against which pupils can judge their own designing;
2 help pupils to find and use essential information efficiently;
3 enable pupils to work independently of their teacher and group for some of the time;
4 supply ideas and guidelines for study and activity.

This textbook has been purposely written to aid the efficient teaching and learning of GCSE CDT and other similar courses. It covers the core areas of all five examination group syllabuses, and where these offer different themes for deeper study every year the book provides a base from which more detailed research can be carried out. Accordingly, it contains themes, information and ideas for activity. It is not offered as a substitute for pupil experience and direct teaching, nor is it a text for completely independent learning. It does not cover making processes which are adequately covered by existing texts.

CDT requires pupils to do and to experience: the importance of direct human contact between teacher and pupil cannot be overstressed here. Yet, pupils must work independently at times as they work through their own design projects. Therein lies the need for such a class text. This book is offered as a resource to enable each pupil to bridge the gap between dependence and independence in the quest for design capability.

P.N. Toft   1987

'Statement of Educational Aims for GCSE Craft, Design and Technology Courses

3.1 The aims of any course in Craft, Design and Technology are set out below.

Most of these aims are reflected in the Assessment Objectives; others are not because they cannot readily be translated into measurable objectives.

1 To foster awareness, understanding and expertise in those areas of creative thinking which can be expressed and developed through investigation and research, planning, designing, making and evaluating, working with materials and tools.
2 To encourage the acquisition of a body of knowledge applicable to solving practical/technological problems operating through processes of analysis, synthesis and realisation.

3   To stimulate the development of a range of communication skills which are central to design, making and evaluation.
4   To stimulate the development of a range of making skills.
5   To encourage students to relate their work, which should demand active and experiential learning based upon the use of materials in practical areas, to their personal interests and abilities.
6   To promote the development of curiosity, enquiry, initiative, ingenuity, resourcefulness and discrimination.
7   To encourage technological awareness, foster attitudes of cooperation and social responsibility, and develop abilities to enhance the quality of the environment.
8   To stimulate the exercising of value judgements of an aesthetic, technical, economic and moral nature.

Assessment Objectives

4.   4.1 The assessment objectives listed below, common to all courses in Craft, Design and Technology, are numbered for reference purposes only and the order in which they are presented does not imply any priority or precedence. It must however be recognised that the emphasis placed upon each assessment objective will be dependent upon the content of the particular course being undertaken. Design, make and evaluate processes are not necessarily linear, but may be cyclic or, at any stage, revert back to different elements. Provision has also to be made for intuitive responses and value judgements.

     4.2 Candidates should be able to:

1   describe and apply facts, principles and concepts related to artefact and/or systems design, realisation and evaluation;
2   demonstrate graphical and other communication skills necessary to give, in a clear and appropriate form, information about an artefact or system;
3   identify problems which can be solved through practical/technological activity;

4   analyse problems which they have identified, or which have been posed by others, and produce appropriate design specifications taking into account technical and aesthetic aspects;
5   identify the resources needed for the solution of practical/technological problems;
6   identify the constraints imposed by knowledge, resource availability and/or by external sources which will influence proposed solutions;
7   gather, order and assess the information relevant to the solution of practical/technological problems;
8   produce and/or interpret data (eg diagrams, flow charts, graphs, experimental results);
9   generate and record ideas as potential solutions to problems;
10 appraise solutions to a design problem relative to the initial specification;
11 select and develop a solution after consideration of the constraints of time, cost, skill and resources;
12 plan the production of the selected solution;
13 demonstrate appropriate skills, make or model the artefact or system;
14 propose or make modifications to a product or system both during manufacture, and after completion and evaluation;
15 compare and evaluate the performance of an artefact or system against its specification;
16 satisfy all mandatory and other necessary safety requirements during the planning and making of an artefact or system;
17 describe the interrelationship between design/technology and the needs of society.'

(From *GCSE The National Criteria, Craft, Design & Technology*, Department of Education and Science and Welsh Office, HMSO, 1985.)

1
WHY ARE YOU STUDYING CRAFT, DESIGN AND TECHNOLOGY?

CONTENTS

1.1 INTRODUCTION

In the modern world enormous amounts of energy, money and time are spent on designing and making things. You live surrounded by things designed and made for you. How often do you stop to ask . . . . . why did they bother?

The answer *may* seem obvious; but read on to see if there's more to it than you thought. You may also find the answer to the question: 'Why are you studying craft, design and technology?'

It is always important to stand back and consider *why* you do things. When you have studied this chapter you should be able to:

1 recognise that people are creative;
2 understand that people have needs;
3 see that the better you are at designing the more you can satisfy your needs and improve both your life and other people's.

You can use the chapter in *two* ways.

1 Study it closely at the start of your course – it explains why you need to succeed in craft, design and technology;
2 Return to it whenever you start a new design project – it will help you to think about who you are designing for.

Humans have evolved – from the time of the first toolmakers 2 million years ago, they have survived by controlling the environment in a way that no other animal has. They even make robots to do their work for them.

1.2 HUMANS ARE CREATIVE

The human race has developed or **evolved** over millions of years. In this time humans have become very different from other animals in many ways.

Can you think of some of the main differences?

Often, animals can do some things much better than people. For example, antelopes can run much faster than humans. Lions use great skill to catch the animals they eat (in their mouths!). Squirrels can climb trees very quickly.

But have you ever seen an antelope drive a car? Or lions store their food in a freezer? Or a squirrel build a ladder? Of course not! But people can do these things. It is this ability to design and make things that makes us different. We are **creative**.

Some animals may use natural objects as tools.

What makes humans different?

The photographs on this and the opposite page show how humans are different from animals. They all show examples of how people are creative.

We use this ability to control our environment, and to improve our natural performance.

For example, a spoon allows us to eat without getting our fingers wet. When we wear a coat we can go out in colder temperatures than when we are not wearing one. A train allows us to travel further and faster than when we walk.

Humans use fire to solve problems such as cooking, heating and making things.

Humans are able to design and make tools to solve a wide range of problems. How many tools can you see in this photograph?

Humans have evolved

Tools
Perhaps between one and two million years ago, the first human ancestors lived on Earth. They learned the skills of holding, using, moving and making **tools**. They learned to solve the problems they came across in their environment.

Fire
Some of their discoveries made a big difference to the way they lived. For example, clothes made from animal skins helped them to move to colder lands. Shelters, like caves and huts kept them safe from dangerous wild animals. Fire allowed them to cook food and so have a much more varied diet. Metals made it possible to make more effective tools like axes.

Farming
About 9000 years ago, people began to make major changes to their environment. This is because they began to settle in one place and to grow crops. They also domesticated wild animals to provide them with milk and meat. Forests were replaced by fields.

The first cities
5000 years ago, people built the first cities, in what is now Turkey.

Humans grow crops and breed animals for food.

Ceremonies are an important part of human culture.

Humans use symbols in language, music, art, movement, etc. No other animal uses this wide range of symbols.

What about the future?

We are now approaching the twenty-first century. People can change whole landscapes overnight. Unfortunately, we have even developed the ability to destroy the whole Earth. Satellites orbit the Earth and astronauts travel in space. More powerful computers are being developed all the time. These are exciting times.

So people are the creators of this progress. We are all born with the potential ability to design and create. But often things that are made do not work as they were meant to. The death of seven astronauts in the space shuttle crash of 1986 is a tragic example of this. We need to learn and practise the skill of designing to reduce this failure. By studying craft, design and technology (CDT) you will be doing this.

1.3 WHAT DO PEOPLE NEED?

This question has puzzled different people for a long time. There is no simple answer.

There are some things which we just cannot do without, such as food.

There are some things which we could do without, like seats; but without them we would get tired.

There are some things which some people feel they need, like cigarettes, which are harmful.

How can we decide what people really need?

One expert sorted human needs into different levels. You can see these in the table. He said that we must be fairly satisfied at the first level before we begin to take the second level seriously. We would then need to be fairly satisfied at this level before taking the third level seriously. And so on. For example, a starving person would be much more concerned to get food (level 1) than to worry about safety (level 2). In fact a starving person might take dangerous risks to get food.

Do you agree with this expert's ideas?

Levels	Needs		Examples of ways of satisfying these needs
1	Needs of the **body**	– to satisfy hunger, thirst, and to be warm, dry and comfortable	Food, shelter, clothes, fire, water supply, furniture
2	Need for **safety**	– to be secure and free from danger	Fences, traffic lights, locks, weapons, doors, etc.
3	Need to **belong**	– to get on with other people	Families, communities, uniforms, fashions.
4	Need for **esteem**	– to have others see how good we are	Prizes, medals, certificates.
5	Need to **know**	– to have knowledge and understanding	Books, computer programmes, schools.
6	Need for **beauty**	– to be surrounded by order, beauty, symmetry	Paintings, sculpture, jewellery, design.
7	Need to **fulfil potential**	– to be able to do things, to the best of our ability	Sports, careers, hobbies.

What influences the levels at which we are able to satisfy our needs?
Generally speaking, the more advanced or civilised we become, the more we can satisfy our needs at the higher levels. A peasant in medieval Europe would have had to accept, if lucky, satisfaction of needs in the lower three or four levels. Today, a lot of people in advanced industrial countries can expect to be satisfied, to some extent, at all levels.

The level at which they are satisfied depends on such things as: how advanced the society is; how wealthy individuals and groups are; how good people are at designing things to meet their needs. By studying Craft, Design and Technology, you will improve your ability to design things to meet your needs, and those of other people, successfully.

Summary

1 We are different from other animals; we are **creative**.
2 We use this ability to control our surroundings and to improve the quality of our lives.
   We do this by designing things to improve our natural performance.
3 We have a variety of needs. The better we are at designing, the better we can satisfy these needs.

Try the following exercises.

1 Think very carefully about what your needs are now. Make a list of these needs. Next, arrange them into order, starting with the most basic needs at the top of the list.
2 Look again at this list: separate what you think are 'needs' and 'wants'.
3 Carry out exercise 1 again, but this time focus on the needs of a newborn baby. Try this again for a particular disabled person.
4 Think about and discuss some of the ways you could find out the exact needs of someone for whom you are designing.
5 Compare how you think the average person living in Britain today, in a town or city, will feel needs which are different from the needs of a peasant farmer in a Third World country.

2
HOW TO DESIGN

CONTENTS

2.1 INTRODUCTION

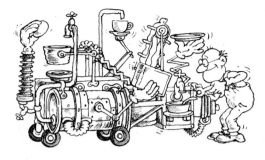

In chapter 1 you learned that you can satisfy your needs by being creative. This does not happen automatically, though. You have to do things! To satisfy your needs properly, you have to make full use of your creative ability. Designing effectively helps you to do this, and it is this that you are going to learn.

When you have studied this chapter you should be able to:

1 understand how designing is made up of a number of skills;
2 practise the skills until you can carry them out well;
3 organise your design projects effectively.

You can use the chapter in *two* ways:

1 Study it as a whole, then take each section at a time and work on the exercises.
2 Refer to it whenever you start a new design project or meet difficulties in a project.

What is designing?

Designing is a way of thinking up solutions to problems . . . solutions which can then be made and tried out. You have to learn five main things in designing. These are shown opposite. The more you practise them, the better you will become.

make the problem clear

think up ideas

develop solutions

make or model the solution(s)

see if the solution solves the problem

2.2 HOW TO SATISFY A SIMPLE NEED: PROTECTING GLASSES

Imagine you have a friend who wears glasses when he is driving his car. He keeps the glasses in a case in the glove compartment. Your friend has just lost this case and needs a new one. You have offered to design and make it for him. How would you go about doing this?

Figure 2.1

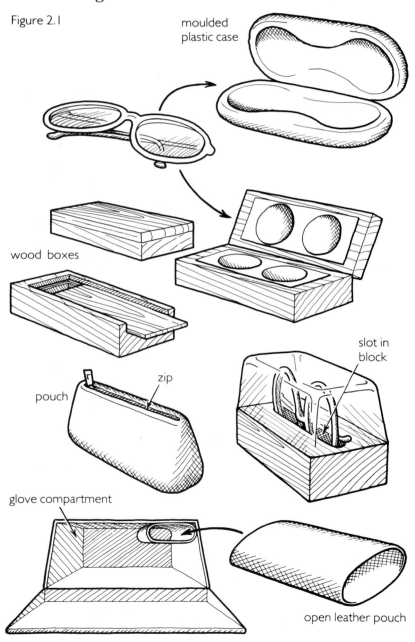

moulded plastic case

wood boxes

pouch

zip

slot in block

glove compartment

open leather pouch

1 Make the problem clear

Your friend needs a new case for his glasses, but why? Without a case the glasses may move about inside the glove compartment. They could get scratched, bent or even broken. They will almost certainly gather dust. Simply putting them inside a hard, rectangular case will not solve the problem as they will just rattle around inside it. Glasses have a complicated shape and the case must fit around them closely enough to hold them still. It must also be soft inside to stop them from getting damaged or scratched due to the movement of the car.

So, you have worked out that you have to design a case with a soft inside that will hold the glasses still. Now you can go on to thinking up specific solutions.

2 Think up ideas

As you think up different solutions to the problem you should begin to draw your ideas, as this may show you problems in your solutions early in the design process.

From the ideas shown, the two that seem to solve the two initial problems the best are a soft leather pouch or a moulded plastic box with a soft lining. So, you can look at these two possible solutions more deeply in the next stage.

3   Develop a solution

Now you must choose an idea, or a combination of ideas, which will solve your problem. But how do you choose? Quite simply, choose by deciding how *well* and how *easily* the idea will solve the problem. Of the two possible solutions chosen, the leather pouch will obviously be easier to make than the plastic container, but it will not be crushproof. As you can see from figure 2.1 you can overcome this by fixing the pouch to the top of the glove compartment.

You have now solved your problem by combining two ideas: *a soft leather pouch* which *fits into the top of the glove compartment*. This is easy to make and fit and will protect the glasses from dust and movement.

Now that you have developed a solution you must start to make it.

Figure 2.2

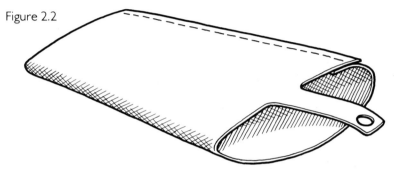

4   Make the solution

First you must work out the size and shape of the pouch that you need, and also the method of construction and fitting. You could make a paper or fabric model to try out your idea in the car. You could stick this temporarily to the glove compartment with 'Blu-tack'. This use of cheap, temporary or scaled-down models, or **prototypes**, is very important in design, and is something that you should get used to. These models can save you a lot of time, money and effort.

When you are satisfied, work out all the design detail and make a working drawing. This should show all the sizes and details. Now you can make the pouch and fit it into your friend's car.

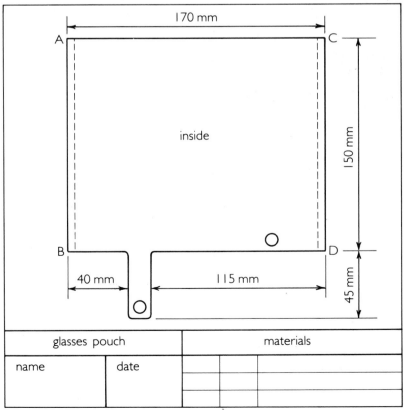

5   Test the solution

Watch your friend use the pouch. Ask for comments on its success. Is it easy to reach? Does it protect the glasses? Do they slip out when the car stops suddenly? Will it stay in place? If your friend is satisfied then you have succeeded in your design solution. If he is not then you should listen to his complaints and start the process again.

However, what you have already done has not been a waste of time, as it will have given you an insight into the problem which you can use in your second solution.

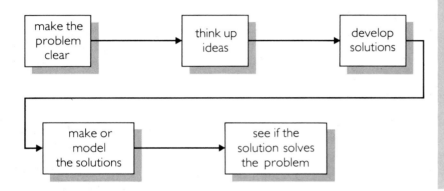

Test yourself

1 Copy the following passage into your notebook and fill in the missing words.
DESIGNING
When I am designing I do
_____ main things. These things are: making the problem _____; _____ up ideas: developing _____;
_____ the solution;
_____ the solution to see if it solves the original _____.

2 Why is it necessary to make the problem clear before you start to develop a solution?

3 In the example that you have just looked at what did the designer consider when choosing the ideas with which to solve the problem?

4 If you test the solution and find faults what should you do?

Try the following exercises

Use the five skills of designing to fulfil the following needs (replacing the making stage with a drawing if you cannot make up your design).

1 Your school has been given 5000 craft-knife blades like the one shown. They should last the school for many years. The firm which made the knives has gone bankrupt and handles are no longer on sale. A set of handles is needed to hold the blades so that they can be used safely.

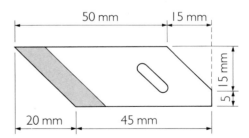

2 The front door of a friend's house has a gap at the bottom. Wind blows in through this gap and makes the house cold. Your friend cannot afford to have a new door fitted. Think of a way of preventing the wind from coming in.

3 A young child has been given a battery-controlled stunt car which is good at moving up and down steep surfaces. The child's parents will not allow the car to be used on the furniture because they know the furniture will be damaged. Some kind of obstacle course would allow the child to play happily with the new car.

4 A group of young people are bored during the long summer holidays. They live on a busy main road where cycling can be dangerous. There is a patch of waste ground nearby, and its owner has given them permission to build a BMX rally course.

2.3 DESIGN CASE STUDY: A FAMILY PROBLEM

Sally got on very well with John, considering that he was her little brother. The only time she did not like his company was when he complained. To be fair, he only complained a little; and only when he was tired. Most of the time they were great friends.

Sally had given John a conjuring set last Christmas, and he had become really interested in performing magical tricks. Sally thought that this might have something to do with their Uncle Richard, who was a semi-professional conjurer himself, and quite well known in the local clubs. With a little help from Uncle Richard, John had become quite skilled at his tricks. Sally and her parents loved to watch him. They were amazed at how quickly and deftly he performed. 'He's a real natural', Sally thought one evening as John performed after coming home from his junior school. His school friends who were watching at the time were equally impressed; but this was the start of the problem.

Not long after, he took his conjuring set to school. His teacher had asked him to show some of his tricks to the class. He did this with great style, and all his friends were fascinated, and wanted to try themselves. But with so many young children around it wasn't very long before the cardboard box for the set was crushed.

When John got home that afternoon he was really annoyed. 'Idiots!' he muttered, 'You'd think they had never seen cardboard before'. When he opened the box, his wand, magic rope and the pack of trick playing cards were missing. They must have fallen out of the crushed box on the way home. John was so upset he cried for half the night.

Sally was furious about what had happened. It was unfair that John's set should have been ruined after he had given a free performance to his school friends. She decided to buy new parts for the set and to remake the box for him – but how?

She thought for a while and examined the box to see how it was made. The next day she bought the new wand, magic rope and pack of cards on her way home from school. That evening, when John was safely asleep, she collected together all the parts of the conjuring set. These were a coin box, three plastic cups, three matchboxes, a wand, a spatula, a dish, two packs of playing cards, three cubes, a box, a length of rope and an instruction manual. She had seen John use them and knew how fragile some of the items were.

Sally had decided that she wanted to make the container small enough for John to be able to carry it easily. This meant packing the items together as closely as possible, so Sally measured them, arranged them and rearranged them until she found an effective layout. She drew this out. She tried out different ways of holding the items still inside the box, and when she was satisfied, she finally got down to making it out of cardboard. Eventually it was finished. Carefully she peeled the labels off the original box and glued them onto the new box, happy with her work.

Just as she was packing away, her father and Uncle Richard walked in. Sally showed her uncle what she had made to solve John's little tragedy and he was clearly impressed. He picked up the box, peeped inside and took out a few items, and in no time at all he was performing tricks. Out of the blue he said ominously, 'You know Sally, this is a fine construction, but what will John do if it breaks again?'.

This had not occurred to her, yet it was really the source of the problem. The cardboard box was just too flimsy to be carried around a lot. Uncle Richard also suggested that professional conjurers need something more than a box. The items have to be laid out in the exact order in which they are needed in the performance. 'Wouldn't it be useful', he wondered out loud, 'if John could have a similar kind of set up? It would be really something if the box could open up into a table so that John could perform the same everywhere without worrying about laying out his tricks'.

Sally now saw the problem clearly. Next day she watched John go through his full performance. She talked to him and her uncle until she fully understood what John did. She

then took the newly-made box and conjuring kit into her CDT lesson. After discussing the problem with her teacher she embarked upon a major project. She set herself some targets which boiled down to producing a box which:

a would hold all the items of the conjuring set
b would stand up to rough treatment
c was capable of opening out into a table to display the layout of tricks
d could be carried easily.

Armed with pencils and felt tips she began to sketch out her ideas. 'Christmas will soon be here again', she thought, 'and I want this to be John's present'.

Sometime later she had developed a solution and made a prototype model in card and polystyrene. Uncle Richard came into school to try it out. He suggested a few minor improvements and Sally adopted them. She drew out the final design and prepared a materials list. She obtained some of the materials from school, and the rest from the local DIY and fabric shops. After a few weeks she had made the box in the school workshops and tested it on a younger pupil who was about John's size. With a few small changes it was ready.

That Christmas John received one of the best presents of his life. With the help of some sharp and careful design thinking and her CDT lessons, Sally had solved a real family problem and John was well on his way to becoming a professional conjurer!

This story shows Sally, a normal school pupil, being creative and satisfying a real need. Now study sections 2.4, 2.5, 2.6 and 2.7 closely. Occasionally, you may want to refer back to the story.

2.4 HOW TO MAKE THE PROBLEM CLEAR

What would you think of someone who went into a
railway ticket office and had the following
conversation?

Person "Can I have a ticket please?"
Ticket clerk "Sure, where to?"
Person "Oh I don't know, anywhere I suppose."
That would be foolish. It would be just as foolish to
try to solve a design problem *before* you try to make
the problem clear to yourself.

Whenever your teacher sets a problem, or you discover one
yourself, you have to start to solve it in the same way. You
must find out exactly what the problem involves. Here are a
few ways of doing this.

I Try it out yourself

One way of making the problem clear is to try it out for
yourself. This may involve joining in with an activity or
using an existing product. Trying it out is not enough
though. You have to be *observant* and *critical*. You must also
make a record of your observations. You can use a notebook,
sketchbook, camera or even a tape recorder to do this. If you
observe honestly, really thinking about the problem, and
trying to put yourself in the place of people who might come
across it, you will be surprised at how much you can learn
and how many ideas will come to you.

Make sure you understand the problem
In Sally's case, she already understood the major problem:
her younger brother was upset about his loss. However, she
still had to think intelligently about her family situation to
make the problem clear. Often, you will not be so clear about
the problem; you will be outside it and will have to find a
way in. How can you do this?

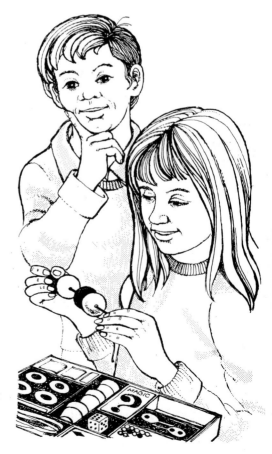

1 Find the area where the problem arises.
2 Decide *how* and *when* you will try it out. Sometimes the
   time of day, week or year, or the weather, will affect the
   situation. If so, try it out at different times and in
   different weathers, and think about the different
   circumstances that your design will have to cope with.
3 If the activity is a familiar one, do not overlook things that
   you normally do not notice. The opinions of others may
   well help in this.
4 Record what you find out and think about it.

Test yourself

1   Copy the following passage into your notebook and fill in the missing words.
    MAKING THE PROBLEM CLEAR: TRYING IT OUT
    I can often understand a _____ if I try it out myself. I need to make a _____ of what I find out. I can
    use a few ways of recording, e.g. _____, _____, _____ or _____.

2   Discuss with a few friends how you can find ways to try out problems that are new to you.

Try the following exercise

A blind person lives alone and likes to clean the house without the help of others. Blindfold yourself and try it
out. What do you discover about the problem? (*NB* Do this with someone watching over you to prevent
accidents.)

2   Ask or watch someone who knows

You may not always be able to try the problem out yourself.
It may occur too far away, you may be too big, too old or too
young to try it or you may not have the right skills.

Sally did not know enough about the problems that a
conjurer faces to be able to think of the whole problem that
she was trying to solve, but she was thoughtful enough to
use her uncle's experience and ask him to point out a few
things to her. You can always gain new views and ideas
about a problem by asking and talking to other people about
it, and it is very important that you get used to doing this.
Here are four ways of getting other people to help you to
solve a problem.

1   The most direct way is to find an area where a need
    arises; then watch a person who is used to the problem.
    Get the person's permission first, though! Look out for
    difficulties and ways in which the person has changed
    things to make them work better. For example, a
    mechanic in an engine room may have wrapped a rag
    around a sharp handle to stop his hands getting cut. Note
    if there are any differences at different times, or in
    different weathers. Talk to the person and ask questions.
    Sally actually observed John in his performance and
    discussed it with both John and her experienced uncle.
    This gave her a clear understanding of the problem.

2   Another way is to find a volunteer who has never come
    across the problem before. Show the volunteer what to
    do, stand back and watch. For example, you may be
    redesigning a handle for a tool. To find the problems with
    the existing handle, have the volunteer use the tool and
    note what happens. See how the volunteer copes and
    does not cope. Listen to the volunteer talk about the
    difficulties. Discuss them.

3   You may gain more information from such research if you try out methods **1** and **2** with a number of people. Each person might show different results. You will then need to compare and explain the differences. When making comparisons, ensure that you measure fairly – see page 84 for more details of this.

4   Finally, some information may not be available from direct observation or discussion. You may be seeking information about events which occurred in the past, or about new materials or processes. Then you will have to use other sources like reading books, journals in a library or writing letters to a company. Chapter 4 gives detailed advice on this.

Whichever method of **research** you use, make sure you record all *relevant* information for future use, and keep a note of where your information came from for future reference.

Test yourself

1   Copy the following passage into your notebook and fill in the missing words.
MAKING THE PROBLEM CLEAR: ASKING OR WATCHING SOMEONE WHO KNOWS
Often I will not be able to _____ the problem myself because it occurs too _____ away. When this is true I may have to ask or _____ someone who knows.

2   Get into a small discussion group with two or three classmates. Each think up an important design problem from outside school which you could not try out yourselves. Discuss why this is so.

3   Explain four ways of finding out information from others.

Try the following exercises

Students are not allowed to go into the staffroom of a particular school. In this room there are often problems at breaktimes when a lot of teachers try to get a drink from a badly laid-out kitchen area. Work out ways in which you could find out about these problems.

3   Make the problem clear

As you are finding out about any problem you will get ideas to solve it. These will not be complete ideas at first, because you may not yet fully understand the problem. But do not reject them because of this. Getting ideas and trying to imagine how they would work is an essential part of coming to understand the actual problem. Sally developed her first ideas around a cardboard box before she fully understood the problem. It was only when she had shown this box to her experienced uncle that the real nature of the problem became clear. However, her original idea of an easily portable box still remained an important part of her final design solution.

Always record these early ideas as they can be easily forgotten. Also record their advantages and disadvantages.

REMEMBER *It is usually impossible to fully understand a design problem until you have made some attempts to solve it.*

Don't tackle the whole problem at once
What happens is this:
You see a problem. Your brain can only handle a few facts at any one time and so you only see parts of the problem at first. You think up solutions and try them out in your mind. These show up other aspects of the problem. You think up better solutions, and so on. After a while you can understand the problem well enough to know what will actually solve it. Then you can prepare a set of targets. This is why it is so important to be patient when trying to design anything, and to follow the five steps given on page 9.

Test yourself

Why can you not always understand a problem until you try to solve it?

4   Set targets

State your targets clearly and accurately. Sally stated hers as:

'Produce a box which:
a would hold all the items of the conjuring set
b would stand up to rough treatment
c was capable of opening out into a table to display the layout of tricks
d could be carried easily.'

When your targets are clear you are able to think up ideas which could solve the problem. Professional designers call this list of targets a **specification**.

Test yourself

What is the point of setting targets?

Try the following exercises

1   Take a design project you have done in the past. Write out in full detail the targets that you set out to reach.
2   Collect a number of newspaper cuttings that highlight any problems from your local newspaper. Take each problem and work out ways of finding out information to make it clear.

2.5 HOW TO FIND IDEAS

The more practice that you get in solving problems, the easier you will find it to think of ideas and to decide how good or bad they are. You are also more likely to come up with more and better ideas the more knowledge and experience in problem-solving you have. For this reason you should never think that a problem is too trivial to think about. You should take every opportunity you get to try to solve problems and to discuss your ideas with other people.

Chapter 1 showed that people are creative and can develop their skills. One of your skills is to be able to think up new ideas. You do this automatically. But you can speed up and control the flow of your ideas and improve their quality. To do this you **a** can use certain 'tricks' and **b** must get lots of practice.

Here are three useful tricks. You can supply the practice!

1 Brainstorm

You can do this on your own but it is much more productive if you do it with three or four friends. Here is one way of brainstorming.

1 Explain your targets or problems to the group clearly.
2 Persuade them to take the problem seriously and to give it their full attention.
3 Have them spend 5–10 minutes writing down a list of ideas about the problem.
4 Ask each person to read out an idea in turn. One person should write the ideas and comments down, say on a blackboard or large sheet of paper that everyone can see.
5 As ideas are read out, new ideas will come out. People who get new ideas should add them to their list and read them out when their turn comes.

Brainstorming should be relaxed and good fun. All ideas are allowed, even crazy ones. The crazier ones may give you a completely new way forward. Try to get as many ideas as possible and make sure that *no-one criticises anyone else's ideas*. Being criticised may make your friends too embarrassed to express any further ideas.

When you have finished you will be left with a lot of ideas. Your job then is to examine them, sort them out and to develop any suitable ones.

2 Make comparisons

An original idea is an idea brought into existence for the very first time. *Very few* ideas are original. No matter what solution you come up with it will probably have been tried somewhere else. This does not matter; **inventing** is concerned with original ideas. Designing is concerned with *finding solutions to problems*. If you can find a solution to a problem by looking elsewhere, do so, but you must make it clear where the idea came from.

Use comparisons to help you solve problems

You can use comparisons to help you to solve a problem in a systematic way. Take part of Sally's problem: 'Making it easy for John to reach his tricks in the right order'. John's tricks had to be easy to see, easy to reach and easy to grip and be in the right order. Who else has this kind of problem? Have you seen a surgeon conducting an operation on TV? Before he starts, all the instruments are laid out in the order they will be used. When he calls for a scalpel, he wants it quickly. The nurse who passes it to him knows exactly where it is and can quickly pass it to him. Sally could borrow two ideas from this method of organisation:

1 she could lay out the parts of John's magic set in order, so that the first item to be used is nearest; or
2 she could arrange for an assistant to pass the items to John during his performance, like the nurse passes the instruments to the surgeon.

There is another way of making comparisons. Take an item that you are concerned with (in this case, a magic set). Take another item and join it to the first thing with 'is like'. So:

Figure 2.3

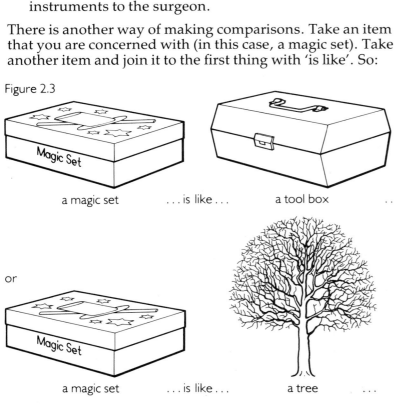

a magic set   ... is like ...   a tool box   ...

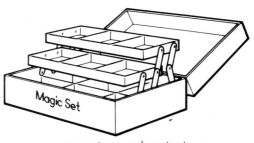

opens to reveal contents

or

a magic set   ... is like ...   a tree   ...

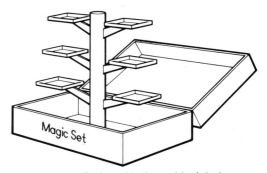

contents displayed in 'branching' shelves

3   Ask questions

Often, asking questions can lead you to examine a problem more deeply. The method is to keep asking 'Why should I do this?'. Sally did it when she was thinking about remaking the cardboard container. She could have asked herself:

Why am I making this container?	Because John needs a new one.
Why does he need a new one?	Because his old one is broken.
Why is it broken?	Because its construction was too fragile.
Why was it made so fragile?	For cheapness.
Do I need to make mine so cheaply?	Perhaps not.
Do I have any alternatives?	. . . and so on . . .

The answer to each question allows you to go on to the next question, and provides a piece of the puzzle that is your final design solution. As you have already seen, it is also very useful to ask other people questions.

REMEMBER *When you are thinking up ideas, you will soon forget them if you do not record them. See the next chapter to find ways of recording your ideas quickly.*

Test yourself

Copy the following passage into your notebook and fill in the missing words.
FINDING IDEAS
Design ideas come from my _____. When a group of people get together to think up lots of ideas they are _____. When I am designing I can find ideas by making _____ with other situations. When I bring together two different ideas I am making a _____. If I keep asking _____ about the design problem, I will come to _____ it more clearly.

Try the following exercises

Using any of the techniques that you have learned think up a range of ideas for each of the following problems. Record your ideas using **a** labels, **b** quick sketching and **c** notes, as is appropriate.

1   A garden hedge grows very quickly and its owner does not like trimming it with hand shears. How can you help her?
2   A hamster lives in an empty cage. He really needs to get some exercise whilst inside this cage. Think of a way to solve the problem.
3   You have over 200 cassettes. It takes a long time to find the one you want to play. Think of a quick method of finding the right cassette.
4   Last night someone crept into your back garden and stole some ladders. You thought you heard a noise but could not see in the dark. If an intruder visits you again you want to be able to see him. How can you solve the problem?
5   Your cousin likes to wear fashionable clothes and jewellery. However, it seems that as soon as an item has been bought, it is out of fashion. This can be very expensive. How can you help?
6   A friend in the flat upstairs plays noisy music. This disturbs you when you are watching television. What can you do about it?
7   A neighbour has designed a way of reducing his heating bills. It involves a device placed outside the back window which gives off smelly fumes all day long. It annoys your family. How can you solve the problem?

2.6 HOW TO DEVELOP SOLUTIONS

As you continue to think up ideas, ask questions about them and test them, they will get clearer and clearer. Eventually you will reach a solution which needs to be developed. At this stage you will probably use a drawing board with drawing instruments and model-making equipment.

Chapters 5 to 11 of this book describe what is important in developing a design solution. The main factors that you must think about include:

a People **b** Function **c** Appearance
d Strength **e** Movement **f** Materials

No one project will be exactly like another; it will be up to you to work out the important factors in any particular problem. Your teacher is always available to help you, of course. You may need to find out a lot of information to decide what is important. Chapters 3 and 4 tell you how to find, record, use and present the information that you may need in a design project.

You should be familiar with a drawing board and instruments.

Prepare a list of materials

Once you are ready to make your design solution you must think about exactly what you will need. You can do this by preparing a **materials list**. This lists the sizes and shapes of all the parts of your design, and the material that you want to make each part out of. For example:

Part name	Number needed	Material	Length (mm)	Width (mm)	Thickness (mm)
Sides	2	Teak	300	75	10
Ends	2	Teak	200	75	10
Partitions	3	Clear acrylic	200	60	4
Base	1	Birch plywood	300	200	4
Locating block	6	Aluminium	25	25	6
Swivel	1	Aluminium	300	25	6
End plate	1	Aluminium	100	50	2

As at all stages of the design process, a little forward planning will save you a lot of time and money. If you make a good materials list, and get hold of all the materials that you are going to need before you start to make your solution, then the construction of your design will be much easier.

To make a materials list you must know about the properties and availability of materials. Chapter 11 will help you.

2.7 HOW TO TEST YOUR DESIGNS

When you have made your solution it should solve your problem successfully and so satisfy the need that you originally identified. How do you judge the success of your solution in fulfilling this need?

Go back to your design targets

Firstly, if you are to judge success, you must define what you mean by success. The best way to do this is to go back to your original **design targets**. This will give you an item (criterion) or items to judge.

Sally's four targets give four things to judge:

1 Does the box hold all the items from John's magic set?
2 How well does the box stand up to the rough treatment that it gets?
3 How well laid out and efficient is the box when it is open?
4 How easy is the box to carry?

How to use your targets
How do you use these targets to measure success?

1 Firstly, you must try the solution out, or watch someone else try it out. This is the only sure way to see how it works.
2 Secondly, you must understand that how well your solution performs must be **judged**, i.e. it will be a **matter of opinion**.

Some targets can be measured with numbers. For example, you could count the number of seconds it takes John to unpack the new container and compare this with the time for the old container. Often, however, numbers mean very little. For example, how could you show how easy the new container is to carry? This is partly a question of John's feelings, and feelings cannot be measured. We can only make an intelligent guess at them.

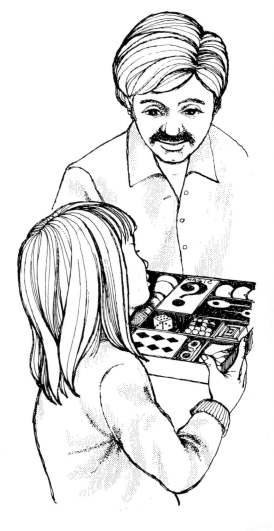

Make a checklist
The best way of judging is to use a scale to guide your own 'intelligent guessing' or opinion. Or it could be used to get other people's opinions. Scales like those on some school reports can be built into a checklist which you can use to test the success of your solutions. Such a scale might include:

A Outstanding	B Good	C Satisfactory	D Weak	E Very Poor

Sally might have made a checklist like the one here:

		A	B	C	D	E
a	Security					
b	Sturdiness					
c	Layout/efficiency					
d	Ease to carry					

Sally might have asked someone else to complete a similar checklist, e.g. John or his magician uncle. In complex projects it may be necessary to break some of the categories in the lefthand column down further. So **a** might become:

a	Security	A	B	C	D	E
	i) Security of contents from falling out					
	ii) Security of contents from crushing					
	iii) Safety					

In order to get a balanced view from these checklists, you may need to fit them into a written report. Guidelines to this are given in chapter 4.

Use the information to improve your design
Use the information from the checklists and the report. You may be able to alter your product to overcome small defects that come to light, or you may have to redesign it if you find any major flaws.

In either case, test the product again after you have remade it. And remember, no solution will be perfect. The more you do the better it should become, but time is a limit to all your work. Eventually you will have to stop one project and start another!

Test yourself

1 Copy the following passage into your notebook and fill in the missing words.
   TESTING
   When I have made my design, I should _____ it to see if it satisfies the original _____. I can use the _____ _____ to judge the design. If I find that my design does not fulfil the _____ need, I should _____ it.

2 How can we judge another person's *feelings* about a design? Take a number of tools that you have to use in your school workshop. Find a friend and discuss each other's *feelings* about how easy it is to use the tools.

Try the following exercises

1 Choose a product that you use in your house. Work out a way of testing how successful it is. Try to get the opinions of other people.

2 Take a design project you have completed. Explain the targets you set out to achieve to a classmate. Ask him or her to judge how well your project met the targets.

2.8 COMPUTER-AIDED DESIGN

Traditionally, designing involves our brains and our hands. For some time designers in the more complex industries have had a new aid to design at their disposal . . . *the computer.* The computer can act as an extension of both the hand and the brain, but cannot replace either. It can tremendously increase the power of our designing. Recently, microcomputers which can be used in design have become available to a wider population. Your school may now have a computer design facility of its own, and your teacher may be able to show you an example of using the computer to aid the design process.

Computers can help you to design your projects.

What is a computer?

As you will probably know, a computer is a device which does things with information. It can handle much more information than people, and it does so much more quickly. It handles information through a massive system of switches. Using microprocessors, very small computers can do very important jobs.

The modern world is a very complex place, and is getting more complex all the time. Every day there is more and more information to handle, and computers have become essential to handle this information. In fact, many aspects of modern life would be impossible without computers, such as air traffic control, some railway controls, modern newspaper production and so on.

How can computers aid our designing?

Things are changing so quickly these days that it is not possible to give a precise answer to this question. Much will depend on the particular kind of computer system installed in your school, and the particular design project that you are working on.

However, there are a few general points which are important for you to understand as a background to computer-aided design. They are given on the next page.

1   Information

Chapter 4 shows you some ways of handling information in your designing. Some of the methods you use to find information take a lot of time, such as searching through magazines or books. It is possible to use computers to allow you to gain the information you need very quickly indeed, by having a well-indexed library system linked to your computer. This depends, however, on whether your computer is programmed to do this or not.

2   Calculations

Many technological design problems need a lot of mathematical calculation. For example, a bridge designer is interested in the bridge span, the conditions of the soil and the rock that the bridge is to be built on and average and maximum wind speeds, among other things. Some of the calculations take a long time when done 'by hand'. The computer is able to make calculations extremely quickly and accurately. It frees the designer for more creative work.

3   Vision

One of the most difficult tasks in designing is to imagine what an object will look like from all angles; to **visualise** it. It is possible to use a computer to draw an object. The computer can then be used to 'turn the picture round' so that you can view it from several angles. See the example opposite.

Try the following exercise

Get hold of the manual for one of your school computers and try to find out exactly how it can help you in designing.

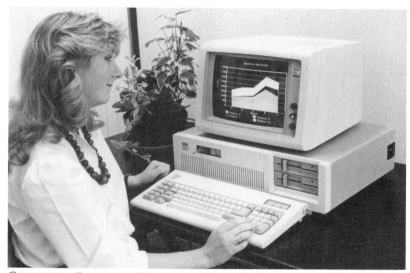

Computers allow you quick access to information.

They make calculations a lot easier!

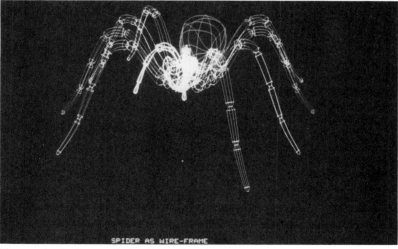

You can look at your design from all angles.

3

HOW TO RECORD AND PRESENT DESIGN IDEAS

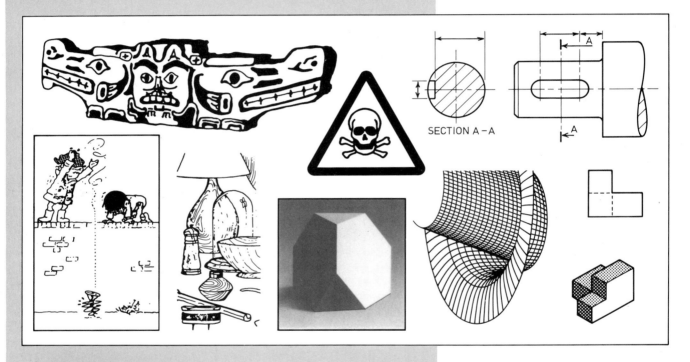

SECTION A – A

CONTENTS

3.1 INTRODUCTION

In the last chapter you read about what goes into designing an object. As you will have found out, design ideas can flow through your mind in a very quick stream. Once you have got started, one idea will very quickly be pushed out by the next. It can be very annoying to think up a good idea only to forget it. You always want to make the most of your ideas, and to do this you need quick ways to capture them before they escape. To do this you must learn how to record your ideas efficiently, and that is what this chapter is going to help you with.

When you have studied this chapter you should be able to:

1 develop your own skills of quick and clear drawing;
2 use these skills to record your design ideas;
3 learn to present your developed ideas by using accurate methods of drawing and by making models.

You can use the chapter in _three_ ways:

1 Study it early in the course to get an overall impression of the skills you must learn.
2 Use it step by step to practise your drawing and model-making skills.
3 Return to it whenever you need help in drawing your design ideas – it will help you to choose the best methods for the project you are working on.

How can you capture your ideas?

When you are thinking up design ideas you need to be able to record them quickly and simply. Words are sometimes useful to describe design ideas. Often, though, drawings do this much more clearly. To be quick you need to use very simple drawing methods, and to get _lots of practice_. This chapter will point you in the right direction, and show you how to use simple methods of recording your ideas to give you a complete record from which you can develop your designs.

3.2 HOW TO MAKE A START

The simplest and quickest way to record your design ideas is through clear freehand drawings. To make a start with freehand drawing you will only need a few simple tools. It is always better to master new skills slowly and in stages. If you start with tools which are too complex you may never master them and will just get impatient and dissatisfied with your work. Leave the complex tools like airbrushes until later.

What drawing tools should you start with?

The tools you need to start freehand drawing with are:

1 a sharp pencil
2 a rubber
3 some felt tip pens with soft, flexible points – these will give thin lines if you press lightly, and thicker lines if you press harder
4 some good quality white paper.

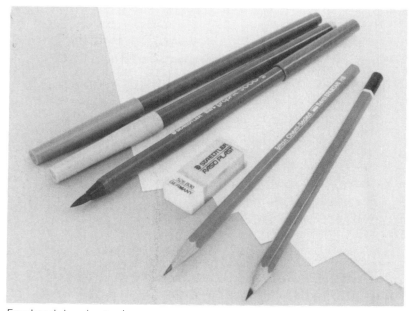

Freehand drawing tools.

Although most objects that you might want to draw look very complicated at first, they can always be simplified into lines. Freehand drawing involves using lines to build up the shape that you want to communicate to other people. So, the first skill to learn is how to draw lines.

How can you draw lines?

The simplest type of line to draw is a straight line. To draw one you should hold your pencil as shown in figure 3.1. Draw straight lines from the centre of your body outwards. If you are righthanded, move the pencil to the right and upwards. If you are lefthanded move the pencil to the left and downwards. Turn the paper so that you are always able to draw lines in this way and try to draw single lines in one movement.

You will find that as you learn to draw single lines in one movement you will avoid making lots of untidily connected lines. Your drawing will rapidly become both easier and tidier.

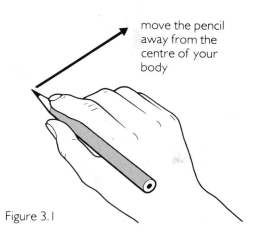

move the pencil away from the centre of your body

Figure 3.1

Try the following exercises

1 Draw a box like the one shown below. Fill the box with straight lines going across. Draw the lines parallel and keep them about 5 mm apart. Repeat this until you can draw such lines really easily and quickly.

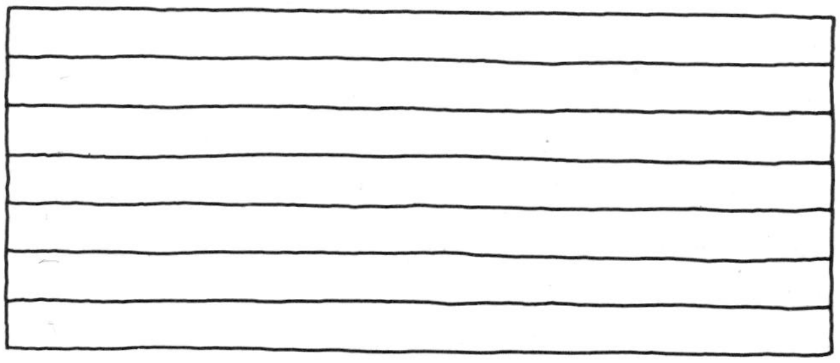

2 Draw a similar box and draw lines 2 mm apart.

3 Try again with lines 1 mm apart.

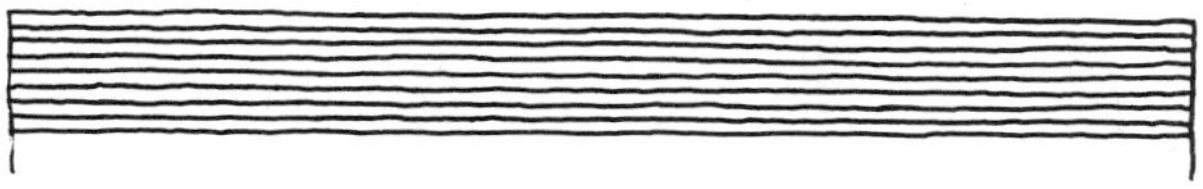

4 Draw sets of intersecting lines like those shown opposite. Fill the spaces with sets of parallel lines. Try to create interesting patterns. Picasso, the famous artist, used to create *very* interesting pictures.

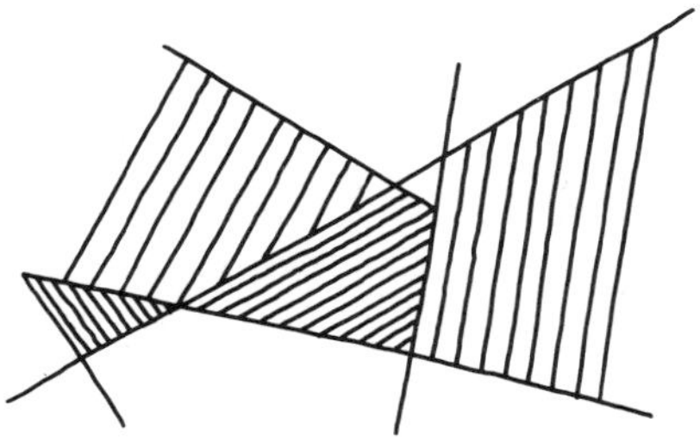

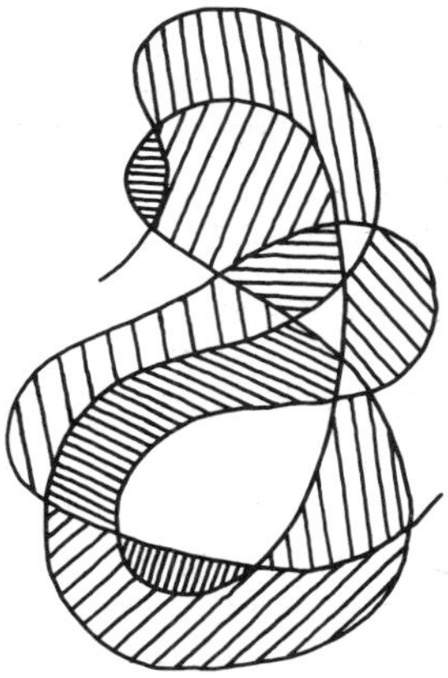

5 When you feel confident, try drawing curved lines in the same way. Some examples are shown below. This skill can be used to portray the feel and form of an object through a very simple drawing.

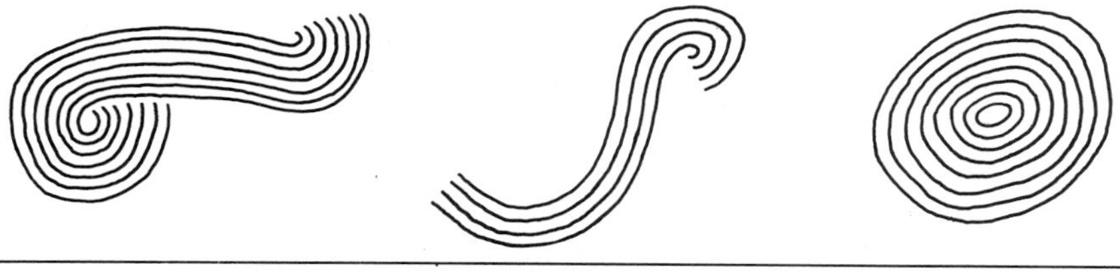

REMEMBER *Keep your pencil sharp, draw continuous single lines and practise whenever you have a few spare moments.*

Test yourself

1 Why is it necessary to practise drawing?
2 Why should you use simple drawing tools when starting to draw?
3 Which is the easiest direction in which to draw lines?

3.3 HOW TO DRAW FLAT SHAPES

How would you draw the front of this house?

Figure 3.2

Figure 3.3

Figure 3.4

Once you have learned to draw lines you want to be able to draw shapes. The photograph opposite shows the front view of a house. If you were asked to draw the front of this house, how would you start? The simplest way is to use lots of boxes, and to link them together to make your final picture.

How can you draw flat shapes in boxes?

Start by drawing the outside box faintly. Get the proportions of the vertical and horizontal lines right.

Next, faintly draw a series of boxes inside to show the main parts of the house.

Then 'line in' the main parts until the drawing is complete. **Lining in** is when you darken the parts of the line that you want to show or make stand out.

Drawing shapes is much easier if you can imagine them to be packed tightly into such a box, or boxes. It helps you to get the proportions right, and to break up complicated shapes into simpler shapes. It is much easier to draw the basic shape of an object and to fill the detail in later, than to be too ambitious and try to get the detail right immediately.

Try the following exercise

Using boxes, draw the fronts of the objects shown in the photographs below.

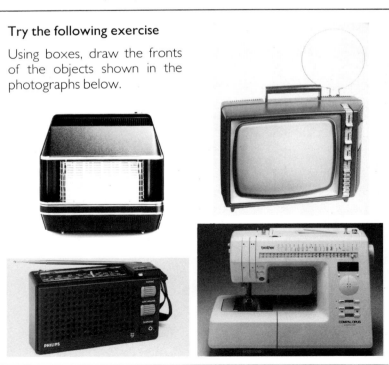

Can you use this method for drawing circles?

It is more difficult to draw circles than to draw straight lines, but you can still use the box method to do it. To draw a circle, start with a square box. Mark the centre of each side of this box. To draw the circle, hold your pencil just above the paper and make circular movements inside the box. Do this until you think you have found the correct place for the circle: it must touch the centre of each side of the box. Then bring the pencil down onto the paper as it traces the circular movement. This is called **ghosting**. Go over the faint 'ghost' lines with a heavier, final line.

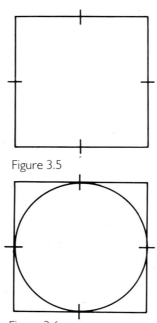

Figure 3.5

Figure 3.6

Figure 3.7

Many flat shapes with curves can be drawn in this way. Look at the pram shown opposite, and how to draw it, shown in figures 3.8, 3.9 and 3.10.

1 First you should draw an outline box.
2 Then you should draw smaller boxes inside the main box to place the various parts of the pram in their correct positions.
3 Finally you should fill in the various parts to give the final shape of the pram.

Test yourself

Why do you think it is easier to draw flat shapes inside boxes, than without boxes to put them in?

Try the following exercises

Find examples of the following and, using boxes, make flat, freehand pencil drawings of each:
1 books on a shelf
2 a cupboard with drawers
3 a radio
4 a window frame
5 a washing machine
6 a block of flats
7 a child's pedal car.

How would you draw this pram?

Figure 3.8

Figure 3.9

Figure 3.10

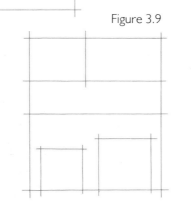

3.4 HOW TO DRAW IN PERSPECTIVE

The drawings that you have done so far have been very simple and have not given the complete shapes of the objects. To give an idea of the real shape of an object you have to do more than draw a flat plan. You have to draw what is known as a *perspective*. Perspective drawing show things as they look in real life.

What does perspective mean?

Stand in front of a window and keep your eyes in one position. Get a friend to hold a box outside the window. Close one eye. Use a wax pencil to trace the outline of the box onto the window.

If the box is right in front of your eye and a little below it, it will look like figure 3.11. The top appears to get thinner as the lines move away. The lines eventually disappear at a single 'vanishing point'. Look down some railway lines or down the length of a footbridge and you will see the same effect (see the photograph below). This is called **one-point perspective**. The one-point perspective box has vertical lines, horizontal lines and perspective lines.

Get your friend to turn the box so that you are now looking at a corner. It will look like figure 3.12. Both sides get thinner as the lines move away. They vanish at two different vanishing points. This is called **two-point perspective**. The two-point perspective box only has vertical lines and perspective lines. There are no horizontal lines.

A perspective view of Windsor Castle.

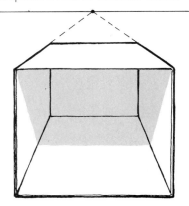

Figure 3.11

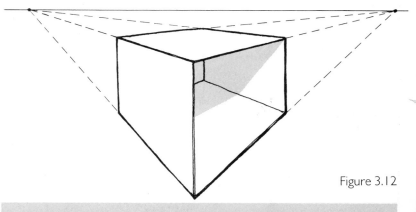

Figure 3.12

One point perspective – the railway lines seem to get closer.

Test yourself

What different kinds of line are found in these two kinds of perspective?

How can you draw freehand in perspective?

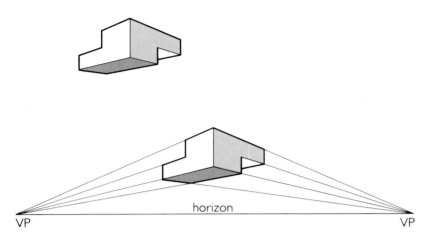

Figure 3.13

1 Two-point perspective

Two-point perspective is the easiest way to draw perspective because there are only two kinds of line: vertical and perspective. There are also two vanishing points. If you join the vanishing points with a horizontal line, the line is called the **horizon**.

Look at the top sketch opposite. It shows a perspective block looked at from underneath. Now look below it.

The same block is shown with its perspective lines traced back to their vanishing points (VP).

2 One-point perspective

One-point perspective has only one vanishing point, but it has three kinds of line: vertical, horizontal and perspective.

Look at the sketch below. It shows a block drawn in one-point perspective. See how the perspective lines all go back to a single vanishing point.

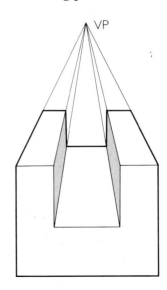

Figure 3.14

Try the following exercises

1   Trace the drawings shown below (figure 1) onto the middle of a sheet of A4 paper. Extend the perspective lines until you find the vanishing points. Draw in the horizon by joining up the two vanishing points.

2   Draw a horizon and two vanishing points onto a sheet of A3 paper. Using figure 2 as a guide, draw transparent cubes with side lengths of 50 mm. Draw them in different places above and below the horizon. Work out the effect of their position on their appearance.

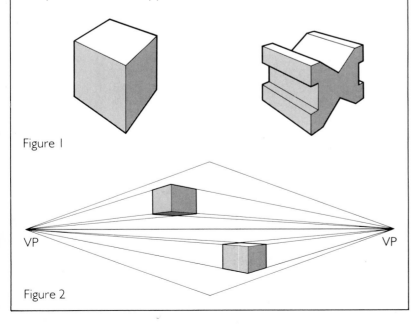

Figure 1

Figure 2

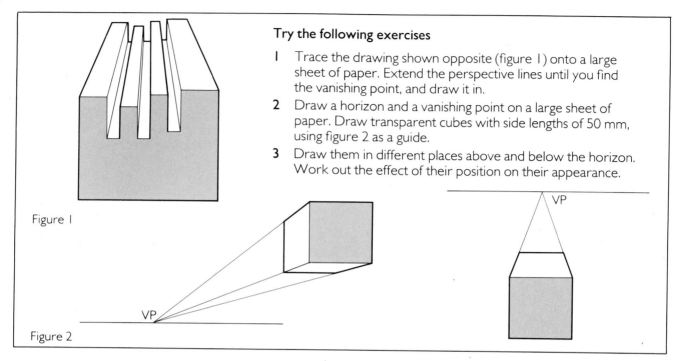

Figure 1

Figure 2

Try the following exercises

1 Trace the drawing shown opposite (figure 1) onto a large sheet of paper. Extend the perspective lines until you find the vanishing point, and draw it in.

2 Draw a horizon and a vanishing point on a large sheet of paper. Draw transparent cubes with side lengths of 50 mm, using figure 2 as a guide.

3 Draw them in different places above and below the horizon. Work out the effect of their position on their appearance.

In both kinds of perspective, boxes were used. For all future drawings, first produce faint boxes, then line in the details. To draw objects which are more complex than simple cubes you will have to either divide cubes up, or add squares and cubes to each other to make up the final shape. You will see how to do this below and on the next four pages.

How can you divide cubes easily?

Study the cube shown in figure 3.15. It is sketched in approximate two-point perspective. How can you divide one of its faces into two equal halves?

This is quite simple. Draw diagonal lines from corner to corner on the face you are dividing up. These lines cross in the exact centre of the face.

Draw a vertical line through this centre point: it divides the face into two. The half cube can then be lined in.

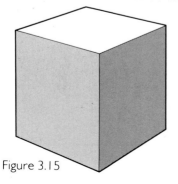

Figure 3.15

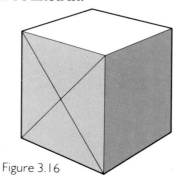

Figure 3.16

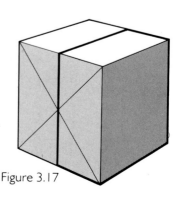

Figure 3.17

Try the following exercises

1 Draw the perspective cube
   shown in figure 1(a).
   Draw diagonal lines on face A
   and divide the cube into halves,
   as in figure 1(b).
   Then draw the cube with the
   corner missing, as in figure 1(c).

2 Use the method shown in
   exercise 1 to draw the blocks in
   figures 2(a) and (b).

3 Draw a large perspective cube
   and create an interesting surface
   pattern on each face. Do this by
   dividing the faces up into smaller
   sections, as shown in figure 3.
   Use colour to emphasise the
   patterns.

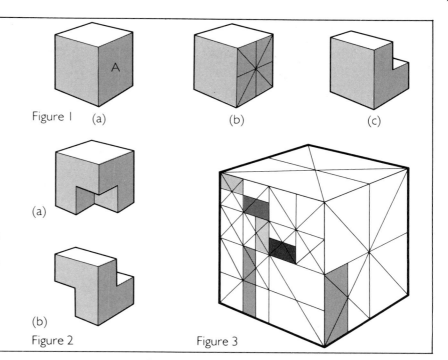

Figure 1   (a)   (b)   (c)

(a)

(b)
Figure 2

Figure 3

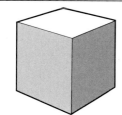

Figure 3.18

How can you add cubes to each other?

Study the cube shown opposite. It is sketched in
approximate two-point perspective. How can you extend it
by adding a series of cubes?

Firstly, use the diagonal line method to divide the face A into
two halves. Then extend the perspective lines 1, 2, 3 and 4
towards the vanishing point.

Next, draw a diagonal of the bottom rectangle on face A.
Draw it from point x to point y and continue until it crosses
line 2. Where it crosses line 2 is the end of the next cube.

You can continue in this way until you have drawn all the
cubes you need. Each cube will look realistic. Stacking cubes
like this can be used for all sorts of drawing, *but first you need
lots of practice.*

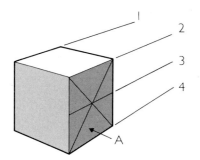

Figure 3.19

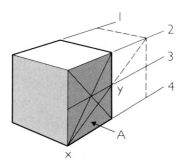

Figure 3.20

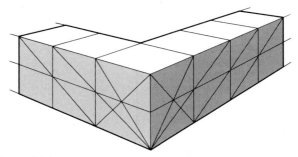

Figure 3.21

Try the following exercises over and over again until you can
do them easily and accurately

1   Draw five cubes, like the one shown
    in figure 1, in the direction of arrow
    A.

2   Draw three cubes in each of the
    directions B, C and D. In which
    direction will the lines not be in
    perspective?

3   Design a kit of cubic building blocks
    for a young child. Make a perspective
    drawing of one object which a child
    might build with your kit.

Figure 2

Figure 1

How can the cube method be used to draw more complex objects?

To be able to start to design any
complex object you need to be able
to see in your mind (to visualise)
what your idea looks like from
different angles. Look at the table
shown opposite; how could you
draw this in perspective from the
simple two-dimensional views
given in figure 3.23?

Three important views of this table
are shown in figure 3.23. A is called
the **top view** (or **plan view**), B is
called the **front view** and C is called
the **end view**.

If the table has proportions of 2:1:1
then it can be drawn inside two
cubes. The next step is to draw a
cube and extend it into another
cube, as shown in Figure 3.24.

Then you sketch the features of the
table which are seen from the three
views.

Finally, pencil in the outlines to the
right thickness, as shown in figure
3.26.

You can use this method to draw all
types of objects. You can also use it
to draw a single object from many
different angles by altering the angle
at which you are 'looking' at the
cubes.

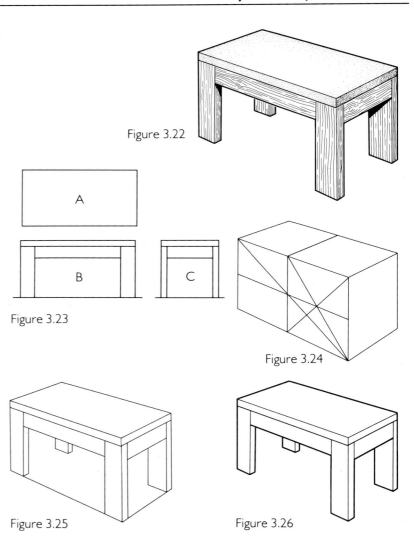

Figure 3.22

A

B   C

Figure 3.23

Figure 3.24

Figure 3.25

Figure 3.26

Try the following exercises

1 Three views are shown of some common objects. Sketch each object in two-point perspective using the cube method.

2 Find a block of flats with a repeating window pattern. Draw the block in two-point perspective using the cube method.

3 Find a picture of a modern fitted kitchen. Use the cube method to draw the kitchen and all its fitted units in one-point perspective.

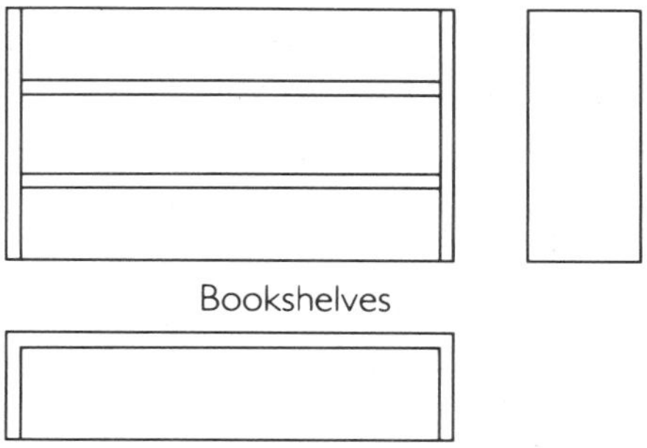

Bookshelves

Figure 1

Chair

Garage

Figure 2

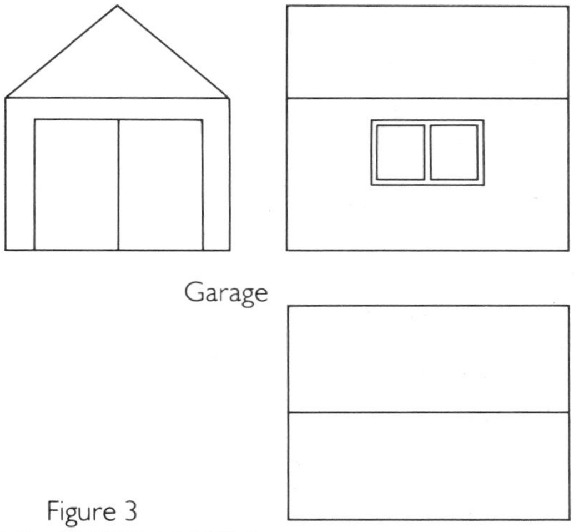

Figure 3

Can the cube method help you to draw curved objects?

Yes it can, and here are some examples.

1 Cylinders

Draw a cube of the correct proportions. On the face where the circle will appear, mark the centre of each edge.

Now draw the perspective circle, making sure that it passes through the centre of each box edge. Do the same on the opposite face of the cylinder, and join up the two perspective circles to form the cylinder.

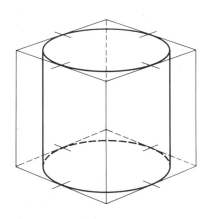

Figure 3.27

2 Cones

Draw a cube of the correct proportions. On the face where the circle will appear, mark the centre of each edge. Now draw the perspective circle, making sure that it passes through the centre of each box edge. Find the centre of the opposite box face. Join this centre point to the perspective circle to form a cone.

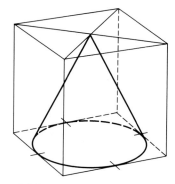

Figure 3.28

Circles drawn in perspective are called **ellipses**. They appear flattened. Hold the edge of a card circle directly in front of your eyes, as shown opposite. It will appear as a thin straight line. Raise the card and the line will become an ellipse. The higher you raise it the wider the ellipse becomes (Figure 3.29).

You can use **ellipse templates** to help to draw ellipses quickly and accurately. A template is a piece of plastic or metal either of regular, accurate shape or with regular, accurate shapes cut out of it around which you can draw.

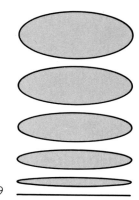

Figure 3.29

Try the following exercises

1   Draw the items shown in figure 1 in two-point perspective using the cube method.

Figure 1

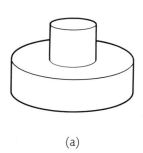 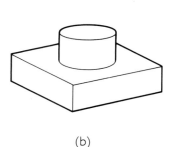 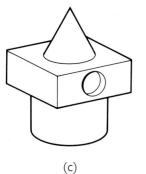 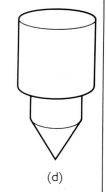

(a)   (b)   (c)   (d)

2   Find examples of the following and draw them using the method stated in 1: a clock; a cup and saucer; a record turntable; a bicycle; a car.

REMEMBER *You must practise until you can draw your design ideas quickly and realistically. Until you can do this, avoid using complex drawing instruments. When you are practising, try to develop your own style; one which is both personal and effective.*

3.5 HOW TO MAKE YOUR DRAWINGS STAND OUT

You will have found out that, often, if you explain an idea badly it will be ignored. The same goes for design ideas. If you do not draw your ideas in a clear and interesting way they will be ignored, or misunderstood. It is therefore very important to make your drawings stand out, and to be able to attract people's attention to the important parts of them. In this section there are some methods to help you to do this.

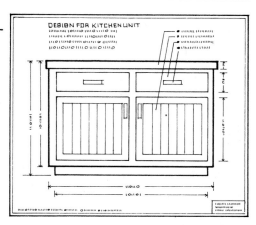

How does line thickness help?

Drawings made from lines which are all the same thickness can be very dull. You can make these drawings more interesting, and more informative, by using different line thicknesses. Thickened lines stand out from the thin lines and make important parts of the drawing stand out. In figure 3.31 the outside lines are thickened and the shape of the object stands out more than it does in figure 3.30.

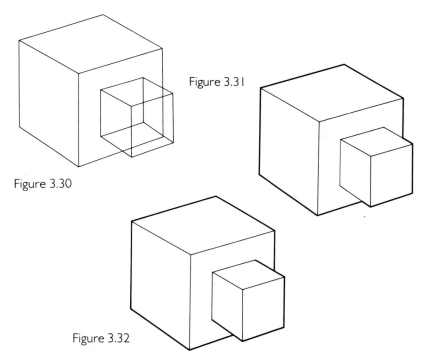

Figure 3.31

Figure 3.30

Figure 3.32

A more realistic method can give even better results. You need to follow two rules:

1 at the meeting of two visible surfaces, keep the lines thin;
2 where a visible surface meets an invisible surface, thicken the line, as in figure 3.32.

How can you highlight objects?

Imagine a design sheet full of different ideas. You want to quickly make some of these stand out from the rest. You can do this by marking a thick, coloured boundary around some or all of each drawing. You can use a felt-tip marker or a brush and watercolour to do this, but be careful not to over-do it and just make a mess of your paper.

Figure 3.31

An aerial view and map of the same area –
note the contour lines.

Can contour lines help?

The most common place to find **contour lines** is on a map, where they are used to show the height and steepness of areas of land. You can also use contour lines in your design drawing to make your ideas appear solid, or three-dimensional. When you are drawing contour lines in your design drawing you must be very clear about the shape of the outer surface of the object you are drawing, as if you get it wrong the effect will be more misleading than not having contour lines at all. You must imagine that each contour line travels over the surface of your object, following all the changes of shape and direction. The closer together you draw your contour lines, the steeper the slope you are showing on your object. The photographs opposite show contour lines on a map and the feature that they are representing, and figure 3.34 shows how you can use contour lines in your design drawing.

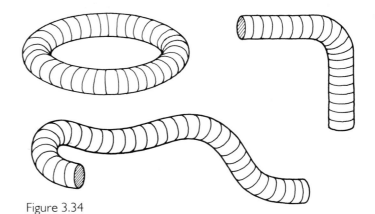

Figure 3.34

What about shading?

In simple line drawings surfaces appear separate because of their boundary lines. Real objects, however, do not usually have boundary lines. Their surfaces appear different because they look darker or lighter. Why is this? You can see objects because they reflect light. You can distinguish between the surfaces of an object because different amounts of light are reflected from different surfaces, and as a result the surfaces look lighter or darker. The darkness of each surface is affected by the position of the object and the source of the light.

You can use the sides of your pencil point to shade your line drawings. You can also use felt tips, but they may stain your paper if you are not careful. For the quick drawing of design ideas you need only four shades. These are: white, pale grey, dark grey and black, as shown in figure 3.36.

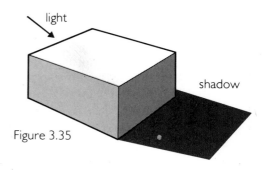

Figure 3.35

Figure 3.36

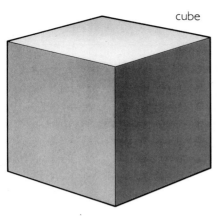
cube

When shading simple, flat-faced objects with sharp corners, the differences between the surfaces are sharp. When shading curved surfaces, the light changes gradually. In these cases you need to gradually merge the four different shades together. The drawings in figure 3.37 show how this can be done on a selection of basic forms.

REMEMBER *with all these methods, you must practise them on simple examples before you try more complicated ideas, otherwise you will only spoil your drawings and make them more confusing.*

Figure 3.37
(shaded using
4 TONES only)

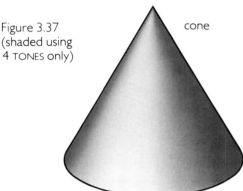
cone

cylinder

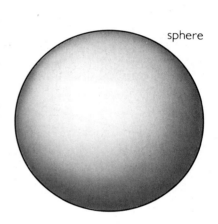
sphere

Try the following exercises

1   Make perspective sketches of each of the objects shown below. The arrows show where the light shines from. Figure 1(a) is shaded correctly. Add the correct shading to all your drawings.

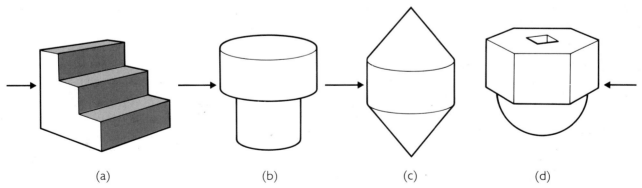

    (a)   (b)   (c)   (d)

Figure 1

2   Imagine the light source in a different position. Redraw the objects using the correct shading.

How can you draw surface texture?

All materials have surface textures. The texture is the *feel* of the surface. Some are smooth, some rough; some are furry, some gritty and so on. You can make your drawings more real if you show the surface textures. Here are some examples of the ways in which the textures of different materials can be drawn.

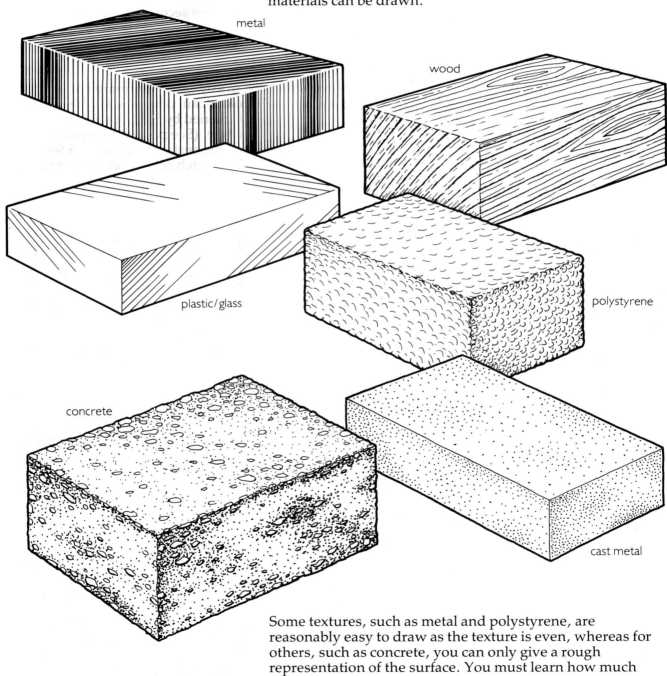

metal

wood

plastic/glass

polystyrene

concrete

cast metal

Some textures, such as metal and polystyrene, are reasonably easy to draw as the texture is even, whereas for others, such as concrete, you can only give a rough representation of the surface. You must learn how much detail is required to convey the texture in your drawing.

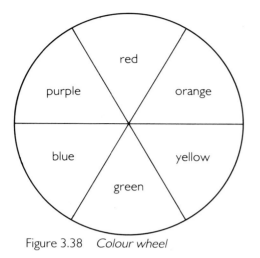

Figure 3.38   *Colour wheel*

What use can you make of colour?

The objects that you make will eventually have colours. In quick sketching, however, you should use colour sparingly. It can be very effective in emphasising features, but if you use too much it can ruin the presentation of your ideas.

There are three **primary** colours: blue, red and yellow. By mixing these, you can make three **secondary** colours:

blue + red   = purple
red + yellow   = orange
yellow + blue   = green

You can make further colours by mixing primary with secondary colours. Each colour can then have varying tones of darkness. They can be darkened by mixing with black and lightened by mixing with white. (See page 118 for more information.) In your sketching, restrict yourself to a few colours, say two or three. Too much colour can reduce the impact of your drawings.

Lettering

You will often need to add words and numbers to your design sheets. Careless and untidy writing can be difficult to read and can clutter up your design. Get into the habit of using a neat, simple and clear form of lettering. You should letter your designs in black ink, and find out which sort of pen you can write with the best. For presentation drawings, you can use dry transfer lettering, although you will soon discover that this also requires a great amount of care and patience, and is very expensive.

ABCDEFGHIJKLMN
OPQRSTUVWXYZ
abcdefghijklmnop
qrstuvwxyz
1234567890

Figure 3.37

Dry transfer lettering is expensive but good for presentation drawings.

3.6 DETAILED DRAWINGS

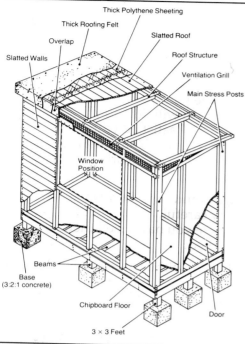

Thick Polythene Sheeting
Thick Roofing Felt
Overlap
Slatted Roof
Slatted Walls
Roof Structure
Ventilation Grill
Main Stress Posts
Window Position
Beams
Base (3:2:1 concrete)
Chipboard Floor
Door
3 × 3 Feet

The earlier sections dealt with capturing your design ideas with quick, simple sketches. As you progress through a design project, you will need to make more careful and more detailed drawings. These will have to contain a lot of information. They will help you to work out the details of your design and to show them to others. This section will show you some of the methods available for making detailed working drawings.

What drawing instruments should you use?

When you go into an art shop you are presented with a huge selection of materials and instruments. Unless you know what you want, and for what purpose, the selection can be very confusing. Here are some of the things that you will need to produce high-quality drawings.

1 Paper

Paper comes in various sizes, denoted by the letter 'A' and a number. Every time the number increases, the size of the paper is halved. Look at the diagram below and the sizes of paper that each 'A' size refers to.

A0		
A1		
	A2	A3
		A4

A0 = 1189 × 841 mm
A1 = 841 × 594 mm
A2 = 594 × 420 mm
A3 = 420 × 297 mm
A4 = 297 × 210 mm

2 Pencils

Pencils are very important in good design drawing. Their leads come in different grades of hardness, each grade being useful for different purposes. Softer leads give thicker, darker lines and harder leads give thinner, lighter lines. At the middle of the range is HB. Soft pencils are B, 2B, 3B and so on. Hard pencils are H, 2H, 3H etc.

... 4H ... 3H ... 2H ... H ... HB ... B ... 2B ... 3B ... 4B ...

To give clear, precise drawings your pencils must always be kept sharp. You can sharpen them in two ways.

a **Conical points** are usually used for pencils softer than H for freehand drawing, lettering and preliminary technical drawing.

b **Chisel points** are used on pencils harder than H for high-quality linework.

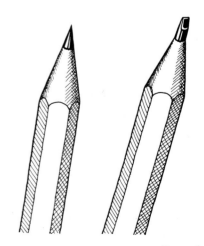

Figure 3.40

Technical pens produce high quality outlines.

3 Technical pens

You can buy technical pens (such as Rotrings) with drawing point diameters ranging from 0.1 mm to over 2 mm. You can use them with many different colours of drawing ink. If used skilfully, technical pens can be used to produce outline drawings of excellent quality. If you are not careful, however, you can easily smudge your work – and mistakes cannot be rubbed out! Usually you will first do your drawing faintly in pencil, and when you are satisfied with it draw over the parts you want to show in ink. You must always allow the ink plenty of time to dry before working on the drawing again.

Technical pens are very fragile (and expensive) instruments and must be looked after very carefully. You should clean your pens thoroughly each time you have used them, or they will quickly become blocked.

Stencils are available for lettering with technical pens, but always make sure that you are using the right size of stencil for the width of your pen, and the size of lettering that you want.

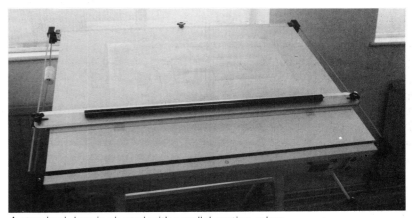

A standard drawing board with parallel motion edges.

4 Drawing boards

Drawing boards are essential for producing accurate design drawings. They vary in size, and their straight edges and flat, smooth surfaces *must not be damaged*. Paper is either clipped or taped securely to the board. Less expensive boards are used with separate tee squares; more expensive boards have parallel-motion straight edges which run smoothly up and down the drawing surface. Set squares are used on the tee-square blade to give vertical and angled lines. Standard set squares give angles of 30°, 45° and 60°. You can also get adjustable set squares which are useful for angles other than these.

Other useful instruments are shown in the photographs opposite. Like all drawing instruments, they are much more effective if well cared for.

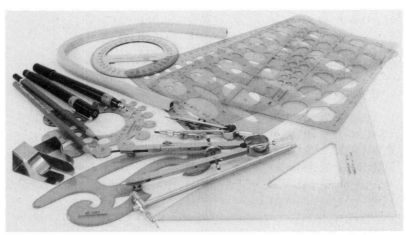

Some useful drawing instruments.

What kinds of line should you draw?

Pencil and pen lines should be even all the way along. For engineering drawings you should use two thicknesses of line, given in the table below.

─────────────	**Outlines** should be thick, straight and continuous
───────────── ──────────→	**Dimension lines, projection lines** and **hatching** should be thin, straight and continuous.
∿∿∿	**Limits of incomplete views** should be shown by thin, continuous and wavy lines.
– – – – – – – – – – –	**Hidden details** should be indicated by thin, short dashes.
─ · ─ · ─ · ─ · ─ · ─	**Centre lines** and the **extreme positions of moving parts** should be thin and chain-like.

You should practise drawing all these types of line as evenly as you can.

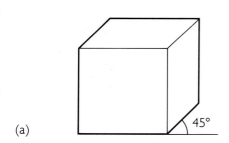

(a)

45°

(b)

45°

Figure 3.41

How do you make detailed drawings?

There are many ways of making detailed drawings. This section will look at three of them: **oblique** drawings, **isometric** drawings and **orthographic** drawings. You can also use perspective to produce detailed, accurate drawings, but a lot of skill is needed to do this.

1 Oblique drawing

Oblique drawing produces a three-dimensional view of an object. First, one face is drawn to its true shape, looking straight at it. The lines of this face are horizontal and vertical. The other faces are then drawn at 45° to the horizontal and usually at a scale of 1:2. A fairly realistic drawing of the object is produced to the correct measurement, but the 45° lines do not close together in the distance as they do in perspective drawings.

It is easiest to start these drawings off with faint cubes, as in sketching. Use a 45° set square over a tee square on a drawing board for this. You can then draw curves on the front face, where they take their true shape, and from there you can project them through the rest of the object by using projection lines.

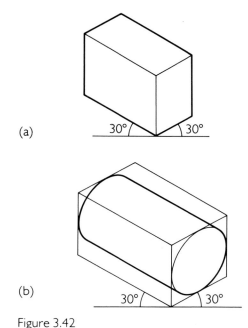

(a)

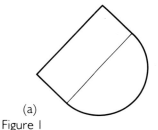

(b)

Figure 3.42

2 Isometric drawing

Isometric drawing also produces a three-dimensional view of objects. It is a little like two-point perspective, although the lines are parallel and do not close together in the distance. In isometric drawings all of the vertical lines remain at 90° to the horizontal and all the other lines are drawn at 30° to the horizontal. A fairly realistic drawing is produced, but lines at the top of the drawing usually appear to be too long. It is easier to start isometric drawings inside outline boxes. Use a 30° set square over a tee square on a drawing board. Isometric grid paper can also be used for quick sketching, although it is expensive and should be used sparingly.

As you can clearly see in the drawing of the cylinder for both oblique and isometric projections, the 'distant' end of the cylinder appears wider than the front end. This is because you are used to looking at perspective drawings, which taper at this end. When drawing or looking at these projections you must be aware of this effect.

Try the following exercises

1 Using a drawing board, tee square and 45° set square (and instruments for producing curves), draw the shapes shown in figure 1 in oblique projection.

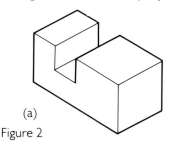

(a)

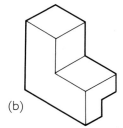

(b)

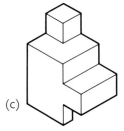

(c)

Figure 1

2 Using a drawing board, tee square and 30°/60° set square, draw the shapes shown in figure 2 in isometric projection.

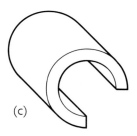

(a)

(b)

(c)

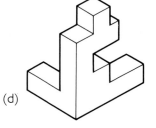

(d)

Figure 2

Test yourself

What are the main advantages and disadvantages of **a** isometric projection and **b** oblique projection? Write them down and discuss them with another member of your class.

3 Orthographic drawing

Orthographic drawing is a method of drawing the true shape of the surfaces of three-dimensional objects. Each main surface is drawn facing the observer, as a **view** or **elevation**. Usually only three views are needed in a drawing. These are the **plan view** (or **top view**), the **front view** and the **end view**. Details which are not normally visible on these views can be shown by using dotted lines (or hidden detail lines). Orthographic drawings are drawn over a drawing board, with a tee square and set square. For quick sketching, orthographic grid paper or graph paper can be used.

There are two types of commonly-used orthographic projection. You need to avoid confusing them if you are going to draw accurately, or understand other people's drawings. The methods are:

a First-angle projection, symbolised by

b Third angle projection, symbolised by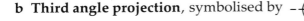

a First-angle projection

The object shown opposite is suspended in a three-sided box. Imagine that images of its front, end and plan views are projected *forward* through the object onto the sides of the box.

Now imagine that the three-sided box is unfolded. The images projected onto its three sections form a first-angle projection of the object. The front, end and plan views are shown as they would appear on the paper.

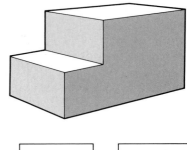

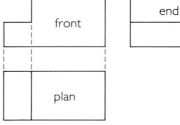

Figure 3.43

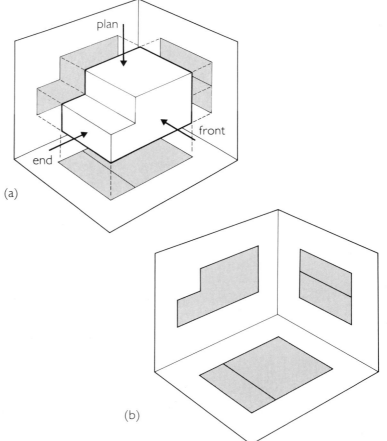

(a)

(b)

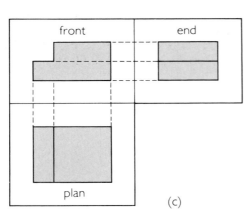

(c)

Figure 3.44

b Third-angle projection

Imagine the same object suspended inside a different three-sided box. In this case, the images are projected *backward* from the object to the box sides, not through the object as in first-angle projection. The object is the same; only the position of the views is different.

These two methods of projection show exactly the same detail, but do so from different directions. In some cases one will be easier to produce, and in other cases the other will. You will have to learn through experience which projection should be used in any particular case.

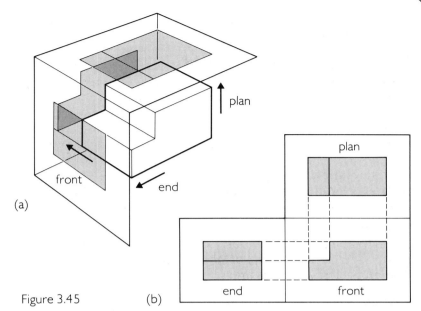

(a)

Figure 3.45 (b)

How can you show hidden details?

If the lines of an object are invisible from one side, they can still be shown on an orthographic drawing. This is called showing **hidden detail**.

The object shown in figure 3.46 has a slot cut in its underneath. This can be shown on a plan view by using two hidden detail lines. These lines are drawn as:– – – – – – – – – – – – .

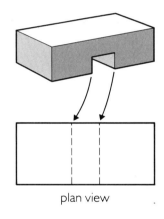

plan view

Figure 3.46 *Hidden detail*

How are dimensions shown on orthographic drawings?

Orthographic drawings are often the main guide to making things. They therefore need to contain all the relevant information about the design. Sizes (dimensions) are obviously very important and should be shown on such drawings.

When you are numbering or lettering your drawings use clear, simple letters and numbers to avoid confusion. You should also use sharp arrow heads which exactly touch the limit lines.

Draw the dimensions so that they can be read from the bottom or the righthand side of the sheet as easily as from the top and the left.

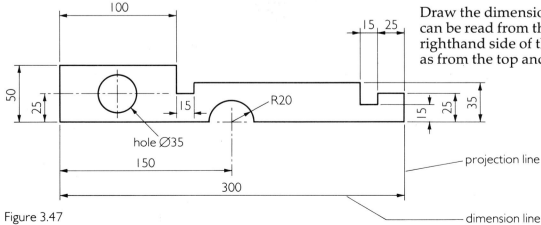

Figure 3.47

How can the insides of objects be shown?

Sometimes outside views and hidden detail do not give enough information about the inside of an object. In these cases a **section** is drawn through the area that you need to show. The cut-through surfaces are **hatched** at 45° to show that they represent a section, as is shown in figure 3.48. These sections can then be looked at along with plan views and other projections to give you all the information you need about the object. The section opposite shows you that the back (hidden) end of the object has a smaller hole in it than the front (visible) end.

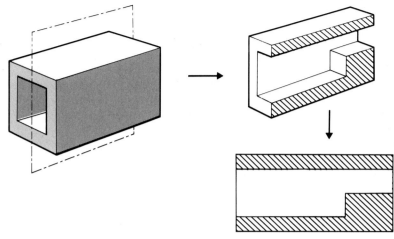

Figure 3.48 *Hatching of the inside of an object*

How can you draw very large objects?

Sometimes you may have to draw an object which is bigger than your paper, such as a kitchen or a wardrobe. Then you have to reduce the size of the drawn object to make it fit your paper. This is called **scaling down**. (You can, of course, scale up as well. Here you draw a small object much bigger than it really is, as you might do with a screw or lock.) You can scale down by different proportions, such as by half, by a quarter, by one tenth and so on. You show this on your drawing by adding 'Scale 1:4' (which means that your drawing is a quarter of the real size of the object). What do these mean? Scale 1:10, 1:3, 4:1.

REMEMBER *if your drawing does not show the correct scale, it will be impossible to read correctly.*

You can also reduce a drawing by removing parts from it. For example, the block opposite has the same section all the way along. To draw it all would be a waste of paper space. You can reduce it, as shown in figure 3.49(c). This is called an **interrupted view**. Again, you must show the full-size dimensions, to allow anyone to understand what you have drawn.

(a)

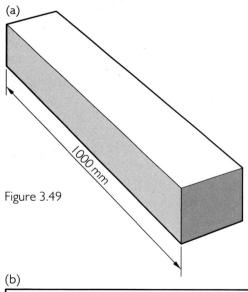

Figure 3.49

1000 mm

(b)

1000 mm

(c) interrupted view of the block

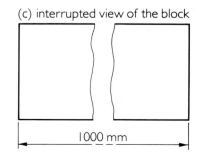

1000 mm

What about really complex objects?

Many objects are too complicated to show the detail of their insides by using either hidden detail lines or hatched sections. In these cases you have to draw the parts of the object 'exploded apart'. These **exploded views** can show all the details of the inside of an object, and how the parts fit together, and are extremely useful for objects which have moving parts. An exploded view of a plane is shown in figure 3.50. (Note that it is drawn in isometric projection.)

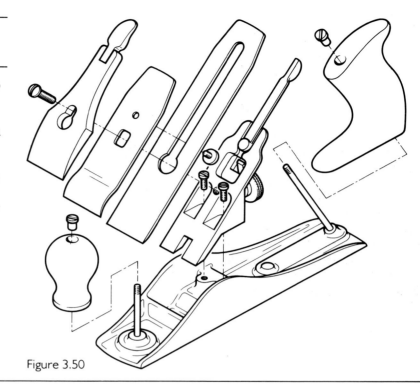

Figure 3.50

Try the following exercises

1   Make accurate orthographic drawings of the objects shown below using either first- or third-angle projection.

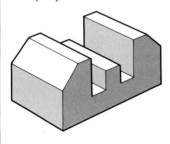   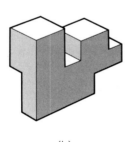   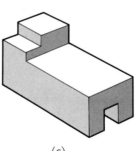   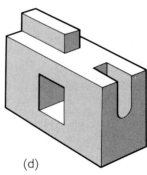

Figure 1   (a)   (b)   (c)   (d)

2   Choose a number of ways of joining wood. Make accurate orthographic drawings of each one, and remember to add clear dimensions to your drawings.
3   Draw sections through the joints you chose in exercise **2**.
4   Take the same joints and draw exploded views of each, using isometric projections.

Test yourself

1   What are the three main elevations in an orthographic drawing?
2   What is the difference between the two types of orthographic projection described in this chapter?
3   Outline the advantages and disadvantages of the three ways of showing the inside of an object on a drawing.

3.7 PRESENTATION AND LAYOUT

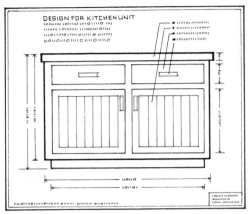

So far you have learned that your drawings need to be well *produced* if they are to show your ideas clearly. To ensure that your ideas really stand out though, they also need to be well *presented* and well *laid out*. There are various ways to help you do this, and they are described in this section.

The most important aid to presenting your work is to have it well organised and protected, so that people can look at it easily and it does not get damaged. Design folders and complete design projects are the best way to keep your work presentable.

1 Design folders

You should keep all your design drawings and notes in a sturdy design folder, which should be large enough to easily accommodate the largest piece of paper that you have. It can be a simple file, a ring binder or a more elaborate artist's portfolio, with flaps and tying tapes. You should get into the habit of filing your work as soon as you finish it or if you are not going to work on it for a while, so that it does not get ruined.

2 Design projects

Your major projects will be made up of many design sheets. They should all be kept, and should be organised in the order in which you produced them, unless there is a very good reason for another kind of organisation. Each sheet should be dated, numbered and headed. A common form of design project organisation is to place the sheets under a number of headings, for example:

Research (making the problem clear)
Early ideas (rough sketches)
Development sketches
Working drawings
Presentation drawings
Evaluation

Sometimes the research and evaluation sections can be presented as separate reports (see section 4.5).

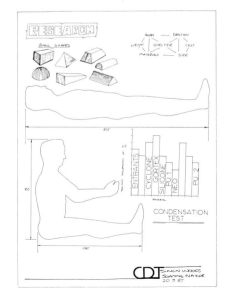

Use notes to explain your sketches

Your early sketches will be done fairly quickly, as ideas spring into your mind, and will rarely be laid out formally. It is always useful to mix notes with your sketches and drawings, not only to explain your design to other people, but to remind yourself of why you chose one design rather than another, what you wanted a particular surface texture to look like and so on. You can also use all sorts of other aids to add to the clarity and interest of your design projects, such as magazine photographs to show a particular idea in its setting.

Although design sketches are mainly a record of your thoughts, you should always try to make them look interesting. Here are some ways of doing this:

1 vary the size of drawings on the sheet;
2 avoid placing objects evenly across the sheet;
3 use different media for contrast, but *do not get over-complicated*.

REMEMBER *if your sketches look boring, others may not look carefully enough at what might really be good design ideas.*

Try the following exercise

Collect magazines and photographs of interesting objects and settings. Make up a scrapbook of those objects, settings and different styles of display that might be of use in your designing. Do this continually throughout your CDT course.

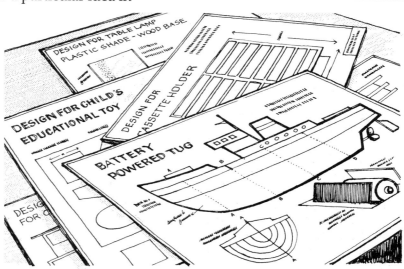

3   Working drawings

For each of your completed design projects you will have a number of working drawings, showing different projections of the design, plan views, hidden details, exploded views and so on. These should contain all the information you need to make your design (or for someone else to make it), such as the shapes and sizes of all the parts, how they are assembled or joined together and the surface finishes.

Plan the layout first

Plan the layout of each drawing before starting it. It is often helpful to make a rough sketch of the layout, and to identify each part of the drawing, its overall size and where it will lie on the sheet. Aim to get the drawing balanced in the centre of the paper, and allow room for any dimension lines and the title block.

Do your drawings in stages

First draw the views in faintly. Then check them and make any corrections. When all is right, fill in the details with a sharp medium line and go over the outlines with a thicker line. Finally add the dimension and limit lines and fill in the title block (see page 57).

4   Presentation drawings

When it is important to convince others of the value of your design, presentation drawings will help. These are attractive, realistic drawings produced in any suitable media and they usually need some artistic skill. Although they have to express what your design is going to look like, they do not have to be as accurate as working drawings. The point is both to give an idea of your design and to immediately interest whoever is looking at it. Thus colour, textures, backgrounds and so on can all be used to improve your presentation drawings. Do not be afraid to experiment with these.

TITLE: PUPPET HEADS
NAME   J.   GROUP   SHEET 2   DATE 20·3·87

5   Design sheets

Design sheets are usually most effective when they are all of the same size, and have their details clearly filled in in the title block. Often they will benefit from a standard form of layout, but on occasion the subject matter will be best communicated in a different way. You should not stop yourself from trying out new layout ideas and methods of presentation. Some examples of design sheets are shown on this and the opposite page.

TITLE : TOTEM POLE   SHEET 4   DATE 20·3·87
DEPARTMENT OF CRAFT DESIGN & TECHNOLOGY   DRAWN BY : J.P

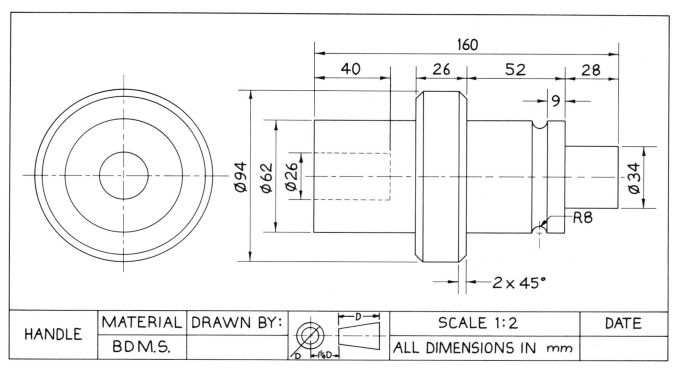

| HANDLE | MATERIAL BD M.S. | DRAWN BY: | | SCALE 1:2 ALL DIMENSIONS IN mm | DATE |

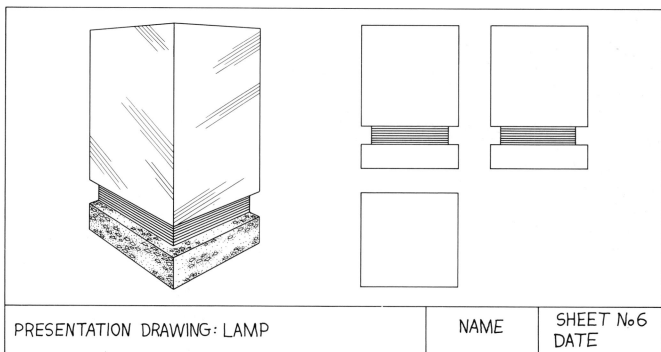

PRESENTATION DRAWING: LAMP   NAME   SHEET No 6 DATE

Try the following exercise and return to it from time to time to see how your ideas are developing

Devise a few different layouts for design sheets. Identify the elements of each which you think are effective, and those that you think are ineffective.

3.8 OTHER MEDIA

So far you have been advised to avoid using too many different media in your designing to avoid unnecessary complication of your work. However, there will be times when the use of artists' media will be of great help to you. This section gives some examples of what media are available to you and how you can use them.

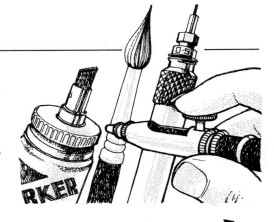

1 Pencil crayons

You can use pencil crayons for colouring and for coloured shading. Hold the pencil almost on its side and shade using a backwards and forwards motion. More pressure will give you a denser colour. To get a sharp edge, shade up to a piece of masking card, which you can cut to any shape that you want to accentuate. Crayons are useful because they can be mixed to produce almost any colour you want.

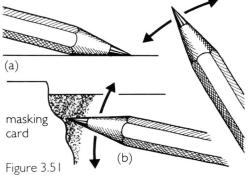

(a)

masking card

(b)

Figure 3.51

Coloured markers for shading and colouring.

2 Coloured markers

You can also use coloured markers for colouring and shading, but they must be used with care to avoid stains. Their tips come in a variety of shapes, sizes and degrees of softness, and you should be sure that you are using the right type of marker for the particular job that you are trying to do. You should avoid spirit-based markers as they can seep right through your paper and destroy hours of hard work.

3 Colour washes

You can mix water colour paints to give a **wash**. When the wash is painted onto a drawing it gives a see-through finish, and lines and other pencil marks are clearly visible underneath it.

When large areas are washed the paper gets very wet and crinkles. To prevent this it should be stretched before the wash is painted on. Wet the paper with clean water and tape it down to a board. As it dries out it tightens up, and, when fully dry, it will not crinkle as a wash is painted on.

Paint the wash in side-to-side strokes. Do not pause, as the wash will dry and show up as a dark patch. When you have finished, dry the brush and use it to soak up any water left in a pool on the paper. For a shaded effect, paint successive layers of wash onto the areas that you want to darken. Wait for the wash to dry before applying another coat.

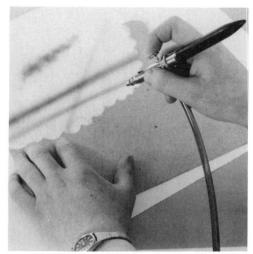

Airbrushes spray ink onto the paper.

4 Airbrushes

Airbrushes are small devices which are held like a pencil and will spray ink or paint from a reservoir. The ink is propelled from the airbrush nozzle by either:

1 a can of airbrush propellant;
2 pressure from a suitably adapted car tyre; or
3 a special air compressor.

Single-action airbrushes are preset so that they will spray a constant supply of ink. Double-action airbrushes allow the spray to be varied during use.

Airbrushes can be used for lettering and for freehand spraying. They are commonly used with stencils to give effective repetition of designs. Such stencils can be cut from stiff paper and can be positive or negative. Positive stencils have what you want to show cut out, so this will appear in the colour of the ink that you are using. Negative stencils have the surround of what you want to show cut out, so that your shape will appear the colour of the paper on which you are working.

Interesting effects can be achieved by spraying the ink through fabrics, such as lace. Shade can be varied, as in colour washing, by applying successive coats to create darker areas. Because the airbrush spray spreads out as it leaves the nozzle, masking is essential. Areas which are not to be sprayed must be masked off using a paper stencil, pressure sensitive film or masking fluid.

REMEMBER *it is essential that these precision instruments are cleaned thoroughly after each use. Follow the maker's instructions exactly.*

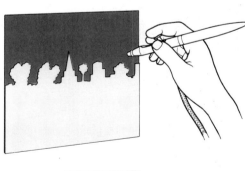
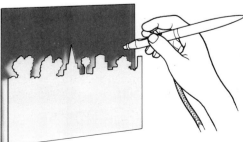

Some airbrush effects.

3.9 PHOTOGRAPHS

So far you have used different methods of drawing to record your design ideas, and, as you will have found out, each drawing takes a long time. Sometimes it helps to record ideas with photographs. Photographs are accurate and can be produced quickly and easily. You can use them in a number of ways; to produce instant (Polaroid) pictures or pictures that have to be processed, and to produce pictures in colour or black and white. This section gets you to think about how you can use photographs to help you in presenting your design ideas.

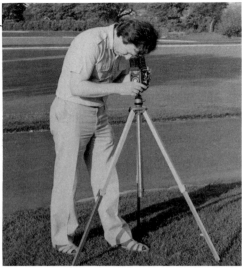

Photographs give an accurate record of ideas.

How do you take photographs?

You will be using photographs primarily to give clear, accurate illustrations of your, or other people's, designs. However, there are a number of things other than the object that you are photographing that you must think about.

The most important factor in taking a photograph is the amount of light. You can use either natural light (daylight), flash or electric light, whichever is most convenient, but whichever you use you must make sure that there is neither too little nor too much. When you become skilled you can start to use the amount and type of light, along with the aperture control, shutter speed and film speed of the camera to produce exactly the effect that you want on your photograph.

The background of the object you are photographing is also important. If, for example, you are photographing a model, put it on a plain surface and make sure that nothing is in the background that you do not want in the picture. When you have set the composition up to your satisfaction, focus the object correctly, set the aperture and shutter speed (although on simple cameras this will not be necessary) and press the button.

REMEMBER *always get close enough to the object, hold the camera steady and make sure that the background is acceptable and the lighting adequate.*

This model is lost agaisnt the cluttered background.

Try the following exercise

Study the photographs opposite and list the good and bad points of each.

3.10 HOW TO MAKE MODELS

Sometimes drawings do not show an idea adequately from all directions, either because the object is too difficult to draw or because the drawings are too complicated to understand on their own. In this case a model can help you. Models are useful to give a sense of proportion, or to show how one part fits or moves against another. They are also useful in showing up faults in your designs before you have put too much work into them. When you are deciding how to make your model, think about how long it will take you and how accurate it will be, as there are many different methods and materials to use.

I Paper and card

You can make realistic models cheaply and quickly from paper and thin card. Always follow these two very important guidelines.

1 First you must draw the model out accurately using proper drawing instruments. Often, solid objects are made from one sheet of card which is folded. Figure 3.52 shows a plan (or **development**) of a cube. It will only eventually fold into a cube if you have drawn it out accurately. Many different types of geometric solid can be modelled if they are first drawn out as developments. Another advantage of drawing models out on a flat sheet is that the surface details can be drawn or painted in before the paper or card is folded.

2 You must cut out and fold the paper or card very accurately. Cutting straight lines is best done with a sharp modelling knife and a straight metal edge on top of a cutting board. Curved cuts can be made freehand with a swivelling modelling knife or a pair of scissors. To bend card accurately you must first **score** it, using a blunt instrument such as the back of a kitchen knife. (See figure 3.52.) It will also help if you bend the card over a straight edge, as in figure 3.53.

Figure 3.52

glue flap

Figure 3.53

Figure 3.54

Thin card and paper can be joined by applying white PVA glue to the flaps. Thick card can be joined by the tissue and paste technique. Here, gummed strips are used to hold the pieces of the model together. Tissue strips coated with wallpaper paste are placed over the joints. They are then overlapped for strength. Although these joints take several hours to dry they are very strong.

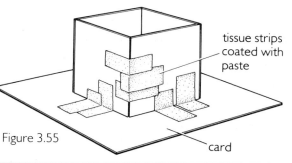

tissue strips coated with paste

card

Figure 3.55

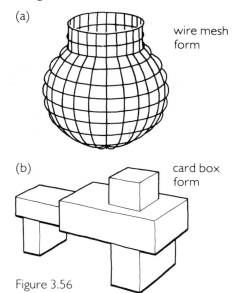

(a)

wire mesh form

(b)

card box form

Figure 3.56

3   Polystyrene sheet

You can use a polystyrene sheet much like card. It will give a smooth, professional finish to any model you make. You can bend it using a strip heater, form it into more complex shapes on a vacuum-forming machine and bond it with polystyrene cement. Experiment with it, but don't expect perfect results immediately.

4   Expanded polystyrene

Expanded polystyrene is light and comes in a variety of shapes and sizes. It is very useful for making large three-dimensional objects quickly. You can use a hot-wire cutter to cut the foam, or it can be cut with a sharp saw or a modelling knife. You can bond it with white PVA glue.

2   Papiér mâché

Papiér mâché models are made by sticking strips of glue-soaked newspaper over a frame. You can make the frame from any suitable material, such as wire, wire mesh, blocks of wood, crumbled newspaper or cardboard boxes. Once you have made your frame into whatever shape you want to model you soak strips of newspaper in wallpaper paste until they go 'pulpy', and then lay them over the frame like a skin. Overlap and build up the newspaper strips until you reach a model that you are satisfied with. Then allow the model to dry for a few days. If you want a hard finish you can then smear plaster of Paris or paint over the surface. The final finish is really up to you. Papiér mâché allows you to build models with complex shapes and of quite large sizes reasonably easily and cheaply.

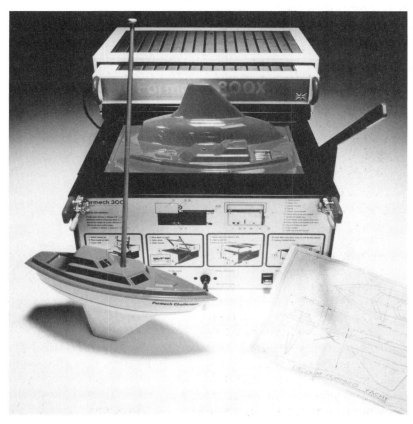

5   Balsa wood

This is a very light, soft and easy-to-work wood. It is available in different sections and sizes, and is very useful for making models of furniture. Balsa cement is used to bond it, but be careful – this cement sets very quickly. Because balsa is easy to work, you may be tempted to assume that accuracy is not important. However, small balsa models must be accurate if they are to be useful.

Balsa wood is soft and easy to work.

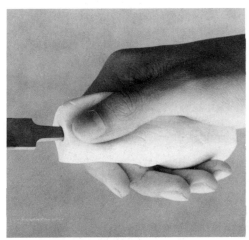

Plasticine is useful for moulds from which to make Plaster of Paris moulds.

6   Plasticine

Plasticine is a very useful medium for making quick, irregularly-shaped models. You can form it in your fingers, or with potters' tools, like those shown below. These are useful for intricate, detailed work. You should use plasticine on a non-absorbent surface so that it stays mouldable. You can make your own tools from wood, metal or plastic scrap. To make the plasticine softer and more pliable, it can be gently warmed up. When it cools it returns to its original hardness. A lot of practice is needed to make really accurate plasticine models, but as with all these materials, you can adjust your results to your skill, and can only improve through practice. Plasticine can be particularly useful in producing master moulds from which plaster of Paris moulds can be made. To make more permanent models you can use clay as a substitute for plasticine.

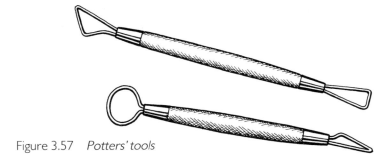

Figure 3.57   *Potters' tools*

7   Wire and rod

Wire and rod can be used to make good models of tubular, or similar, designs. Gas welding rod is easily bent, comes in different diameters and can be soldered easily. Again, experiment and practise to see what can be done with these materials.

8 Scenery

Sometimes you may need to model your designs within the environment in which they will be used. You can buy trees, shrubs and similar aids from model shops. Alternatively, you can create lots of scenic effects, such as hills, valleys, plants and trees, as well as animal and human figures with combinations of wire, wood dust and shavings, papiér mâché, plasticine, Lego and so on. The only limit is your imagination!

This model railway layout includes scenery.

9 Models which move

If your designs include moving parts, it will be all the more difficult to model them using the methods so far shown. It is much easier to make accurate working or moving models from kits than to try to make the moving parts yourself. There are useful constructional kits such as Meccano and Technical Lego which enable you to model all sorts of mechanical movements. They are quick to use and give realistic versions of design ideas.

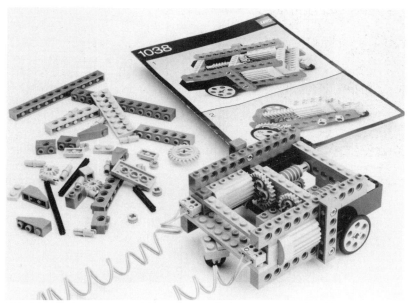

Working and moving models can be made from construction kits.

REMEMBER *models are not easy to make. You should plan what materials and tools you will need before you start, and practise as much as you can, because this is the only way you will improve your skills.*

Test yourself

1   Give two reasons for making models of your design ideas.
2   Name materials which would be suitable to make models of design ideas for: a telephone receiver; a cylindrical torch handle; a dog kennel; a park landscape to show off concrete furniture; packaging for a toy; a metal walking frame; an aeroplane food tray. Explain why you chose each material.

4
HOW TO USE
INFORMATION
WHEN DESIGNING

CONTENTS

4.1 INTRODUCTION

Designing is not all about drawing and technical skills – the things you learned about in chapters 2 and 3. At various times in all design projects you will have to find and use pieces of *information*. Investigating a new problem will involve finding facts, sorting them out and, eventually, judging them. In major projects there may be so many facts to deal with that you have to reduce or summarise them before you can really grasp them. When you have made your design you will have to judge how well it performs. This will also involve finding, sorting out and judging facts. There are many ways to help you handle this information. This chapter will introduce you to some of them.

When you have studied this chapter you should be able to:

1 understand some basic methods of handling information;
2 choose suitable methods for your own project work;
3 know how to start looking for the information you need.

You can use the chapter in *two* ways:

1 Study it quickly until you have a general understanding of how to use information.
2 Return to it when you need help in a particular project: that is use it for reference.

4.2 HOW TO FIND INFORMATION

One of the most difficult parts of researching a subject is to find the information in the first place. You may look for information on your own or within a group, but either way you must plan your search well to avoid wasting time. The following sequence and methods of how to look for information will help you in your search.

Look in magazines for ideas.

How should you plan a search for information?

1 Identify the topic you are working on.
2 Collect together as much information as you can from nearby sources, i.e. from school or home.
3 Read as much as you can, *but set a time limit*. Make brief notes of the relevant facts and try to get a 'feel' for the topic.
4 Then decide what further information you need. Talk to your teacher about it.
5 Work out how to find this, usually more detailed, information. The following sections will show you some important methods.

How do you use the library?

Most libraries have three sections: fiction; non-fiction and reference. You will find the non-fiction and reference sections the most useful. In these two sections books are **classified** so that you can find what you want easily. Most libraries use the **Dewey system** of classification. This system has ten sections, and each section has a number range (see figure 4.1). Within the range, each book has its own number which is usually stuck onto the spine of the book. For example, a book about wood materials might have the number 674.2. Some number ranges which are important in CDT are shown in figure 4.2.

If you know the exact topic that you are interested in, you can look through the **subject catalogue**. This will tell you which books the library has on your topic. If you are looking for a particular book, and you know its title and author, you can look it up in the **author catalogue**. Both catalogues will tell you the Dewey book numbers. These numbers will tell you where the books are on the shelves. For example, the book 'Design and Form' by J. Itten has a Dewey number 707.1. You find the shelf which holds books of this number and look for the book. Ask the librarian if you get stuck.

Figure 4.1   *The ten Dewey sections*

000	General Works	600	Technology
100	Philosophy	700	The Arts
200	Religion	800	Literature
300	Social Sciences	900	History
400	Language		Geography
500	Pure Science		Biology

Figure 4.2   *Some numbers of use in CDT*

620	Engineering
643	The Home and its Equipment
645	Household Furnishings
669	Metallurgy
671	Metal Manufactures
674	Wood Technology
678	Plastics Technology
690	Building
730	Sculpture
735	Modern Sculpture
736	Carving
739	Art Metalwork
740	Drawing
747	Interior Design
749	Furniture
760	Graphics
770	Photography

How can I get information from books quickly?

First you must be sure about the kind of information you want. If you have chosen a reference book, read the instructions on how to use it. Otherwise use the table of contents and the index carefully to find the topics that you are interested in. Make notes of the facts which are *relevant*, but do not waste time copying whole passages unless they are definitely needed. Always make a note of the book's details in case you need to find it again, e.g. 'Nature as Designer' by B. Bager kept at 581.3 in the public library.

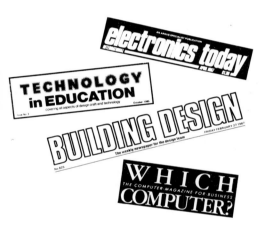

What about magazines?

There are many magazines and journals in libraries which you may find useful. They are usually kept on a stand in the reference section. Back copies will be on the shelves, so ask the librarian if you need them. The best way to look for the information you want is to use the contents page. 'Scanning', or quick reading, of articles is another way to try to find the information you want.

What if the information is not in the library?

Sometimes you may not find exactly what you need in the library. Then you may have to interview or write a letter to someone who knows the facts, or you may have to observe the problem yourself, or even set up an experiment.

How can you interview people?

You can interview people by asking them a set list of questions which you and your teacher have prepared, or you can be more informal and chatty. You should write down or tape record the responses that you get and the facts that you learn. Always be well prepared and polite. Do not waste people's time by asking vague questions, and do not try to force people to answer your questions if they do not want to.

What about letters?

You may need facts which only a company or other organisation has. Then you may have to write a letter to them. Only write to someone if you have clear questions to ask. A vague letter will get a vague reply, or no reply at all! Write to a named person if you can find out beforehand who the person most likely to be able to help you is. Lay out your letter in a businesslike way. Have your letter checked by your teacher, and typed if possible. Keep a copy yourself and enclose a stamped addressed envelope for the reply. Here is an example.

```
                              Craft, Design and
                              Technology Department
                              Holbroody School
                              Jamesham   JS6  8GB

                              12/1/87

Director of Research
Bradwin Adhesives Ltd
Tortonly  TL1  2DZ


Dear Mr Smith

     I am researching into the design of
children's sledges.  I want to laminate
layers of 2 mm thick hardwood using your
X1-3B Resin to form the sledge runners.
Could you please tell me how the strength
and durability of this resin are affected
by snow and freezing temperatures?

          Yours faithfully

          B. J. Skipton

          B J Skipton
          (5th form pupil)
```

Have you ever observed this problem?

How can you observe?

The facts you need may only be available where the design problem is. You may then have to go out and make your own observations. This can take a lot of time. There are two stages in observing:

1 watching the behaviour or problem;
2 recording the facts and thinking about (analysing) them.

For example, consider the problems of opening shop doors. If a customer is carrying bags, pushing a pram or using a walking stick, all sorts of problems crop up. One way to find out what they are and how often they arise would be to watch the shop for a given time to see the ways people open the door, and then record these ways in different categories, using the sort of chart shown in figure 4.8. See section 4.3 for more details.

What about experiments?

The only way to find out certain facts will be to run your own experiments. For example, you may have been given some scrap materials with which to make a lot of outdoor containers. You do not know how these materials will stand up to rain. It may be necessary to set up an experiment with samples of the scrap material exposed to rain for a period of time. This will tell you whether or not the material meets your needs. In experiments, you must decide exactly what information you need before you start. Work out how to find and measure the information and then interpret your results. For complex experiments you may get help from your science or social studies teachers. Time spent planning your experiments will always save you time later on.

Test yourself

Copy the following passage into your notebook and fill in the missing words.

FINDING INFORMATION

When I need to find information for a project I must carefully _____ my search. The library is often a useful place to start. Here, books are _____ in the Dewey system. This means that books are placed in one of _____ sections. Each book has a number belonging to its section. I can save time looking for the book I want by using either the _____ or _____ catalogue. If I cannot find the information I need in the library I can _____ people, observe them, write _____ to them, or even carry out _____.

Try the following exercises

1 Use your school or public library to find the following information:
   a the names and qualities of five plastics which can be used outdoors;
   b ways of making metal surfaces flat;
   c standard measurements for dining furniture.
2 Write letters to relevant organisations to get information about:
   a methods of polishing a new material;
   b gaining permission to place concrete street furniture outside your school premises;
   c gaining entry to a playgroup to observe children at play.
3 Work out a sound method of finding out the problems young pupils face when using certain hand tools in your school workshops.

4.3 HOW TO REPRESENT INFORMATION

Sometimes facts do not mean very much unless they are arranged in a special way. Representing information carefully can make it easy to see just what the facts really mean. Here are some useful ways of representing information in CDT.

Suppose that your class has made some benches for the school playground. You have asked 100 pupils to sit on these benches and tell you whether they were *comfortable*, *fairly comfortable* or *uncomfortable*. Suppose that a group of 26 found the benches comfortable, a group of 59 found them fairly comfortable and the remaining group of 15 found them uncomfortable.

How can you present these numbers so that the size of each group shows up clearly?

Sets of numbers like that given above can be shown very clearly in **charts**. Here are three types of chart that you can use.

The bar chart uses heights on a bar to show the size of each group.

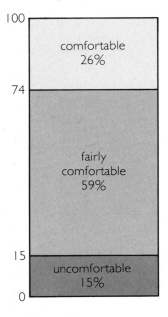

Figure 4.4

The horizontal bar chart makes comparisons between the groups easy, but does not show the total number of people in each group as clearly as the bar chart does.

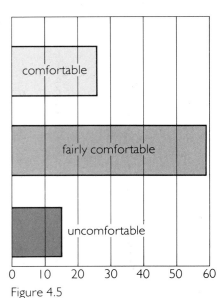

Figure 4.5

The pie chart shows the groups as segments of a circle. The full circle represents all the groups, i.e. the 100 pupils. Therefore 100 pupils are shown by the 360° that there are in a circle, and any group of pupils is shown as a percentage of 360. The 'fairly comfortable' group of 59 pupils makes up 59% of the total. Now 59% of 360° is 212°. Therefore this group has a segment on the pie chart of 212°. The other segments are worked out in the same way.

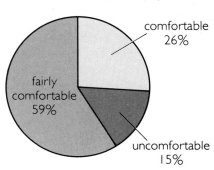

Figure 4.6

How can you represent more complex sets of facts?

The three charts shown on the previous page can show certain facts very clearly, if the facts belong to just a few groups. However, some projects may need a lot of facts which may belong to a lot of groups. Suppose you measure the heights of 50 young children. You may end up with the heights shown in figure 4.7.

Figure 4.7

99	100	96	102	100	104	99	96	105	99
100	97	96	101	98	100	103	100	103	100
98	101	100	99	98	101	100	98	103	101
99	104	98	98	97	97	100	99	97	103
101	101	99	96	101	96	101	101	98	105

Make a frequency distribution chart
This table of numbers does not mean very much as it stands. To produce a clear picture in your mind you can arrange the numbers in a **frequency distribution chart**. On the chart each height is represented by a 𝍷. When you get up to 𝍷𝍷𝍷𝍷, instead of going on to 𝍷𝍷𝍷𝍷𝍷, you strike through the 𝍸. This now represents five children. The heights in figure 4.7 are shown much more usefully in the frequency distribution chart in figure 4.8.

When using this sort of chart to analyse the sort of information described on page 70, about supermarket doors, you must choose your various frequency headings very carefully to give you any useful results.

Figure 4.8

96	𝍸	5
97	𝍷𝍷𝍷𝍷	4
98	𝍸 𝍷𝍷	7
99	𝍸 𝍷𝍷	7
100	𝍸 𝍷𝍷𝍷𝍷	9
101	𝍸 𝍷𝍷𝍷𝍷	9
102	𝍷	1
103	𝍷𝍷𝍷𝍷	4
104	𝍷𝍷	2
105	𝍷𝍷	2

Can complex sets of facts be represented even more clearly?

A frequency distribution can be shown graphically on a **histogram**. A histogram is a set of rectangles. Each has the same width, but their different heights show the frequencies of what you are measuring very clearly. The numbers from figures 4.7 and 4.8 are shown in a histogram in figure 4.9.

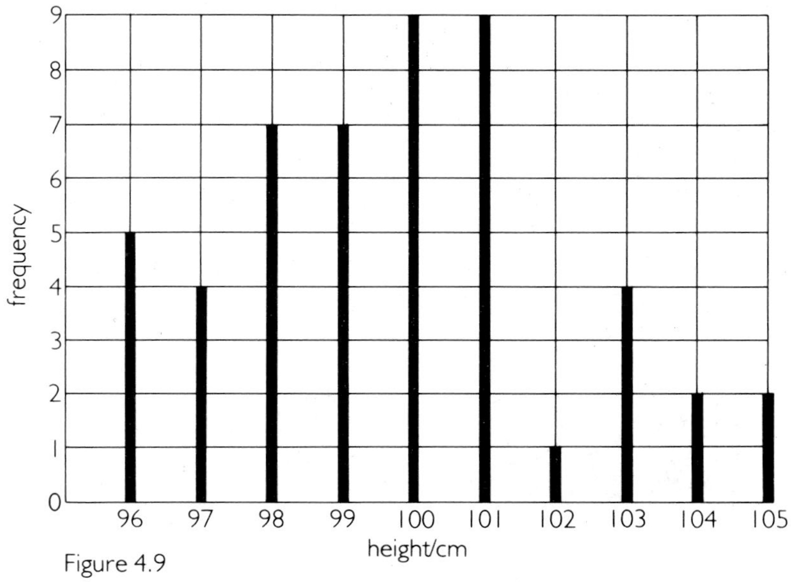

Figure 4.9

How can we represent facts which vary?

When the facts you collect vary in time, e.g. a temperature range or the elongation of a material being tested, they can be represented on a graph. The time axis will be horizontal. The graph then shows the values of your variable at different points in time. The areas between the points can be estimated by joining up the points on the graph. Figure 4.10 shows a graph of a material being tested for creep.

Graphs can also be plotted without a time axis. Figure 4.11 shows the change in impact strength of polypropylene as its temperature rises. Impact strength is plotted against temperature. On these graphs you have to control the variable that is shown on the horizontal axis very carefully to get any sensible results.

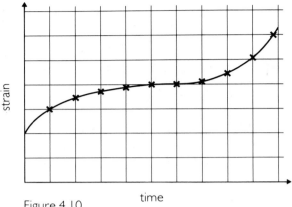

Figure 4.10

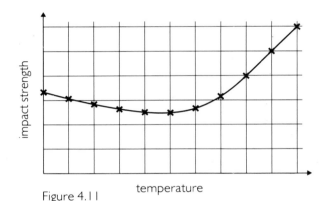

Figure 4.11

Test yourself

Copy the following passage into your notebook and fill in the missing words.

REPRESENTING INFORMATION

If I represent facts carefully, it is easier to see what they really _____. I can represent groups of numbers in _____. There are _____ kinds of simple chart: the _____ chart, the _____ bar chart and the _____ chart. If there are lots of numbers involved, I can use a _____ distribution chart, or a histogram. If the facts I am representing vary at all, they can sometimes be shown on a _____.

Try the following exercises

1 Find a simple object made from three or more materials. Estimate the proportion of the object made from each material. Represent your results in a bar chart, a horizontal bar chart and a pie chart. How effective is each chart in showing the facts quickly and clearly?

2 Choose a body measurement you might need for a design project, e.g. knee height. Find a sample of 30 people and measure them. Represent your results in a table, a frequency distribution chart and a histogram. How effective is each in showing the facts quickly and clearly?

3 Carry out a material strength test. Choose a variable such as the area of cross-section. Test the strengths of samples with different areas of cross-section. Draw a graph of your results with the area variable along the horizontal axis. How effective is the graph?

4.4 HOW TO REPRESENT OPERATIONS

Not all of the information that you will have to show people will consist of numbers. You may want to describe operations or processes, such as why you chose a particular metal to make a garden chair. In these cases *flow charts* are very useful. Flow charts show the steps in an operation, with each individual stage shown by a symbol. They can help you to represent and organise a complicated process in an easy-to-understand way.

A **flow chart** is a method of breaking down a process into its constituent parts and writing it down in the order that you did it. Each operation and decision is shown, along with the possible choices available to you at each stage. It gives a very clear picture of the entire problem, and can be used either to describe an operation that you have done or to understand an operation that you are going to have to perform.

 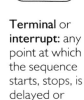

Terminal or **interrupt:** any point at which the sequence starts, stops, is delayed or interrupted.

Process: any kind of process, function or operation.

Decision: any point at which a decision has to be made from a number of alternatives.

Modification: any change in the process.

Figure 4.12

What are the main flow chart symbols?

The main flow chart symbols and the operations that they describe are shown in figure 4.12.

Figure 4.13 shows an example of a flow chart to describe the process of making a line bend on a sheet of acrylic.

Try the following exercises

1 Choose a simple process of working a material, e.g. cross-cutting a board of wood. Draw a flow chart to show the main stages in the right sequence.

2 Draw a flow chart of how you worked through a recent design project.

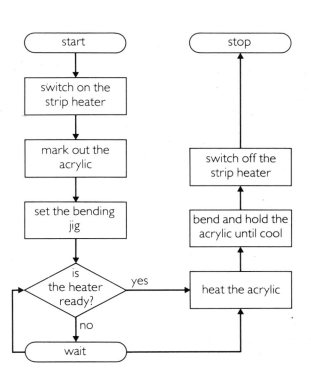

Figure 4.13

4.5 HOW TO WRITE REPORTS

As well as the quick ways of recording information that you have already looked at, there are times when you will have to provide more detailed information about parts of your design projects. You can do this by writing a *report*. There are two main times when you may need to write a report in CDT. These are when you are collecting facts in investigating a complex design problem and after you have tested the design you have made. In both cases, your report will be much better if you follow the guidelines given below.

How can you write clearly?

A report is a statement of fact for someone to read and understand easily. You should represent your facts as simply as possible through the use of words and illustrations. You can also use other aids, such as tape or video recordings if these will help you – but do not use them just for the sake of it. You should avoid using long-winded words or expressions and only record what is relevant, as people don't have time to read irrelevant facts.

Look at the two sentences below and say which you think is the best and why.

The tube container held all the tubes neatly, securely and with no waste of space.

During the final testing process it was found that the device designed and made to contain these tubes actually held all the aforementioned tubes in a way which was at the same time neat, secure and economical of space.

What is the report for?

Before you start to write, decide on the report's exact purpose. This will guide you in **a** the kind of facts you will include, **b** the amount that you will include and **c** how you will present the information. This is called setting the **terms of reference** of the report.

How should you arrange the report?

When you have collected and sorted out all your facts arrange the report under the following headings:
1 the purpose of the report (terms of reference)
2 a summary of the facts
3 conclusions
4 recommendations for future action.

Before writing the report out finally, weed out any irrelevant or incorrect facts. Go over your conclusions and recommendations to see how sensible they are. Never be afraid to change your opinions or admit that you have been wrong in the light of the information that you have found, as this is the point of collecting it in the first place.

Test yourself

Copy the following passage into your notebook and fill in the missing words.
WRITING REPORTS
I may need to write a report firstly, when _____ a design problem and secondly, after I have _____ a design solution. In my reports facts should be written clearly and simply. I can write the report under four headings:
a _____
b _____
c _____
d _____ .

Try the following exercise

Write reports on:
a a recently completed design project, including detailed conclusions on how far your solution solved the original problem;
b the performance of any one tool in your school workshop;
c an investigation into the behaviour of a certain kind of pet which needs a new cage;
d the value of this chapter in helping you to handle information.

REMEMBER *time spent planning your report, as with all methods of presenting information, will save you time in the long run and will lead to a much better end product.*

5

HOW TO DESIGN
FOR PEOPLE

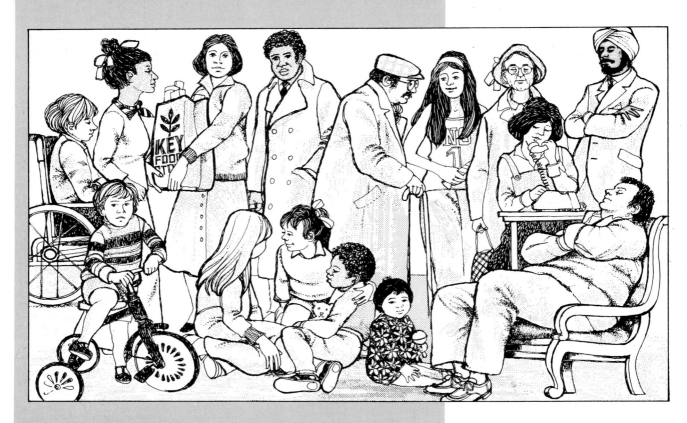

CONTENTS

5.1 INTRODUCTION

Most of the things you make will be used by people. Imagine trying to design a chair or a suit if you had never seen what people looked like! People are much happier if they can use things easily, in comfort and safety. If it is possible to use things like this they have been well designed, or, to say this more accurately, they have been designed for people. This chapter shows you what to think about when you are designing for people.

When you have studied this chapter you should be able to:

1 work out ways of finding out people's sizes;
2 recognise how important body movements are in designing;
3 design things which are suitable for the people who will use them.

You can use the chapter in *two* ways:

1 Look up individual topics to help in your designing.
2 Study the whole chapter to give you knowledge for future designing.

Comfort

The chairs we sit on need to be comfortable. They must be of the right size, shape and springiness. They should not have dangerously sharp corners or edges.

Have you ever sat for a long time in a chair which is too low? Or have you had to sit on the back seat of a car which did not have enough leg room? When was the last time you rode a bicycle with a seat which was too high? Have you ever had an aching back caused by bending over a low work bench for a long time?

Safety

These questions are about your comfort. But what about your safety? Have you ever cut or scratched yourself with a sharp-edged toy? Until a few years ago, it was possible to buy wooden toys which were finished with lead-based paint. When young children sucked these they became very ill. The toys had not been *designed for people*. Many things are designed and made with faults like these. This chapter will help you to avoid such faults in your designing.

5.2 THE HUMAN BODY

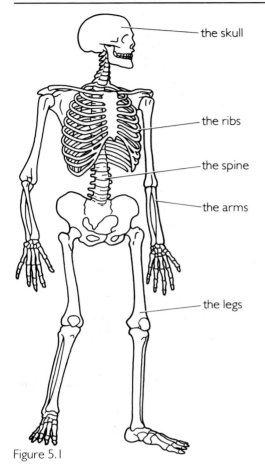

Figure 5.1

The human body is built around its skeleton, which is made up from the five parts shown opposite. You must keep all the parts of the skeleton in mind when you are designing things for people.

When you are designing you must think about the comfort and safety of each part of the body. Each part is important for different reasons.

The head
The head holds the brain and the major sense organs – the ears, the eyes, the mouth and the nose.

The spine
The spine holds the body upright. It also holds the nerves which channel signals to and from the brain. These signals control the way our bodies move. Find someone who suffers from back ache, and ask them about the problems that they face in using everyday objects, like chairs and desks.

The arms and legs
The arms and legs are limbs which help us to do things like move, hold things, lift things, use tools and so on. The arms in particular are important ways of controlling things. You have to try to design things so that you keep your arms and legs as comfortable as possible, even when they are not being used.

Bones and muscles
Many of our bones are hinged together so that they can move. They move when our muscles **contract**, or shrink, and **relax**. Our muscles make these movements when they are told to by the brain. You want to design things both to keep people's muscles comfortable, and to allow them to operate to their full potential.

So, you can see, there are various parts and functions of the body that have to be considered. When you are designing an object for people there are two main factors to think about:

1   the sizes of the people who will use them;
2   the movements they will make.

Sections 3 and 4 of this chapter deal with these factors.

Ergonomics and anthropometrics
There are names given to the study of designing for people.
1 Ergonomics – this is studying ways in which objects, systems and environments can be made suitable for people to use efficiently.
2 Anthropometrics – this is the science of measuring people.

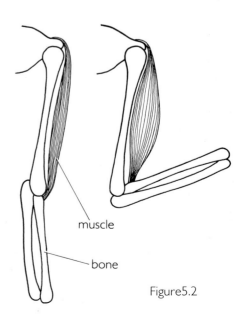

Figure5.2

5.3 BODY SIZES

The human body comes in all sorts of shapes and sizes. People can be short or tall, thin or fat, light or heavy. Some people may have long legs, others may have short legs. Children grow into adults, and some adults get fat! Women are different from men. Because body sizes vary, you will sometimes need to find out sizes in your design work.

Table of average sizes (mm)		
	Men	Women
Height	1730	1600
Sitting height	915	815
Buttock to back of knee	483	457
Lower leg length	419	394
Buttock width	356	368

The easiest way of finding out body sizes is to look them up in a **table**. Whilst this can save a lot of time, tables do not always give all or the exact information that you need. In many cases you will have to measure people yourself. Look at the design problem below. It will give you an idea of how to measure people, and how to use the measurements you make to help you in your designing.

A design problem

You are going to fix a shelf to a corridor wall. It must be above the heads of those people who will pass by. But it should be as low as possible so that items can be easily reached. Before starting to build the shelf you should:

1 Find out who uses the corridor.
2 Decide whether you can measure all of these people, or just a few of them.
3 Decide who will do the measuring.
4 Devise a way of accurately measuring people's heights.
5 Either measure all the people, or a sample chosen at random.
6 Record the heights.
7 Decide whether to place the shelf above all of these heights, or just above a certain number of them. Remember, the higher you place the shelf, the more difficult it will be for the shorter people to reach things. As an alternative you may place the shelf low enough for most people to reach and expect the 'giants' to bend.

Person	Height (mm)
1	1841
2	1606
3	1599
4	1991
5	1423

You can't please everybody!

Many of the things that we buy, like clothes, come in a range of shapes and sizes to fit different people. But very large or very small people often have to have clothes specially made for them. This is because so few are needed that it is not worth setting up factory production to make them. In the example on page 81, one person was taller than 1900 mm. Everyone else was smaller. In this case you may decide to fix the shelf lower than 1900 mm to make it easier to reach items on it. Those few people who are taller than 1900 mm will simply have to bend down a little when passing by! It is often not possible to *satisfy everyone's needs* when designing for groups of people. A **compromise** may be necessary. In this case, the few people who are taller than 1900 mm will have to bend a little so that the many shorter people are able to reach things on the shelf easily. There may also be a few people who are too short to reach the shelf even at this height.

What methods of measuring can you use?

Some methods of measuring are shown in the drawings opposite and the photograph below. You may have to invent your own measuring method. Whatever method you use, you must follow the *basic rules* of measuring. If you are going to use a ruler or a tape measure you must make sure that the markings, or **graduations** are in close contact with what you are measuring. If the ruler is thick you must position your eye directly over the required graduation. If you have time, take more than one reading of each measurement. If possible, get someone to help, as this may help to remove any error. Make sure that you are measuring exactly the part of the body with which you are concerned, and are measuring it in the way that is most useful to you.

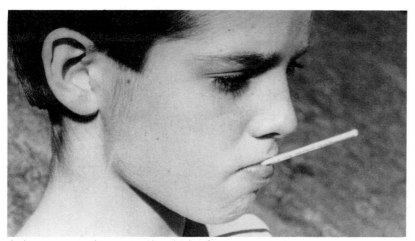

A thermometer is a measuring device for temperature.

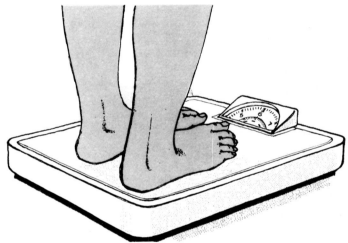

Different ways of measuring people.

Try the following exercises

1 Read the problem on page 81 and then think about a new coffee bar which is to be fitted in a leisure centre. Customers will stand at the bar. Work out a way of finding a suitable height for the bar. Use the procedure given in the example.

2 Devise a way of accurately measuring the length and width of people's hands for glove fitting.

3 Outline how you could try to find a range of heights for an ironing board which could be used widely by adults.

4 Find out what measurements are needed to design a well-fitting pair of spectacles. Devise a way of accurately finding out these measurements for a range of people.

More notes on body measurement

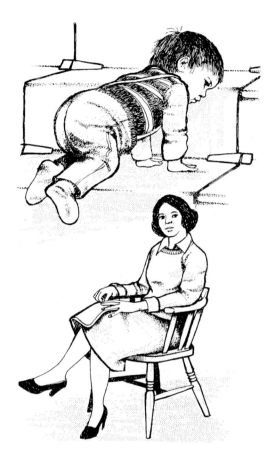

Individuals

You have already read about the many ways in which people differ. Sometimes this does not matter, e.g. when producing an individual piece of equipment for someone, or a dress for a particular large person, or an aid for a child with a specific handicap. You simply determine the person's needs, make the necessary measurements and proceed to design.

Groups

When designing for more than one person, however, the problem is more complex. This is even truer when you are designing for a large group of unknown people, such as customers who will buy a finished product in shops.

Identify the target population
In the case of designing for a large, unknown group you must identify the **target population**. You must think carefully about the type of measurements which are relevant to your designing. Make sure that you do not confuse these with irrelevant measurements. You could measure:
a all of the target population; or, if this is too large,
b measure **samples** from the population.

Work out your measurement range
In either case, you can then work out:
a average measurements; or
b a range of measurements from the smallest to the largest; or
c a range of groups, e.g. 'small', 'medium', 'large'.

Measurements should be taken several times on each person to increase accuracy. Better still, more than one person should do the measuring. This will take longer but the results should be more *reliable*.

How ro record your measurements
A **histogram** is one useful way of recording your measurements (see page 73). It will give you a clear picture of the distribution of the various measurements that you have made. The example opposite will illustrate this.

Example: School Home Economics room worktop

The problem
Imagine that you had to arrange for a worktop to be installed in your home economics room. Many people will have to use this worktop. Assume that the best height for the worktop is the one shown opposite. How do you work out this height? A number of decisions have to be made.

Decision 1
How do you measure the height to the elbow? You could stand each person in the working position and take a number of measurements from elbow to floor with a tape measure held vertically. For extra accuracy, someone else could repeat the measurements.

Decision 2
Who do you measure? If there were only a few users the answer would be measure everyone. However, if, say, five hundred people worked in the room it might be impossible to measure them all. You would have to decide how many you could measure and then choose a **sample** from the whole group. If the sample were not **representative** your results would be useless. For example, if by accident your sample included all of the short pupils and few of the tall ones, your measurements would be biased towards the short pupils. You would then place the worktop too low. Statistically, you can reduce this possibility by **a** making a **random** sample choice and **b** by measuring as many potential users as possible.

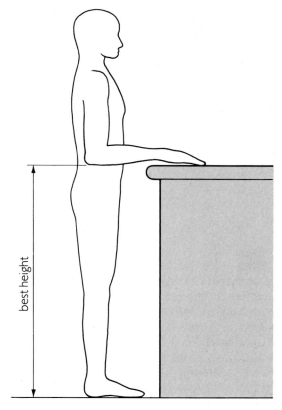

Figure 5.4

Decision 3

How do you record the results? You could use a histogram, as shown opposite. This can give a very clear picture of the distribution of heights of the sample that you have measured.

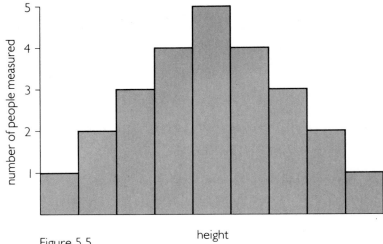

Figure 5.5

Decision 4

How do you interpret the results? The ideal solution would be to make an adjustable worktop. But assuming that other design requirements prevent this (e.g. cost, storage space below the worktop and so on), what can you do? If you install the worktop for the '520 mm person', all the others will find it uncomfortably low and may even get back ache. Similarly, if you place it high enough for the tallest people, the short ones will have to stretch and will develop muscle fatigue.

In designing this is a very common problem. If you cannot develop an adjustable solution, the simple compromise is to satisfy the **average** person. In this case the worktop height would be 560 mm. This is known as the **mean** height of the sample. The tallest and shortest people will be uncomfortable but the majority of users will find it satisfactory. You will find that many design problems have to be solved with a **compromise**. All you can often hope to do is to accommodate as many people as possible.

Scientists and designers working in the fields of anthropometrics and ergonomics (see page 80) use more sophisticated versions of these ideas. They also use quite complex statistics.

5.4 BODY MOVEMENTS

When you are designing for people you must remember that they can, and will, move in many ways, both voluntarily and involuntarily. If you bear these movements in mind you will improve your designing. If you don't, people will find it very difficult to use your designs.

When you design you must aim to make:
1 equipment and objects of the right size and shape for people to use; and
2 spaces large enough for people to move about in.

How do we move?

The human body contains over 200 different bones. These are sometimes fixed firmly to each other, and are sometimes connected by moving joints. There are two different kinds of moving joint. Some can **flex**, like the elbow and finger joints, and others can **rotate**, like the shoulder and hip joints.

This section deals with those movements which are of most interest to designing, i.e. those of the head, arms and legs.

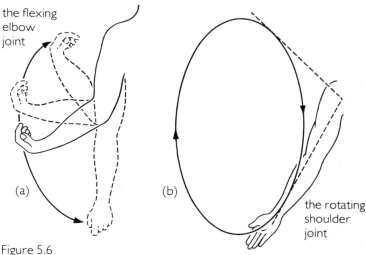

Figure 5.6

How does the head move?

The head can move in the directions shown below. The eyes can swivel even further than this, so your range of vision is greater than your range of head movement.

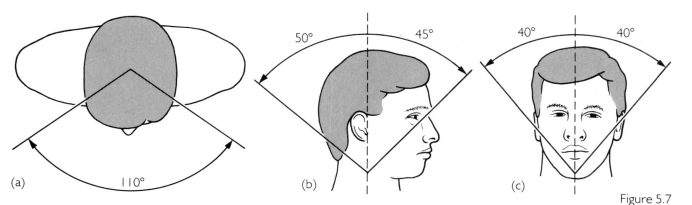

Figure 5.7

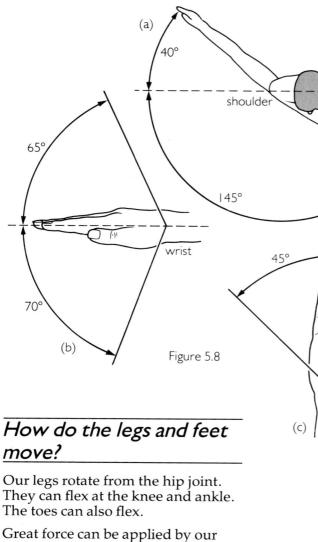

Figure 5.8

How do the arms and hands move?

The arms and hands have a very wide range of movement. Because of this they are the most useful parts of the body for doing things.

At the shoulder the ball and socket joint has the widest range of movement of any joint. At the elbow the arms can flex, and can also rotate. The hand can flex at the wrist. The fingers can flex at the knuckles. When all these are combined, many movements are possible.

How do the legs and feet move?

Our legs rotate from the hip joint. They can flex at the knee and ankle. The toes can also flex.

Great force can be applied by our legs. They are not as good at complex movements as our arms; they are not very good, for example, in the use of delicate machine controls. But they are excellent for heavy jobs, such as digging with a garden spade, or pressing car pedals.

Some possible leg and foot movements are shown opposite.

Sketches like these may not give you all the information you need for particular design work. Sometimes you may have to make your own study of body movements. The following is an example of how you can do this.

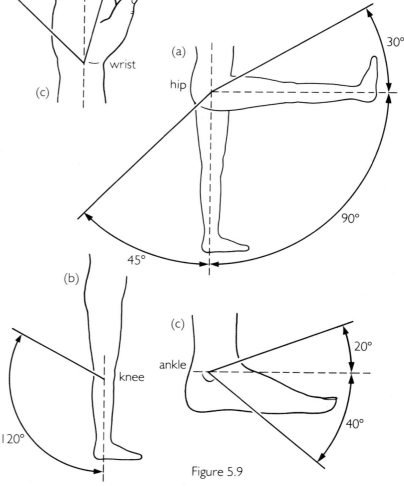

Figure 5.9

Example: A worksurface

A group of individuals sit upright in front of a worksurface. They have to use many objects on this worksurface. They need to be able to reach them quickly and without stretching. You need to find out the lowest, highest and average arm reach of this group. How would you go about it?

1 Find out which people use the worksurface.
2 Decide whether you are going to measure all of the people or just a representative sample.
3 Attach a large sheet of drawing paper to the worksurface, directly in front of where the people work.
4 Draw a vertical line down the centre of the paper.
5 Place the chair in position; mark this position and make sure it is the same for every person in your sample.
6 In turn seat each person in the chair.
7 The person draws two arcs across the paper, one with the left hand and one with the right. Both arcs start on the vertical line. The person must not stretch, but must have fully extended arms, as is shown in figure 5.10.
8 Identify from the paper the shortest, longest and average reaches.

Consider the 'best' radius for the positioning of objects round the worksurface. Allow all, or a specified number, of the people to reach them without stretching. Try to do this whilst leaving as much clear working space as possible in front of the seated person.

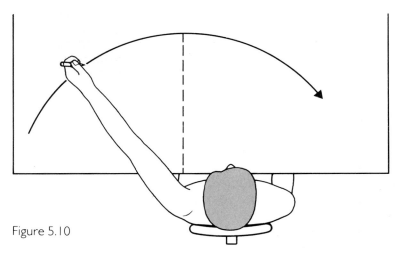

Figure 5.10

Try the following exercises

1 Design a brush which a bather can use to scrub all of his or her own back.

2 Investigate some of the ways in which handicapped people without the full use of their legs can move around unaided by others.

3 A pedal-driven toy is to be made for four-year-old children. Devise a strategy for finding out a range of minimum and maximum pedalling movements for the legs of children of this age.

5.5 HOW TO DESIGN FOR PEOPLE'S BODIES: SOME EXAMPLES

Since the different parts of people's bodies move in different ways you have to design everything specifically for the task it is supposed to satisfy. This involves taking careful measurements of particular areas of the body. Some examples are given below.

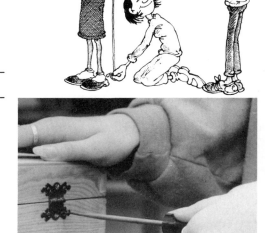

I Grip

The hand is capable of a great deal of movement. It can also vary between delicate control and applying great pressure. Many objects have handles which do not fit the hand well. Usually, the hand can adapt to use them fairly effectively. Sometimes, however, objects have to be used with great hand power, in which case their handles need to be very carefully designed.

The screwdriver is a good example of a tool that often has to be used with a great deal of power. Try to get hold of as many screwdrivers as you can and you will see that there are many different types of handles used on them. The best are those with a lot of contact between the hand and the handle. You can see this from the following experiment.

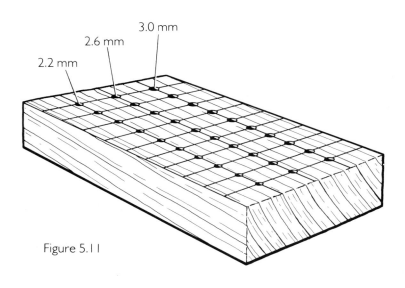

Good grip is important when using a screwdriver.

How can you find out how the power of a screwdriver is affected by the area of contact between the hand and the handle?

To do this experiment you have to find two things out about a number of different screwdrivers. Firstly, you need to find out the area of contact between the hand and the handle of the screwdriver. Secondly, you have to find out the power of each screwdriver. To set up the experiment you will have to find a few screwdrivers of the same blade size but with different handles. Also find some *washable* paint and a brush, some clay, some graph paper and some No. 8, No. 10 and No. 12 steel screws. Take a piece of *even-grained* hardwood and drill pilot holes of the right size for the screws, i.e. 2.2 mm, 2.6 mm and 3 mm respectively.

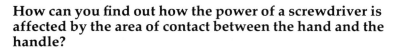

2.2 mm   2.6 mm   3.0 mm

Figure 5.11

How can you find out the area of hand to handle contact?

1 Paint the screwdriver handles one at a time with water paint.
2 Whilst the paint is still wet grip the handle tightly, as if you were tightening a difficult screw.
3 Uncurl your hand and place your flat palm down onto a sheet of graph paper. This will leave a print of the area of hand to handle contact. Wash your hand and the handle.
4 Repeat this for all the screwdriver handles.
5 To work out the contact area, count the number of graph paper squares covered by the paint.

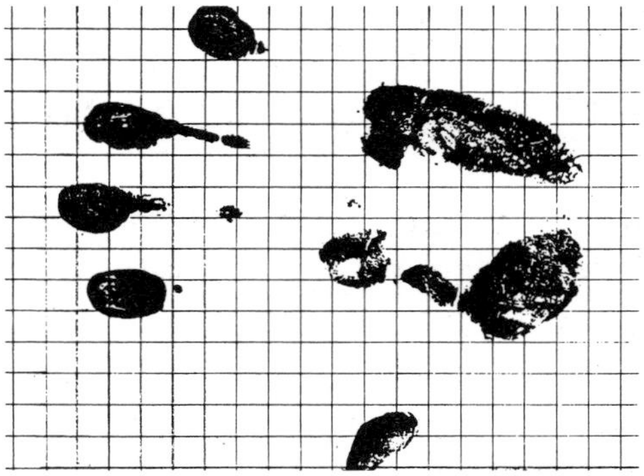

Figure 5.12

How can you find the power of each screwdriver?

1 Take each screwdriver in turn and drive a No. 8, a No. 10 and a No. 12 screw home into the correct pre-drilled pilot hole. Drive them as far into the wood as you can with one complete twist of the screwdriver.
2 Measure the distance from the screw head to the top of the wood to find out how deep you have been able to drive it.
3 Record the heights of the screw heads above the wood. You could use a histogram for this.
4 Also, use a five-point scale to rate each screwdriver on how easy you found it to use.

Figure 5.13

Compare your results with the hand to handle contact results. What relationships can you detect?

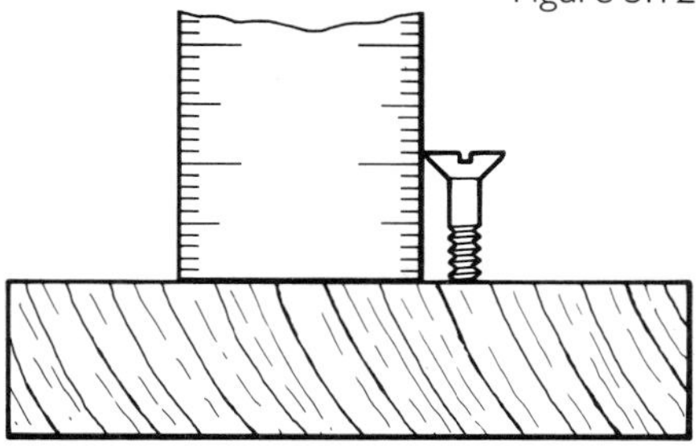

Figure 5.14

	very easy	easy	moderate	difficult	very difficult
1	✓				
2			✓		
3			✓		
4					✓
5				✓	
6		✓			

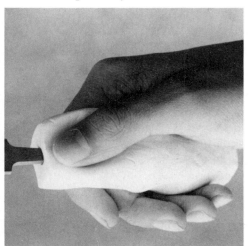

You could model a handle in Plasticine before making a mould.

How can you use this knowledge?

You can use the knowledge gained from the experiment to design a new screwdriver handle. You can use clay or Plasticine to try out different ideas for the form of the handle. Try to satisfy the two following needs:

a produce a high hand to handle contact area;
b ensure that the handle is not limited to one kind of grip.

You can devise ways of testing the handle. The tests will be more effective if you actually make up a working prototype from your model. You could use a plaster of Paris mould to produce a polyester resin handle. Alternatively an aluminium casting could be made. These could be attached to steel tool blades and tested for power in the way already described.

You can use this kind of approach for other design problems which are based on hand grip, e.g. handles for doors, pans, brushes, bags, pens, wheelchairs, control devices and so on.

2 Seating

People sit down in a number of ways and for a variety of reasons, like writing, resting and watching TV. When sitting people change positions often to stop parts of the body getting too tired. A good chair design will allow people to move about like this.

Seats can be badly designed in a number of ways. Seat A is too high. The front of the seat presses into the back of the thigh at X. The thigh is not meant to bear a lot of weight and will soon get tired.

Seat B is too low. The legs either slide forward or the body has to crouch. Both positions soon become uncomfortable.

Seat C is too long. Either the sitter has no back support or has to lean back too far. Both positions can cause back ache.

An unusual seat!

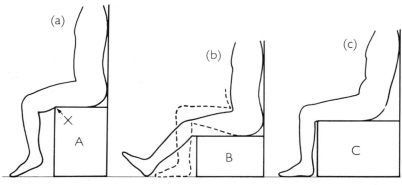

Figure 5.15

How can you decide upon seating size and shape?

1 First you must decide exactly what the seat's purpose is. An easy chair will have to be very different from a desk chair.
2 Then you must take measurements of the relevant parts of the body (see below).
3 In complex cases you should use a test rig, or prototype model, to test your design.

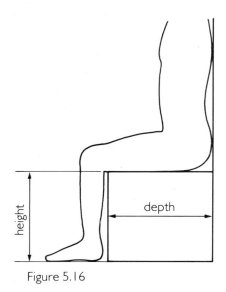

Figure 5.16

What needs to be measured?

1 **Seat height** depends upon the distance between the lower heel and the back of the knee. In adult men there is a range between about 370 mm and 470 mm. For women the range is 355 mm to 455 mm. Therefore, overall the range is between 355 mm and 470 mm. An ideal solution would be a seat with an adjustable height. If you cannot make this, a reasonable height for, say, a dining chair would be between 390 and 420 mm. The ideal height would be lower for an easy chair.

2 **Seat width** is not so critical, unless the chair has arm rests. The seat needs to be wide enough to hold the spread of the buttocks. It must also allow for small changes of position. For long periods of sitting a minimum width is 435 mm.

3 **Seat depth** depends on the distance between the back of the knee and the buttocks. The minimum for adult women is about 405 mm and the maximum for an adult man is about 505 mm. A common work chair seat depth is 380 mm, which will be suitable for both men and women.

4 **Seat angle** usually slopes down towards the back of the chair.

5 **Seat hardness** needs to be soft enough for comfort but firm enough to support the body. For short periods of sitting the seat can be hard, but for longer periods some sort of padding has to be provided.

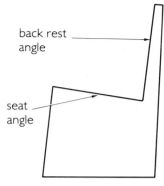

Figure 5.17

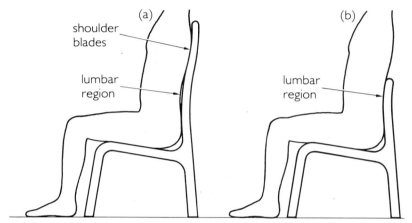

Figure 5.18

6 **Back rests** are generally used for chairs in which a person is to be seated for more than a short time. A rest which tilts backwards is more comfortable than a perfectly upright rest. The angle of tilt varies.

A leisure chair will tilt more than a work chair, for example. Why do you think this is? A good back rest will support both the lumbar region and the shoulder blades. For working chairs, the shoulders are normally free and only the lumbar region is supported.

How are these seats designed for their purpose?

Try the following exercises

1 Find as many different kinds of chair as you can. State their main purpose. Try them out, measure their height, depth, angle and so on and describe how successful you think they are.

2 Find an adjustable chair. Study it until you understand how it works. How could you improve the design?

3   Equipment and furniture

There are countless pieces of
equipment and furniture which
have to be designed to suit people.
This book is not long enough to give
all the sizes you might need when
designing. Often you will have to
find out the sizes for your own
design projects, so the example
below shows a way of doing this for
a piece of kitchen furniture.

Is this sink at a comfortable height?

How can you find out the best height for a kitchen sink?

Sink height is very important. Have
you ever thought about it as you
were washing dishes? If the sink is
too high you have to stretch, and
this can make you tired. If it is too
low you have to bend, and this can
cause back ache.

We do not usually expect a kitchen
sink to fit one particular person
only. More than one person
normally uses a sink. These people
will probably be of different sizes,
but it is not practical to have a
kitchen sink which can be moved up
and down. The most obvious
solution is to find a height which
most people find comfortable.

How can you do this?

1   Collect a washing-up bowl,
    dishes and a dish mop.
2   Choose a sample of people to
    test.
3   Do the following for each
    person. Get two people to hold
    the bowl (without water in it!) at
    different heights in front of the
    person being tested. This person
    then pretends to wash the dishes
    and decides how comfortable
    each height is. In this way, find
    the *lowest* height at which the
    dishes can be washed in comfort.
    Also find the highest.

4 Do this with all the people in your sample and plot your results on a chart. This will then show the range of sink heights which all users will find comfortable.

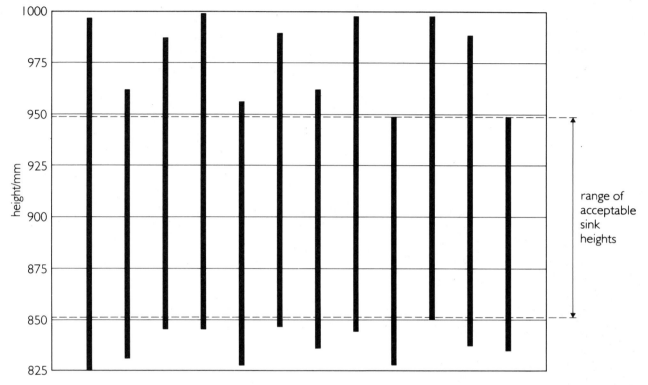

Figure 5.19

As you can see, ideal working heights will vary. When no one height is suitable for all the people involved, choose the lowest acceptable height. A lower worktop is usually less uncomfortable and less dangerous than a higher one. For worktops like those in a kitchen, elbow height is most comfortable. If the person needs to use lots of force, say whilst chiselling on a workshop bench, a height lower than the elbow is best to give the user the leverage that he will require. Here are some dimensions which will be useful. Remember, however, that often you will need to make your own measurements from your own sample group.

Item	Minimum height	Maximum height
Door	1880	1980
Reaching up	1525	1675
Kitchen worktop	840	870
Craft worktop	760	790
Table/desk top	740	760

4   Room layout

There are many different kinds of
room in many different types of
building, such as houses, schools,
offices and factories. Most of these
rooms have to cater for more than
one activity. Sometimes one activity
gets in the way of another. For
example, young children jumping
and running about may make it
impossible for adults to listen to
music. Therefore, rooms often have
to be designed to allow different
things to go on at the same time.

When solving design problems concerned with room layout
you first have to find out exactly what goes on in the room.

How you can find out what activities go on in a room?
1   Choose the room you are going to study.
2   Choose a method of finding out the activities that take
    place in it. You could watch and make notes, either for a
    long, continuous period or for a number of short periods
    of time, or you could ask others to do the same. You
    could ask people what they do in the room, or what they
    know goes on there, or ask them to take notes of
    everything that they do and any problems that they come
    across in doing these things.

3   When you have done this you can see if the activities
    have anything in common. You should be able to place
    them in groups, with each group holding similar kinds of
    activity. For example, in a living room there might be:
    a writing, sewing, reading, model-making;
    b watching television, talking, playing the piano;
    c playing on the floor, playing table tennis;
    d moving around, cleaning.

When you have grouped the activities, you will be in a better position to decide what furniture is really needed, how it will be used and how it should be arranged for maximum efficiency.

There are no simple ways of accommodating activities which interfere with each other. Sometimes equipment for multi-purpose use can be designed to help, or sometimes the room layout can be changed. There are no hard and fast rules other than that in most cases you are wise to plan each room individually. Below and opposite are some common layout sizes for household activities. For other activities you can carry out your own investigations, and try to plan your own layouts.

(a) making meals

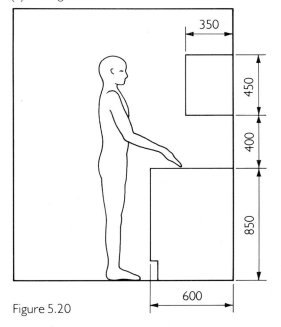

Figure 5.20

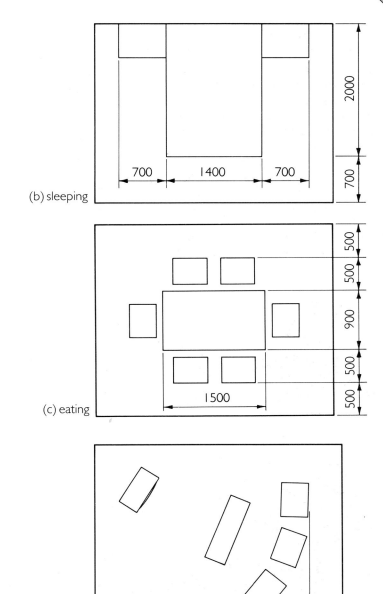

(b) sleeping

(c) eating

(d) watching TV

Try the following exercises

1 Design a room layout which will permit all of the following: using a computer; doing homework; eating; engaging in quiet hobbies like sewing and model-making.
2 Choose a room you know which is used for activities which interfere with each other. Suggest ways in which the conflicts could be reduced or eliminated.

5.6   VISION, COLOUR AND LIGHTING

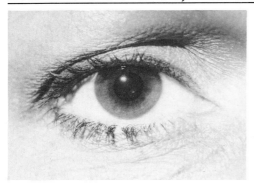

Most activities require you to see what you are doing. Therefore your eyes are very important to you. They send information from your surroundings to your brain. The brain can then use this information to control your actions. So the way that people can see in a room is very important to them. You are going to look at three things which influence this: vision, colour and lighting.

I   Vision

Your eyes can move over a large field of vision (see page 87). You can get a lot of information in this way. Sometimes you have to take in a lot of information very quickly, for example when riding a bicycle through a busy town.

In such cases it is easier for the viewer if the information has been well displayed. Information can be displayed in a number of ways, such as by indicators, readouts, labels, direction signs, display panels and gauges.

How to design displays

When designing such displays, you must pay special attention to:

a   how clear the visual elements are;
b   whether the symbols you use will be readily understood or will have to be learned;
c   the speed at which people will have to read them;
d   who will have to read them;
e   what information they will contain.

A car dashboard displays a lot of information.

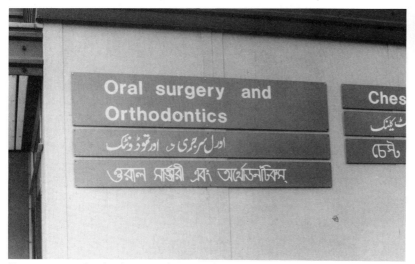

Signs may need to be in more than one language.

Try the following exercises

1   Design a signposting system for visitors to your school.
2   Design a signposting system for visitors to a large public building in a town centre.
3   Evaluate motorway signs from the point of view of a non English-speaking driver.

2 Colour

Colours such as yellow, orange and red can create a sense of warmth in a room. On the other hand, colours like blue, grey and green can give a sense of coolness.

Narrow, long rooms appear wider when the side walls are pale and the end walls dark. Dark colours absorb light and seem to move inwards, so large areas of dark colour can make rooms seem smaller. Illusions can be used in various ways to make apparent improvements to the shape and size of rooms.

Colour can also have a strong unifying effect. It can be used to split a room into areas with different functions or to unify an awkwardly-shaped room.

Lighting affects colour

The colour of an object depends on two things: its **pigment** and the **light in which it is viewed**. The type of lighting used has a great effect on the way you see colours. A green light shining on a red pigment will make the object appear black because all the light has been absorbed.

Colour creates mood

So, you can see that, although people may not always think about the colour of rooms, colour can be used to give certain effects and to create the right sort of mood for the activities that take place in a room. Hospital wards are often painted yellow or orange because these colours are meant to give a soothing effect, whereas operating theatres will be white or pale blue to give a cool, clean appearance.

Dark colours absorb light. They make a room seem smaller.

Bright colours reflect light. They make a room seem larger.

3 Lighting

Our ability to see an object is affected by:

1 the amount of light falling on the object;
2 the contrast between the object and its surroundings; and
3 the absence of fierce dazzling light.

When designing a lighting system you have to take these factors into account.

Sources of light

The amount of light shining on an object or room will depend on where the light is coming from. There are two sources of light:

1 **Natural light** (daylight) comes through windows, doors and skylights. The larger the opening the more light there will be. In this country openings which face southwards, towards the Sun, get more light than those facing in other directions.

2 **Artificial light** from standing lamps, ceiling or wall lights, candles, fires, televisions and so on. Most artificial light is now from electrical sources. The amount of light given off depends mainly on the number of light sources and their electrical power.

We can only see objects when they appear to be distinct from other objects. You can ensure this **contrast** by using different colours, shapes, angles and textures of objects in a room. For example, when two objects are of different colours they reflect light differently and you can tell them apart.

Glare

This is caused mainly by strong sunlight beaming directly through windows at a low angle. It can be very annoying as it reduces vision, as you will know from watching television under these conditions. Its effects can be reduced by curtains or blinds. Moving to other parts of the room whilst the Sun glares is also possible. What might stop you from moving a television to another part of the room? How could you solve this problem?

How to choose the right lighting

Different activities will need different *levels* of lighting. For example, sewing or model-making may need more light than writing, and writing may need more than watching television.

Different activities will also need different *types* of lighting. For example, sewing or model-making may need a **spotlight** whereas watching television may be more pleasant with a **diffused** light.

When designing household lighting you need to consider the following factors.

1 What activities will take place in the room?
2 What levels and types of lighting will these activities need?
3 How can natural and artificial light be used to support each other?
4 Which walls, areas and surfaces of the room will need particular levels and types of light?
5 Where are the electrical sockets? Can more be fitted?
6 And, of course, how much money can be spent to provide the lighting?

Bright lighting in a shopping arcade.

This tiny tungsten spotlight is economical and does not heat up like ordinary lamps.

Test yourself

1 Name *two* sources of light.
2 How can you ensure *contrast* between the objects in a room?
3 State six factors to consider when designing lighting for the home.

Try the following exercises

1 Design an electrically-powered light source which can be varied to provide two or more of these kinds of lighting: general, directional (spot), diffused, coloured and moving.
2 Design a table lamp which can give out variable levels of lighting.

5.7 HOW TO DESIGN FOR SAFETY

People's bodies are remarkable. They can do the most complicated jobs and can adapt to many different surroundings, but they do have limitations. There are many dangers for people in everyday activities and it is very important for them to be safe from these dangers. You can increase safety by careful designing.

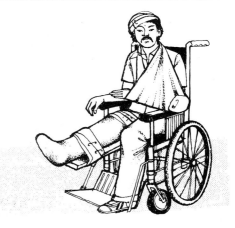

There are many ways in which careful design can help to ensure people's safety. Whenever you design anything you need to consider possible accidents. Some consequences of accidents are:

bruises;   falls;   suffocation;
burns;   injury;   swallowing;
collisions;   poisoning;   trapping.
cuts;   skin irritation;
electric shocks; slipping;

Accidents in the home are commonly caused by poor design in the following:

fire guards;   trailing wires;   shelves;
floor surfaces;   toys;   electrical goods.
lighting levels; stairs;
loose mats;   handrails;

You can reduce the chances of accidents by good design. Pay particular attention to:

strength;   moving parts;   hot surfaces;
durability;   surface finish;   electricity;
wear;   sharp edges/   combustible materials.
balance;   corners;

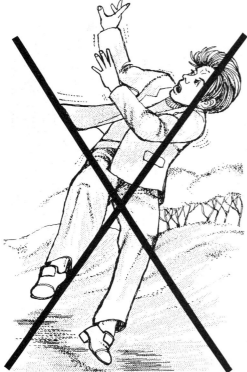

Example: How can workshop layout improve safety?

If you observe a workshop being used you will recognise a pattern of activities. You will probably notice:

1   lots of movement between various areas of the room, such as the sink, worktop and acid bath. You can record the frequency of these movements on a plan view of the workshop. In the plan opposite each line represents one movement from one part of the room to another;
2   objects which may be hot, sharp or heavy have to be carried round;
3   people have to stretch and bend to reach things;
4   people get in each other's way;
5   many activities need bright lighting.

You should carry out an analysis of the movement and activity that goes on in a room yourself. When you have analysed the activities you may notice that certain of them require more effort than they need to. For instance, in the above example there may be a lot of movement between the sink and the acid bath. If this is true then perhaps they ought to be closer together. Some items used a lot may be stored on high shelves. It would make sense to store these where they can be reached more easily. Try this with your own school workshop and then redesign the layout to reduce the chances of accidents occuring.

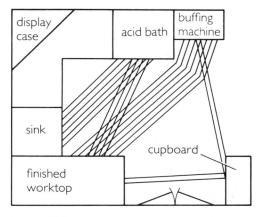

Figure 5.21

Try the following exercise

Take some of the following and for each one make a list of their dangers and suggest ways of overcoming them: roads; cars; playgrounds; bathrooms; classrooms; gardens; cycling; ironing clothes; playing with toys; carrying shopping; power drills; staple guns; sewing machines; rocking chairs and tents.

Which of these two children's slides is the safest?

5.8 HOW TO DESIGN FOR GROWTH AND AGEING

People change in many ways as they get older. The quickest changes take place in childhood and adolescence. After this comes a period of little change during early adulthood and then, during middle and, in particular, old age another period of rapid change takes place. These changes have to be designed for.

How should you design for children?

As children grow older they become more mobile. They also develop skills and get better at manipulating things. You need to watch them to find out what they can do, and that they can't get hold of anything which could hurt them.

Children change shape as they grow. This is because some parts of the body grow faster than others. For example, the head grows very quickly in early life. The brain reaches 80% of its full size before the child is five years old.

Make your designs flexible

When designing for children do not simply scale down adult measurements. You have to measure children of the age in question to know what shape to make things. You will also have to recognise that variations in body size are greater in children of a certain age than they are in adults. They also grow very quickly! Your designs, therefore, may have to cover a wide range of shapes and sizes, and be much more flexible than designs for adults. Young children also do not understand about how fragile things are, so you will have to design things that much stronger for them.

You may need to consider growth or ageing in your designs.

What about adolescents?

During adolescence the physique of boys becomes very different from that of girls. The differences are visible in height, shoulder and hip widths, breasts, and bone and muscle size.

When designing for growing people it is essential to make your own observations and measurements. This will help you to take account of the variations that develop.

How to design for old age

Ageing is gradual: it is difficult to see when it starts. In old age joints become less movable and bones get weaker and more brittle. If they break they take longer to heal: accidents can therefore be extra serious for an ageing person.

Older people slow down and their mobility and flexibility are reduced. They tend to stoop and find it more difficult to hold their bodies erect. Higher work surfaces and seats can help – they cut down the need to bend. As ageing reduces strength people find it more and more difficult to grip things.

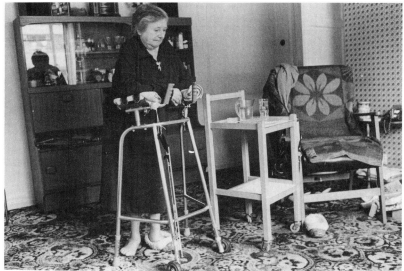

A walking device.

Special aids

The lives of older people can be made more comfortable and dignified by the design of special aids to help them overcome their problems as they arise. Some examples of such aids are:

1. aids for walking on the ground or upstairs;
2. mobility aids for people who cannot walk;
3. gripping devices, e.g. tap and can opener handles;
4. special seating which makes it easier for people to get out of chairs and stand up;
5. alarm and communication systems;
6. trolleys to carry things like shopping or luggage;
7. access to storage cupboards;
8. exercising equipment.

One old person's problem is likely to be very different from another's. It is extra important, therefore, for you to observe, measure and discuss specific problems before attempting to design and make solutions. If you can arrange it, talking to medical experts and social workers can be very enlightening. This may be possible if your school or college runs a community service scheme. If not, ask your teacher how you might get into contact with such people.

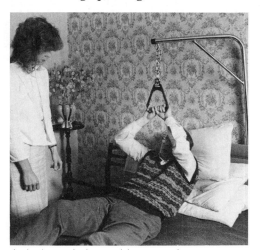

A device to help an old person sit up.

A gripping device.

Try the following exercises

1. Talk tactfully to an old person to find out what difficulties they have in doing things at home.
2. Make a list of these problems.
3. Work out design ideas that might solve these problems and sketch them clearly.
4. Discuss the ideas with this old person and find out his or her opinion of them.

5.9 HOW TO DESIGN FOR PEOPLE WITH SPECIAL NEEDS

Children and old people have their own special needs, but there is another group with quite striking special needs. In this group are people with all sorts of disabilities. They have design problems of a very special nature which require special thought and care in trying to solve them.

You probably know someone who is disabled. People can be disabled in three ways: emotionally; mentally and physically.

Often a person may be disabled in more than one way. More people than you probably realise are disabled. They can be born disabled, or suffer disabilities through illness or accident.

Everyone needs the skills of the designer in helping with their life. Disabled people need extra help beyond this. They need chances to join in with 'normal' life. They need to get involved and do the sorts of things that other people can do quite naturally. Sensitive and thoughtful design can make very big improvements to the life of a disabled person.

Stevie Wonder is blind.

How can you design for people with special needs?

To design aids for disabled people needs very careful study. You must try hard to understand disabled people's *feelings* as well as their *physical needs*. It is essential to make your own special study before attempting to design anything for a disabled person. This would benefit greatly if you could get advice from medical or social workers.

On the next page are some examples of ways in which design can improve the lives of disabled people.

A disabled person may still take part in sport.

1 Signposting

The international symbol of accessibility to buildings for disabled people is shown opposite. Many public buildings are now being adapted so that disabled people can use them. To show people what facilities for the disabled are on offer, signposting systems are needed. A signposting system should:

a show suitable entrances, routes and lifts;
b show cloakroom and toilet facilities;
c advertise special services in the building for disabled people.

Figure 5.22

> **Try the following exercise**
>
> Take a building you know and design a signposting system which shows:
>
> a directions to a particular room, e.g. the cafeteria;
> b the location of the room;
> c information about what the room contains.
>
> Use the international symbol of accessibility where appropriate.

2 Water taps

For people with weak or disabled hands a normal screw-down water tap can be very difficult to use.

For such people a 'lever-action' tap fitting is much easier to use. There are various kinds. Each gives good leverage when the tap is being turned.

(a)

screw-down tap

(b)

single lever-action tap

(c)

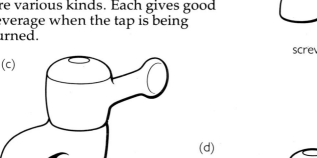

quarter turn lever-action tap

(d)
constant spray lever-action tap

Figure 5.23

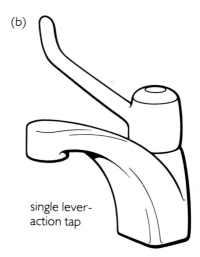

> **Try the following exercise**
>
> Get permission to use a wheelchair. Describe the problems you face in trying to use a bathroom wash basin from the wheelchair. In what ways can design overcome or remove these problems?

6
HOW TO DESIGN
FOR FUNCTION

CONTENTS

6.1   INTRODUCTION

In chapter 5 you saw that you must always consider people's needs in the design process. Sooner or later, though, you will have to concentrate on the actual product or system that you are designing. The product or system will have a *function*, or a set of functions. In this chapter you will look at the idea of function, and think about the function of things that you are designing.

When you have studied this chapter you should be able to:

1   understand the meaning and importance of 'function';
2   work out functions that your designs must perform;
3   work out the functions of existing products or systems, and judge how well the systems perform.

You can use the chapter in *two* ways:

1   Study it closely as a unit — it will help you to think clearly about function.
2   Do the exercises from time to time to get practice. As you progress through the course your thinking should get clearer — try to judge how much this is happening.

What is function?

Quite simply, the function of something is the way that it does its job. Being clear about function is one of the most important parts of your designing activity.

Try the following exercise

Examine a pen and think carefully about its function. Write down as many of its functions as you can think of.

'To enable me to write' will probably be your first answer to the exercise given above, as it was mine. What about the importance of these other functions, though?

To deliver the right amount of ink to the paper.
To prevent the ink leaking.
To prevent the ink drying up.
To show how smart or well off you are.
To act as a straight edge when you cannot find a ruler.

Also, what about the things you do with the pen which the designer perhaps did not intend, like fiddling with it, or tapping the desk top when you are bored? Even a product as simple as a pen can have numerous functions, as well as unintended uses!

6.2 LOOKING AT EXISTING FUNCTIONS

This section is very short. If you are to benefit from it you will need to do a lot of thinkinng. You will need to think specially carefully about those familiar objects which you take for granted, and all of the ways that you use them without thinking about it.

On the previous page you saw that a simple pen can have quite a few functions. Now consider the chair shown opposite.

The chair is in my study. At first sight its function seems to be to allow me to sit comfortably whilst working at my desk. For most of the time I use it like this.

At other times, when I tidy up, it becomes a surface on which I rest my books for a while.

Often I have to reach high for a book. The chair then becomes a kind of ladder on which I stand.

When we have lots of visitors, the chair is taken into another room and used for all sorts of things, like sitting at the dining table.

On occasions, I have found my cat sleeping on it!

It has even been used to support sheets so that my small children could pretend that they were playing inside a tent!

This list could go on and on. The important point, however, is that *the things you design may have more than one function.* Some of these will be more important than others. In this case you will need to list them in order of importance. My list above shows the six functions of my chair in their order of importance. *Sometimes functions will be in conflict*, and then you have to decide which function to cater for. If I stand on my chair wearing wet shoes the seat will get too dirty to sit on. Conflicts of function are a big problem in more complex design projects.

Try the following exercises

1   Take each item listed below in turn and make a list of all the possible functions you can think of. Also make lists of any possible uses for the items which you think were not intended by the designer.
   Comb; eraser; nail; oil painting in a gallery; paper clip; saucer.

2   Take three of your lists of functions and place the functions in order of importance.

3   Look again at each list. Try to identify functions which conflict with each other.

6.3 HOW TO MAKE FUNCTIONS CLEAR

You have had a chance to think about the function of existing products. You should now be able to sort out the functions that your designs will have to perform. Here are two examples of how to do this.

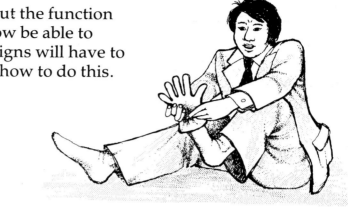

1 Play

A single parent lives in the country. Getting to the shops involves a long, slow bus ride. Two young children usually have to be taken on this bus ride, and they often fidget, argue and create a great deal of noise. The other passengers are often disturbed by this. The parent needs to find some way of reducing the arguments and noise.

Make a list of functions

I think you will agree that the need here is quite clear: the children have to be occupied. Imagine that you have been asked to design a product which will fulfil this need. What will its function be? How about these?

1 To stop the children arguing and making a noise . . .
2 by attracting and occupying them on the bus . . .
3 separately or together . . .
4 in ways which are safe . . .
5 busy and interesting . . .
6 and preferably help them to learn . . .
7 and be compact and portable enough for the parent to carry it along with the shopping.

Once you have listed these functions you can put them in order of importance. As you go deeper into the design project, more functions may spring up. Include them in your list. Sometimes you may find it helpful to think up separate design ideas for each function and then combine them in your final design to best satisfy the complete problem.

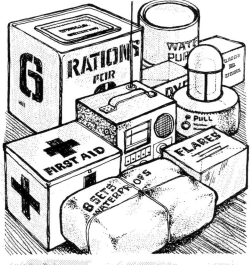

2   Survival at sea

An adventure-holiday group has bought a sea-going ship. The ship contains a lifeboat. If the ship begins to sink all the crew will have to board this lifeboat and live there for a time until they are rescued. In the panic of a ship sinking the crew will not be able to take all the things they might need onto the lifeboat. Therefore the ship's owners have decided that the lifeboat will be fitted with a permanent survival kit.

What will the survival kit's function be? The simple answer is *to save life*! However, this depends on whose lives are to be saved, under what conditions and for how long.

1   Suppose that the boat would carry up to six people for a week in cold, wet and stormy conditions. What would these people need under these conditions? The first step in clarifying the functions of the survival kit would be to make a list of these needs. It might include food, drink, warm and waterproof clothing, medicines and first aid equipment, a signalling device or radio, evacuation of body waste and so on. A main function, then, would be to *contain these items* so that they could be *used effectively* in the lifeboat.

2   If the designer left it at that, though, it probably would not help anyone very much in an emergency. The kit must not only contain, but it must *protect* its contents. It must therefore be *waterproof*, *strong* and *well laid out* inside.

3   As it will be carried in a lifeboat it will also need to be *compact* and *light*. Perhaps it would need *to float* just in case it were washed overboard and had to be pulled back.

4   If the kit were to be useful in stormy conditions, it would have to be as *simple as possible*. Cold, tired and possibly injured crew would not be able to handle a complex device with stiff locks. It might need a built-in light so that its contents could be seen. Its location in the boat would also affect its usefulness in an emergency.

5   Furthermore the kit would need to be *secure* and *reliable* for long periods when it was not in use. It would also need to be *checked* and *refilled* at regular intervals.

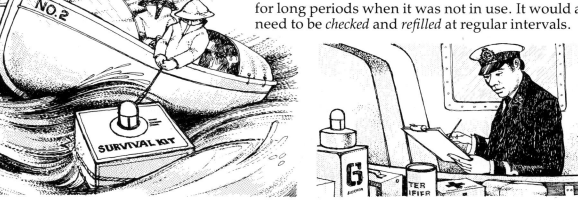

Draw a bubble diagram

This all adds up to a complex list of functions. It may help you to get a clear picture of all the functions by sketching them out. One way of doing this is to use a **bubble diagram**. This will also help you to see which functions are in conflict; for example, making the kit light and unsinkable may conflict with including all the items needed for survival.

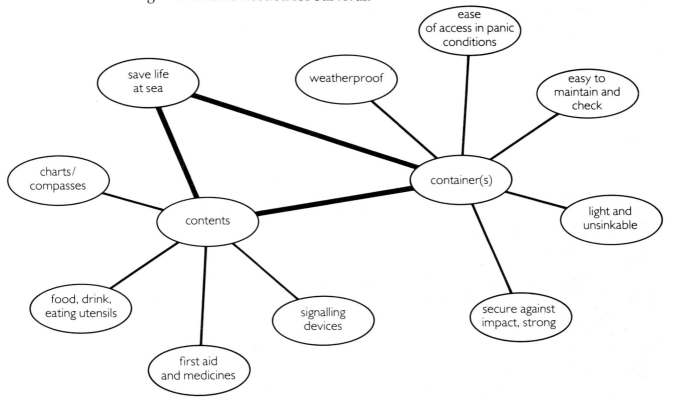

In this case, being clear about function is a matter of life and death. As you work through such a complex project new functions may spring to mind; or you may see the original functions in different ways. If this happens you must build the new ideas into your bubble diagram. At first you will probably find it convenient to design for each function separately. In the end, however, you must consider all the functions together if you are to produce a design which works. As soon as you are clear about the function(s) needed, you can write them up as design targets. Re-read section 2.4 to remind yourself about these.

Try the following exercises

Each situation below contains a need which might be satisfied by a specially-designed product or system. For each one, make a list of the functions which would completely fulfil the need.

1 Opening a can whilst camping.
2 Enabling visitors to announce their arrival at a house.
3 Watering window plants.
4 Carrying a baby.
5 Shopping from a distant supermarket.
6 Birds eating newly-sown seed.
7 Dispensing adhesive tape in a busy office.
8 Keeping fish in an outside garden.
9 Slicing bread with one arm in a sling.
10 Helping a dog warden to catch stray dogs.

7

HOW TO DESIGN FOR APPEARANCE

CONTENTS

7.1 INTRODUCTION

In your everyday life, you take a lot of things you see for granted. Some of these things may please you, or look attractive; some may displease you, or look ugly. Appearance does depend a lot on personal tastes and opinions. In designing, however, you have to think very hard about appearance. You need to simplify what you see, and break it up into parts that you can examine. This will make it easier for you to develop your own attitudes to appearance. Many of the objects that are made do not look very attractive. This chapter will help you to produce attractive designs.

When you have studied this chapter you should be able to:

1 recognise what makes up the appearance of things;
2 design things which look attractive;
3 make up your own mind about the appearance of the things you see.

You can use the chapter in *two* ways:

1 Study the whole chapter to give you knowledge for future designing.
2 Look up individual topics to help in your designing.

This demolition site is not aesthetically pleasing!

There are two names given to the study of appearance. They are:

1 **Aesthetics** – this is the study of the nature of beauty.

2 **Visual** – this describes things that we can see.

You should think about both of these when looking at something to assess its appearance.

7.2 SOME ELEMENTS OF APPEARANCE

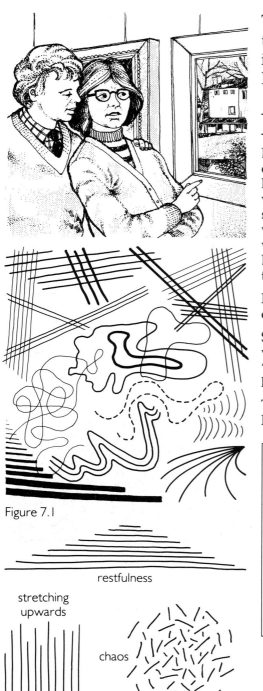

Figure 7.1

The idea of appearance is a big one. It will help you to understand the idea to break it up into smaller ideas. You can then think about these separately. Here are some of the main elements of appearance.

1 Lines

Lines are the basic elements you use when you try to organise a representation of an object. Individually, however, lines do very little. In fact, lines do not even exist very often in real life. Much of what you see is made up of shapes rather than lines. However, in designing, lines are very useful. Most of your drawing will consist of lines, which you have to join and link together to create shapes. Learning to use lines to create certain appearances is therefore important.

Firstly, you need to consider the many types of line that you can use. Figure 7.1 gives some examples of these.

Secondly, lines can be used to organise space into things that we recognise. They can also be used to create certain 'feelings'. Figure 7.2 gives some simple examples of how lines can be used to represent feelings.

Thirdly, lines can be used to organise space by enclosing it. In this way, **shapes** and **forms** are created.

Try the following exercises

1 Draw patterns using as many different kinds of line as you can.

2 Make pattern designs using one from curved lines, straight lines or radiating lines.

3 Use lines to create the following feelings: relaxation; confusion; fear; anger; continuity.

4 Make line patterns on materials using some of the following: a plough plane; a saw; dowels; veneers; etching; scribing lines on acrylic.

---

restfulness

stretching upwards

chaos

distance

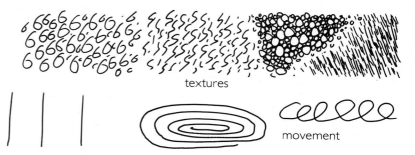

textures

movement

Figure 7.2

2   Shape

A shape is an area enclosed by lines. It is two dimensional and has a length and a width, but no thickness. There are many possible shapes.

Free shapes are not governed by any rules. The number of free shapes you can draw is limitless. When looking for ideas, a quick way to trigger them is to draw straight or curved lines at random and fill in any interesting shapes which are produced (see figure 7.3).

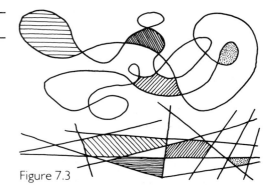

Figure 7.3

Natural shapes occur all around us. Plants, animals, people and landscapes are all rich sources of ideas for shapes. **Man-made shapes**, like cities, buildings and structures, are another rich source of design ideas.

Geometrical shapes are regular shapes, and are very important in designing. A great deal of the man-made environment has been created from such basic shapes, some of which are shown in figure 7.4.

When a number of shapes lying in different planes intersect they produce **forms**.

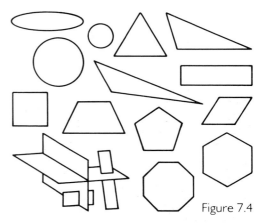

Figure 7.4

Try the following exercises

1   Cut some geometrical shapes from paper, e.g. circles, squares and triangles. Cut each shape into parts and rearrange the parts in as many interesting ways as you can. Make drawings of some of them.

2   Make patterns with similar shapes which are of different sizes and draw some of them.

3   Create geometric shapes by one or more of the following methods: cutting sheet metal or veneer; boring into wood; cutting sections of tube and bar. Make drawings or take photographs of any that you think are interesting.

A Henry Moore 'free form' sculpture.

3   Form

A form is three dimensional, whereas a shape is only two dimensional. Like shapes, forms can be found in nature, the man-made environment and in geometry. It is also possible to create free forms. Some examples of forms are shown in figure 7.5.

Forms become very important to you when you are designing things, but they are often very hard to visualise. It may help you to try to break down any forms that you want to use into their component shapes, draw these, and make your measurements on them before trying to work on the three-dimensional form itself.

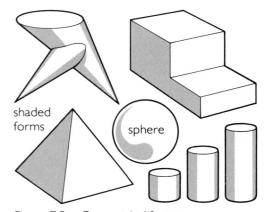

shaded forms

sphere

Figure 7.5   *Geometrical forms*

4 Colour

You can get an immense variety in the appearance of basic shapes and forms by using colour. Colour can also be used to create various illusions and moods (see section 5.6).

In section 3.5 you looked at the three primary colours – red, blue and yellow – and how they could be mixed to produce the three secondary colours, and then any other colour you might want. The colour wheel in figure 7.6 shows how the basic colours mix.

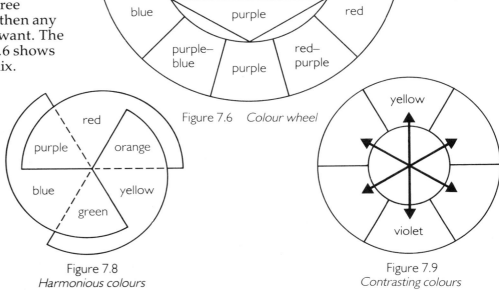

Figure 7.6   *Colour wheel*

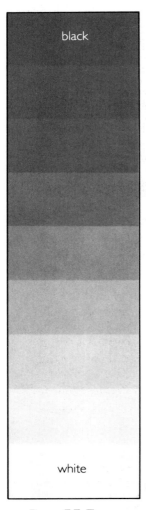

Figure 7.7 *Tones*

Figure 7.8
Harmonious colours

Figure 7.9
Contrasting colours

Section 3.5 also told you how the colours can be mixed with white or black to produce either lighter or darker tones. A tone chart between white and black is shown in figure 7.7.

Complementary colours
Colour provides the simplest and most striking way of giving a mood, or feeling, to anything. It can be used to create either a sense of harmony or of contrast in an object. Some colours relate **harmoniously** to each other. This means that parts of a design can be made to look closely related. Other colours, however, contrast with each other. These are called **complementary colours**.

Look at figure 7.8. A simple colour wheel is shown divided into three semicircles. At the centre of each semicircle is a primary colour. Immediately next to each primary colour are two secondary colours, one on either side. For example, purple and orange lie on either side of red. Colours within each semicircle are harmonious; they belong to the same family and can be used together to build up a sense of harmony in your designs. So blue can be used in harmony with green or with purple. The other colours contrast.

5   Texture

Surfaces can also be varied by the use of texture. A texture is the feeling and appearance of a surface. You can see a texture because of the differences in light and shade created by its surface relief. All materials have their own particular texture which plays a large part in how you recognise them. Metals are often smooth and 'cold', plastics smooth and 'warm', wood not quite so smooth but very 'warm' (see chapter 11). Textures can also be *added* to materials and you should look into the sort of textures that you can apply to surfaces.

You can use textures to make your designs interesting. For example, smooth can be contrasted with rough. They can also be used for functional reasons. For example, hospital equipment has to be smooth so that it can be easily cleaned.

Experiment to produce the best appearance
With all these elements of appearance you have got a huge number of possible ways in which to make your designs visually and aesthetically pleasing. You should experiment with the ways that you can change the appearance of your designs, as the more practice that you get, the easier you will find it to produce things the way that you want them to look.

Try the following exercise

Take a range of materials that you are familiar with. Experiment with ways of *changing* their surface textures. Keep a record of what changes you have made, the methods used and the effects produced. Work safely and be careful!

7.3 ARRANGEMENT

You have seen that appearance is a very personal matter. What I think is ugly, you may think is pleasing. However, there are certain ways of *arranging* things which most people find attractive. Here are some examples of attractive arrangement for you to think about.

There are various ways of giving an object a unified appearance that the eye can take in and give a pattern to. This pattern allows the brain to gain an overall feeling of the object, and thus to make judgements about it. Three ways of producing this unified appearance are through rhythm, symmetry and proportion.

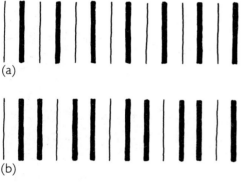

(a)

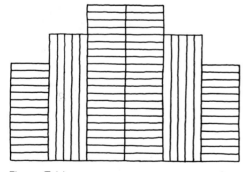

(b)

Figure 7.10

1 Rhythm

When things are repeated at intervals they are said to have a **rhythm**, and they create a sense of order. This repetition can be exactly the same, as in figure 7.10(a), or can contain only partial repetitions. Part of the pattern might be emphasised at regular intervals, missed out or modified in some other way, as in figure 7.10(b). However it is used, rhythm gives the eye a pattern to rest on, from which it can absorb other, possibly irregular, things about the object. A very good example of rhythm is in the patterns that you will often see made from bathroom tiles, or on wallpaper.

2 Symmetry

When a shape is the same on either side of a central line it is called symmetrical. Symmetry is a way of producing **balance** in an object and, again, helps to create a sense of stability and wholeness, from which more subtle details of an object can be studied.

3 Proportion

A system or object which is made up from a number of parts will have certain qualities of proportion. Proportion is a way of describing the relationship between the various parts. It is concerned with whether the relationship *looks right or not*. Of course, this is partly a matter of personal taste.

Figure 7.11

Try the following exercise

Take some of the following: a room; a building facade; a piece of furniture; a large machine; a necklace. Study each in turn and try to judge how its designers have achieved rhythm and balance. (They might, of course, not have achieved it.) Make notes and sketches of your judgements.

The golden section

However, there is a way of working out proportions for rectangles which dates back to ancient Greece. It is called the **golden section**. A golden section has a ratio between the ends and sides of 1:1.6 (see figure 7.12). The Parthenon is a famous Greek building in Athens in which golden section proportions were used, and is shown below.

Figure 7.12

The Parthenon in Athens has golden section proportions.

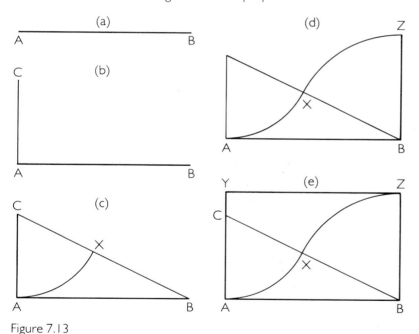

Figure 7.13

One way of calculating a golden-section ratio is to use geometry:

1 Decide on the length of the base of your rectangle and draw it as line AB.
2 Draw a line AC at right angles to AB, such that AC = ½ AB.
3 Set your compasses to length CA and draw an arc from A to X.
4 Draw a second arc from X to Y with your compass set at length BX.
5 ABZY is then a golden-sectioned rectangle.

A quicker method is to use the **Fibonacci number series**. Each number in this series is the sum of the two previous numbers:

0, 1, 1, 2, 3, 5, 8, 13, 21, 34, 55, 89, 144, 233, . . .

If you take any connected pair above 1 and 2 they will give an approximate golden-section ratio, e.g. 3:5; 13:21.

What lengths would complement each of the following numbers: 2; 21; 55?

Try the following exercise

Study a room that you are not familiar with. Judge its proportions and then measure them. What elements in the room give a sense of **a** harmony, **b** rhythm and **c** symmetry? Think about any other elements of appearance, such as colour, that have been used to produce the overall appearance of the room. Discuss your ideas with other students in your class.

4   Repetition

A particular shape can be repeated over and over again to give a form to your designs. This repeat pattern can be either regular or irregular. In a regular pattern, the basic shape or **motif** is repeated in a predictable way. However, more than one motif may be used in any pattern.

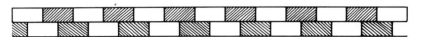

A simple way to start any regular pattern is to draw a grid. This may be made up of squares, triangles, hexagons and so on (see figure 7.14). Then you can apply a motif to the grid in any pattern that you want. Obviously, using this method of design many combinations are possible.

> **Try the following exercise**
>
> Draw some different kinds of grid. Devise a single motif which can be fitted into each grid. Produce as many different repeat patterns as you can by using the same motif in different ways.

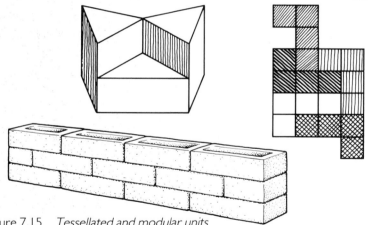

Figure 7.15   *Tessellated and modular units*

These children's playbricks are modular units.

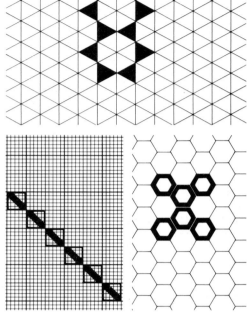

Figure 7.14

Tessellations

The idea of repetition can be developed into **tessellations**. These are geometrical shapes which interlock, often in different ways. Once you have chosen a shape you can make a **template** of it. This will allow you to draw the shape accurately over and over again.

A further extension of this idea is the **modular unit**. A module is a standardised unit, i.e. it is the same size and shape as other units. Many modern designs are built up from modules. The most common example is the builder's brick. The photograph shows an example.

> **Try the following exercise**
>
> Find examples of commercially-produced designs which are based on tessellations or modular units. Work out exactly how they fit together. Can they be rearranged in different ways?

7.4 SOURCES OF IDEAS

Ideas for shapes and forms do not spring from thin air; you have to search for them. Sometimes you can use ideas that you are already familiar with, but often you will have to look for ideas that are new to you. There are many things in the surrounding environment that you can use to try to prompt and develop your ideas. Some ways of using your surroundings to help with ideas are discussed here.

How to take ideas from your surroundings

Natural and man-made surroundings can give us a wealth of ideas for shapes, forms, rhythms and patterns. By taking forms from nature or man-made objects, and drawing them, an endless source of ideas can be created. You will need to look carefully for these sources. Plants, insects, animals, fish, rocks, buildings and collections of items are starting points. Magnified views of cellular structures, microscopic photographs of plant life and close-up views of bubbles are some examples of where you could look. Once you have found an interesting example, make detailed analytical drawings and from them develop visual design ideas. Try, for a day, to study as many things as you can while leading your normal life, and you will notice how much you usually miss, and how many ideas you get if you really concentrate on your surroundings.

Look around you for ideas about form.

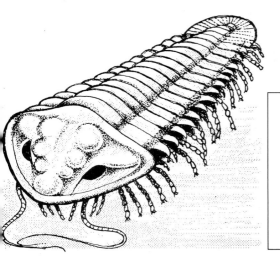

Try the following exercises

1   Find pictures of interesting patterns, shapes and forms. Alternatively, take photographs from real-life objects. Draw the elements that you find interesting and keep them for future designing.

2   Make a scrapbook in which you can collect interesting pictures. Keep adding to the book. Use it as a source of design ideas for future projects.

8
HOW TO DESIGN
FOR STRENGTH

CONTENTS

8.1 INTRODUCTION

How can you make strong objects? Imagine you were asked to design and make a really strong chair. One way would be to carve it out of a solid lump of stone or wood. This has often been done in the past. However, this way of making is not very sensible nowadays. For one thing, the materials would cost too much. A solid stone chair would also ruin the floorboards! A much better way would be to make the chair by joining parts together. This chapter is about ways of joining parts together strongly . . . it is about *structures*.

When you have studied this chapter you should be able to:

1 understand the important ideas of strong structures;
2 judge how strong a design will be;
3 begin to design strong structures yourself.

You can use the chapter in *two* ways:

1 Study it closely as a unit – it will help you understand why structures are strong.
2 Return to it whenever you need information in designing. Use the index to find the topic you need to learn about.

What is a structure?

Quite simply, a structure is an *arrangement of parts*. Of course, this could mean anything. Most objects are arrangements of parts. In chapter 11 you will read about the structures of materials. You will see that they are arrangements of parts such as atoms, crystals and cells. Here, though, the word structure is being used in a different way. You are going to look at the ways you can arrange the parts in the objects that you design to create solid structures.

Structures are designed to stand up to certain loads without distorting or breaking. What do you think causes a structure to be strong? There are four answers to this question:

1 the strength of the materials making up the structure;
2 the quality of the joints between the parts;
3 the shape of the parts;
4 the way the parts are arranged together.

This chapter is concerned with answers **3** and **4**. You will need to read chapter 11 for information on the strengths of materials.

There are four types of load which structures have to stand up to, which are described below.

Compression

This is where a load squashes objects, e.g. when you lean on a desk you put its legs under compression

Tension

This is where loads pull objects apart, e.g. when you pull a rope tight you put it in tension.

Torsion

This is where loads cause an object to twist, e.g. when you tighten the handle of a vice you put it in torsion.

Shear

This is where loads push at right angles to the surface of an object, e.g. when you cut paper with scissors you shear it.

Figure 8.1   Compression

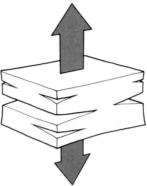
Figure 8.2   Tension

Figure 8.3   Torsion

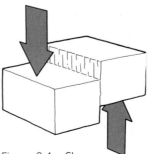
Figure 8.4   Shear

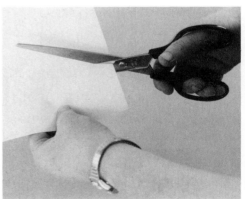

8.2 STRUCTURES IN NATURE

A spider's web is fine but strong.

There are lots of very strong structures found in nature which have to stand up to all four of the loads described on the previous page. They also have to withstand wind and other moving forces. Designers have always been able to copy or adapt design ideas from nature's sources. Here are three examples of strong, light natural structures.

1   The royal water lily

The royal water lily has huge, round floating leaves, often up to two metres in diameter. They are very thin, yet they manage to keep their shape. How do they do this? If you look underneath the leaf you will see a web of ribs which radiate from the centre to the outside. They are like the spokes of a bicycle wheel. In the centre the ribs are deep, and they flatten as they spread outwards. They also split into forking branches which are joined together by struts. The ribs and struts act as beams to support the water lily platform.

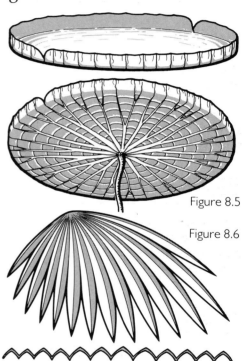
Figure 8.5

Figure 8.6

2   Palm tree leaves

Some palm tree leaves can be over ten metres long and a metre across. Yet they have to be very light so that their stalks can support them. They also have to be stable enough to stand up to storms. How do they do it? The leaves are light and strong because they are thin sheets folded into corrugations. The cross-section of the leaf opposite shows a zig-zag pattern. This pattern of folding makes the thin leaf very stiff and hard to tear apart or shred.

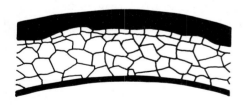
Figure 8.7

3   Honeycomb structures

Plants often have thick areas which are light because they are hollow. But they are also strong. How can this be? The drawing opposite shows a magnified cross-section through a blade of grass. The gap between the two outer surfaces is filled with a mesh or honeycomb of very thin material. It is strong and stable, yet light in weight.

Try the following exercises

1   Find man-made structures which support platforms in the way the that the royal water lily does. Sketch them and make notes to explain how they work. Try looking at: a sports stadium; a multi-storey car park; a modern factory roof.

2   Find man-made structures which are made like the palm tree leaf. Sketch them and make notes to explain how they work. Try looking at plastic trays, shed or garage roofs, cardboard boxes and models.

8.3 BEAMS

As you have seen, there are many ways to add strength to structures. Beams are one of these. A beam is a strip or section of material used horizontally to support a load. It may be very small, as in a model bridge, or may make up a large part of a building. In all cases, however, beams are designed to support structures, in the same way as the ribs and struts of the water lily. You are going to look at how beams work.

This bridge is made of beams.

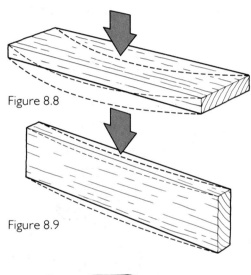

Figure 8.8

Figure 8.9

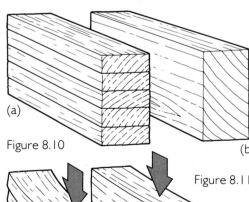

(a)

Figure 8.10

(b)

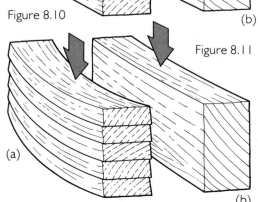

(a)

Figure 8.11

(b)

How are beams designed to support?

Take a thin strip of wood with a rectangular section. Apply a load to its wider edge, as shown in figure 8.8. Now apply the same load to its narrow edge, as shown in figure 8.9. You will find that the strip of wood, or beam, bends much less in the second case than in the first.

Now imagine taking several strips of wood. When they are added together (figure 8.10(a)) they have the same cross-section as the single strip in figure 8.10(a). If you press the same load down onto both beams, the beam made up of strips would bend more. It would not be as **stiff** as the single solid piece. Why is this?

What happens to the strips in figure 8.11(a) is that each thin strip bends and slides under the load, just as the strip in figure 8.8 bends. In figure 8.11(b) the wood is thick and solid and it resists the load.

Beams that are placed with their sections 'upright' like this are much better at resisting loads than when placed 'flat'. They are said to be **stiffer**.

What happens to beams which are under a load?

Look at figure 8.12. It shows a beam bending under a downward load. If you examined the beam carefully, it would show two quite different things happening at the same time. At the bottom the surface is being stretched . . . it is under **tension**. At the top it is being squashed . . . it is under **compression**. Moving from the bottom to the top, the beam changes from tension to compression. Somewhere in the middle very little is happening. This is called the **neutral axis**. (See figure 8.13.)

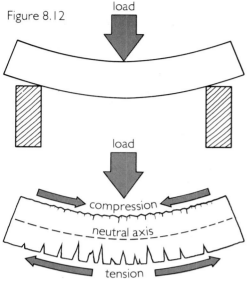

Figure 8.12

load

load

compression

neutral axis

tension

Figure 8.13

Different types of beams

How do you think this is important? If you want to save material, or reduce the weight of a structure, it is very important. At the neutral axis, the beam is doing very little. At the top and bottom it is working hard to resist the forces of compression and tension. It would therefore be sensible to design beams which have their strength concentrated at the top and bottom. This is exactly what structural engineers do. The drawings below (figures 8.15, 8.16 and 8.17) show how this idea is used in building. Where the beam is doing little work (the middle) the material has been thinned down. Where it is doing a lot of work the material has been left in place, or even reinforced. In this way beams can be made both light and strong. The particular cross-section of a beam can be designed to best withstand the particular loads that it is going to be under.

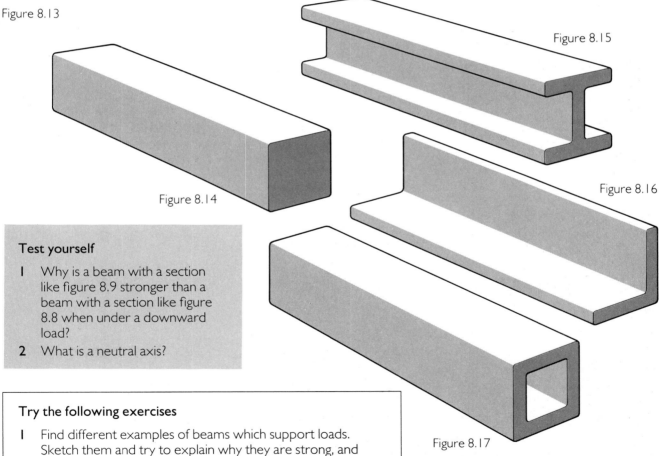

Figure 8.15

Figure 8.14

Figure 8.16

Figure 8.17

Test yourself

1 Why is a beam with a section like figure 8.9 stronger than a beam with a section like figure 8.8 when under a downward load?
2 What is a neutral axis?

Try the following exercises

1 Find different examples of beams which support loads. Sketch them and try to explain why they are strong, and how they are specifically designed to do their jobs.
2 Take some everyday objects which have to stand up to downward loads, e.g. stools, chairs, benches. Redesign them by making their beams lighter without losing strength.

8.4 FLAT SHEETS

A palm tree leaf is thin but strong.

There are many cases when you will want to use flat sheets which are strong in your designs, such as partitions, roofs and other coverings. You saw from the palm tree leaf that thin sheets of material can be strong. You are now going to look at ways that you can make strong but light structures from thin sheets of material.

How can flexible sheets be made rigid?

Take a sheet of paper. Hold one edge; the other edge flops. Wave it in the air; the sheet bends and flutters. It is very **flexible**. Because it is flexible it does not seem to be a good material with which to make a **rigid** structure. But the very sheet you hold can actually be made much more rigid. How?

Fold the paper in half. You will now find that it is more rigid. You have made a kind of beam. The more thoughtfully you fold the paper, the more rigid it will become.

Now, it is possible to use this idea to make different kinds of sheet more rigid. Metals can be folded and deformed in a variety of ways. Plastics can also be bent and formed in a variety of ways. Thin plywood and veneer can be laminated. The photographs below show some examples of thin sheets made rigid in a variety of ways.

Car doors are made of thin sheet metal.

Corrugated iron makes a rigid roof.

Why does the flexible sheet become more rigid?

When you fold or form a thin sheet you make a kind of beam. If you increase the material away from the neutral axis, as in the I-sectioned girder on page 129, you will gain even more rigidity. Because of this, you will find that the **castellated**, or rectangularly-bent sheet in figure 8.18 is more rigid than the simple triangulary-bent version. More paper is concentrated at the top and the bottom of the castellated beam, but, of course, more material is needed to make a sheet of equal thickness.

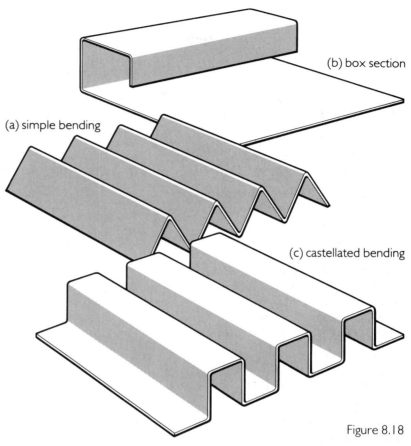

(b) box section

(a) simple bending

(c) castellated bending

Figure 8.18

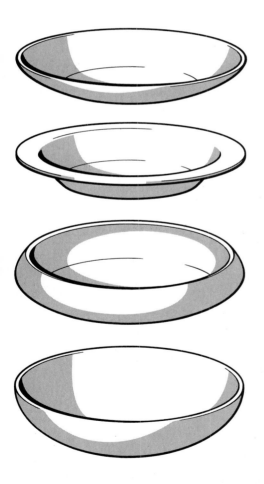

Figure 8.19 *Beaten metal forms are also rigid because they act like beams*

Test yourself

1 Why does folding make a thin flexible sheet more rigid?
2 Give one advantage of using folded sheets in your designing, and think of a simple design that would benefit from their use.

Try the following exercise

Take four A4 sheets of cartridge paper. Fold and cut them to make four sheets which will span a 150 mm gap. Test to see how much load each will take before distorting. Try to explain your results. Observe exactly how each sheet distorts and try to explain what you see.

8.5 FRAMES

Frames are structures made from thin sections of material. They are used to enclose spaces without filling them full of heavy solid material. Some examples are picture frames, gates and stools. They are very important parts of a lot of the things that you are going to have to design.

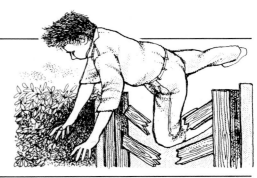

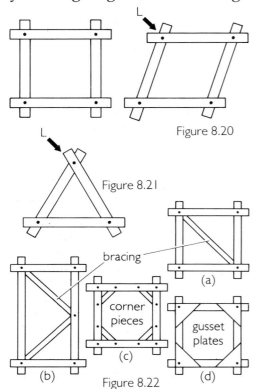

Figure 8.20

L

Figure 8.21

bracing

corner pieces

gusset plates

(a)

(b)

(c)

(d)

Figure 8.22

Are frames rigid?

Frames can be light, but when they are made from four or more pieces, like those shown opposite, they may not be very rigid. Try the following experiment. Get some thin strips of card or balsa wood, and some straight pins. Make up a frame like that shown in figure 8.20. Press the frame at L and you will see that it will distort. Square or rectangular frames are not rigid in themselves – they often rely on the strength of their joints for rigidity.

Now remove one piece and make a triangular frame, as in figure 8.21. Press at L again. What happens this time? The triangle does not distort. Even though the pin joints can still swivel, the triangle is quite rigid. Triangles are the most *stable* and *rigid* structures in nature. Making use of this idea in designing is called **triangulation**.

Square, rectangular or other frames can be made more rigid by **bracing**. Here diagonals are added to create triangulation. Where diagonals cannot be fitted, you can fit gusset plates or short corner pieces instead, as is shown in figure 8.22.

Test yourself

1   What does triangulation mean?
2   Explain three ways of bracing a square frame.

What about three-dimensional frames?

Here, the same ideas apply. A load can distort frameworks made up only of square or rectangular frames because they are not in themselves rigid. Take the cube shown in figure 8.23(a). Each of its six faces could distort. However, if each face is given a diagonal brace, as in figure 8.23(b), the whole cubic frame becomes very rigid.

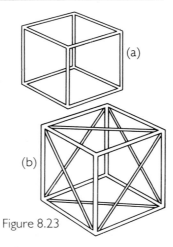

(a)

(b)

Figure 8.23

Try the following exercises

1   Make sketches of examples of triangulated structures. Look at modern structures like electricity pylons, roof trusses and space frames which support roofs in certain large buildings.

2   Take examples of frames which are not rigid. Use triangulation to increase their rigidity. Sketch your solutions.

8.6 BOXES

One of the most commonly used shapes for providing storage space is the box. You use them every day. However, boxes are very prone to distort, through heavy treatment or from resting on uneven floors. You may not be able to see this distortion, but it causes problems like sticking drawers and doors. As boxes are so useful in your everyday life you want to know how to stop them from distorting.

Open boxes

Open cabinets, like the one shown in figure 8.24, will tend to distort as in figure 8.25. Triangulation would, of course, prevent this; but a cabinet constructed like that would not hold very much!

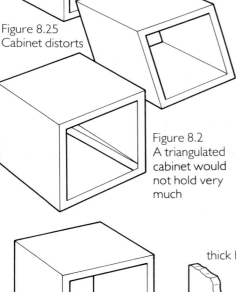

Figure 8.24

Figure 8.25
Cabinet distorts

Figure 8.2
A triangulated cabinet would not hold very much

How can boxes be stiffened?

There is another way to make box cabinets stiff. It assumes that the cabinet has four sides, a back and an open front. Any load will work to twist the cabinet's sides. However, if one side is prevented from twisting and the corner joints hold firm, none of the other sides will be able to twist. The whole cabinet will then be rigid. One way of stiffening a cabinet side relies on the beam idea explained in section 8.2. The outer surfaces of a box cabinet are, in effect, beams. You can therefore make the cabinet stronger by increasing the strength of one of them. You can make the surface thicker, i.e. increase the thickness of the beam, by using a variety of methods. Some possibilities are shown in figure 8.27.

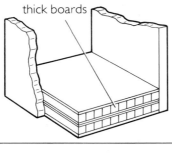

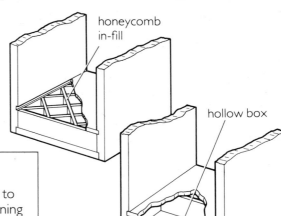

thick boards

honeycomb in-fill

hollow box

Figure 8.27

Try the following exercise

Find examples of cabinets which seem to have distorted. Try to work out why they have distorted. Devise ways of strengthening them by stiffening one of their sides. Make sketches of your solutions.

9
HOW TO DESIGN
FOR MOVEMENT

CONTENTS

9.1 INTRODUCTION

You may have designed and made many objects in the past; but how many of them moved? If you look around, you will see lots of things that move and do work. Simple examples include safety pins and doors. More complex devices include washing machines and cars. In fact you are surrounded by things that move. You are also surrounded by things that should move, but do not. They fail for a number of different reasons. One of these is poor design. Good designing for movement involves producing movement and allowing this movement to continue. This chapter deals with moving things.

When you have studied this chapter you should be able to:

1 understand the main ideas of movement;
2 recognise where these ideas might help you in your designing;
3 begin to design objects which can move.

You can use the chapter in *two* ways:

1 Study it closely as a unit – it will help you to understand how and why things move.
2 Return to it whenever you need information in designing. Use the index to find any topic you need to know about.

Cars are designed for movement, but sometimes the design fails to work!

9.2 HOW TO PRODUCE MOVEMENT

Imagine a brick resting on the ground. It is quite still. Why is this? It is held still by the force of gravity. Stillness is the normal state of affairs – movement has to be produced. How can you force things to start moving?

You need energy to make things move
To make the brick move, you have to apply a force to it. Another way of saying this is *you have to do work on it*. It is only possible to do work if you have **energy** that you can apply; without energy no work can be done.

What is energy?

In simple terms, energy *is the ability to do work*. Energy exists everywhere, and although it cannot be seen you feel its effects all the time. You may have learned about the law of conservation of energy in your science lessons. This law states that energy exists and cannot be destroyed; but nor can it be created from nothing.

Energy comes in a number of different forms. Three of these are:

1 **Mechanical energy** – e.g. which allows a car engine to run.
2 **Electrical energy** – e.g. which allows lights to be turned on.
3 **Heat energy** – e.g. which provides warmth from a fire.

A car engine uses mechanical and electrical energy.

Windmills convert wind energy into mechanical energy.

How are the different forms of energy important?

All the energy we use already exists in one form or another. Making things work often involves *converting one form of energy into another form*. Energy conversion is very important in designing. For example, windmills were once used to convert wind energy into mechanical energy to drive flour-milling machinery.

Common sense tells us that we rarely get something for nothing. We can start with one form of energy, say the water energy in a river, and try to convert it into another form, say the mechanical energy of a water wheel. It is impossible to get more energy out of the water wheel than is put in through the moving river. Unfortunately, some energy tends to 'disappear' in the change over. The energy does not simply disappear, but is converted into other forms, such as sound and heat. During all energy conversions there is an **energy loss**. When you are designing moving objects you need to consider ways of minimising this loss. A very common way of doing this is to reduce the heat loss which accompanies friction (see section 9.3).

Here are some examples of other energy conversions:

From \ To	Mechanical	Electrical	Heat	Chemical
Mechanical	Gear box	Electricity generator	Friction	Nuclear energy
Electrical	Electric motor	Transformer	Electric fire	Electrolysis
Heat	Heat engine	Thermocouple	Heat sink	Methane production
Chemical	Car engine	Battery	Fire	Chemical processing

A waterwheel converts the water's energy into useful mechanical energy.

What is power?

The more successful you are in transferring energy, the more power you will get from your designs. Power is *the rate at which energy is converted from one form into another*. That is:

$$\text{Power} = \frac{\text{Energy}}{\text{Time}}$$

All moving objects and machines have only limited power. They might be able to handle lots of energy, but they can only do this at a certain rate.

The amount of power that a machine can produce is not the only important factor to take into consideration when you are designing things which move. You must also think about the **efficiency** of the machine.

What is efficiency?

Moving objects and machines are devices that convert energy from one form into another. Some machines are very efficient because *they lose little energy*. For example, electric motors can convert over 95% of incoming electrical energy into mechanical energy for movement. Some machines are less efficient because they lose heat through friction. Friction can be reduced, but can never be got rid of altogether. Consider the pendulum in figure 9.1. If you lift the pendulum bob and then let go of it, it drops, because lifting it has given it gravitational energy. Gravity pulls things down. As the bob drops, the gravitational energy is converted into movement energy, and so it swings back up again. Then the cycle is repeated. Eventually the bob will stop because it gradually loses energy through friction. There will be friction at point A, from where the pendulum swings, and there will also be energy lost due to air resistance.

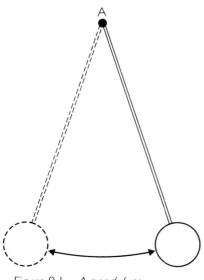

Figure 9.1   *A pendulum*

Where does all the energy come from?

Quite simply, it comes from the Sun. The diagram below shows you a way of breaking down the energy of the Sun into the various different forms that we use.

```
                          sun
                           │
        ┌──────────────────┼──────────────────┐
        │                  │                  │
 earth's atmosphere   solar radiation        life
        │                  │                  │
   ┌────┴────┐        ┌─────┴─────┐      ┌─────┴─────┐
   │         │        │           │      │           │
wind      water  temperature   solar  solid fuel   food
energy    energy                energy  energy       │
   │         │        │           │      │      ┌────┴────┐
   │         │        │           │      │      │         │
 yacht    hydro-   heat pump   solar   turbine muscle   horse
        electricity            cell            power    power
```

Are energy sources permanent?

Many of them are not. Much of our current power comes from the burning of fossil fuels such as oil and coal. These cannot be replaced; eventually they will run out. Recently, the idea of **conserving** our energy sources has become important. Ideas are developing for the wider use of solar, water, wind and nuclear energy sources. You will return to this in chapter 10.

Test yourself

1 What is energy? What is power?
2 Identify some examples of energy conversion.
3 Give an example of energy loss in your kitchen.

Try the following exercises

1 Study one of your school workshops.
2 Try to identify all the forms of energy which go into workshops.
3 Try to identify all the energy conversions that take place there.
4 Suggest ways in which any energy loss could be reduced.

How can you use electrical energy to power your designs?

Many of today's moving devices are powered by **electrical energy**. Electricity is the movement of **electrons**, each of which carries a very small amount of energy. You need to understand some aspects of this movement if you are going to use electricity to power your designs. Some terms used in talking about electricity are defined below.

CURRENT is the rate of movement of the electrons. It is measured in **amperes**, or **amps** (A).

THE ELECTRO-MOTIVE FORCE (e.m.f.) is the force which causes the electrons to actually move. It is measured in **volts** (V).

CONDUCTORS are the paths that the electric current moves along. They are usually wires. Some metals, such as copper, are good conductors. Some other materials are poor conductors. They resist the flow of electrons.

RESISTANCE is the ability of materials to resist the flow of electrons. It is measured in **ohms** (Ω). A resistor is a component used to control the flow of electrons. Some resistors are fixed at a certain level of resistance. Some can be varied by turning a knob: these are called variable resistors, rheostats or potentiometers.

INSULATORS are materials, such as rubber or plastic, which have very high resistance. They are used to stop electrons flowing, often to keep people safe from being electrocuted.

CIRCUITS are rings of conductors or wires with electrical components attached to them. When the circuit is closed electrons are able to flow: the circuit is switched on. When the circuit is open or broken the electrons stop flowing: the circuit is switched off. Look at the two circuits shown in figure 9.3. What is each doing?

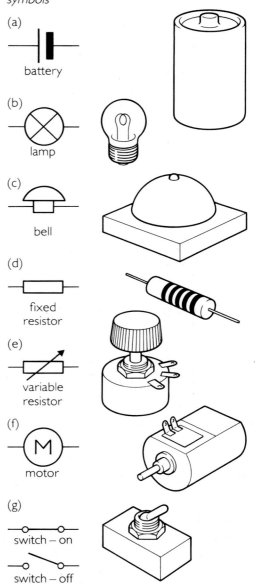

Figure 9.2 *Some electrical components and their symbols*

(a) battery

(b) lamp

(c) bell

(d) fixed resistor

(e) variable resistor

(f) motor

(g) switch – on

switch – off

The amount of current flowing in a circuit depends on the voltage (V), and the resistance (R). You can express it as:

$$\text{Current (A)} = \frac{\text{Voltage (V)}}{\text{Resistance (R)}}$$

or

$$\text{Resistance (R)} = \frac{\text{Voltage (V)}}{\text{Current (A)}}.$$

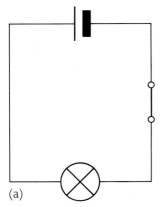

(a)

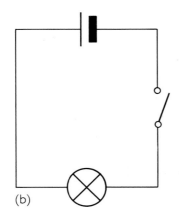

(b)

Figure 9.3

9.3 WAYS OF MOVEMENT

You read on page 136 that making things work often involves converting energy from one form into another. A *machine* takes in one form of energy and changes it into a form which is more suitable for the job it has to do. So, an egg whisk will convert your muscular energy into mechanical energy to drive the whisk blades which beat the eggs. A machine therefore converts energy into work.

A steam engine is one form of machine.

What are the basic machines?

There are many types of machine in use today. No one person could know them all. How many can you name? Learning about how machines work, though, is made easier because there are only a few different kinds of working part. The tremendous variety of machinery is simply created by arranging these few parts in many different ways to do different jobs. These kinds of working parts are called **mechanisms**. You need to understand each type of mechanism if you are going to design and make things which move. We are going to examine five mechanisms.

I Levers

Imagine lifting a rock with a crow bar resting on a smaller rock. Now imagine having to lift the rock with your bare hands. Using the crow bar is much easier. A crow bar enables you to lift things which you would not be able to lift with your bare hands. The crow bar is called a **lever**; the small rock is called a **fulcrum**.

Using a lever and fulcrum like this enables you to lift a load (the rock) which is greater than the effort you put into the lifting. The lever gives you a **mechanical advantage**. The larger the mechanical advantage, the easier it is to lift an object. Mechanical advantage can be calculated by the following formula:

$$\textbf{Mechanical advantage} = \frac{\textbf{Load}}{\textbf{Effort}}$$

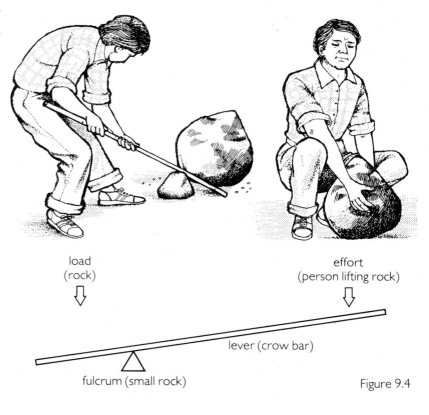

load
(rock)

effort
(person lifting rock)

lever (crow bar)

fulcrum (small rock)

Figure 9.4

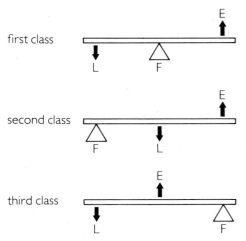

first class

second class

third class

Figure 9.5   *The three types of lever*

In this case the rock (load) might weigh 2500 newtons and the effort you need to lift it might be 500 newtons. The mechanical advantage will therefore be:

$$\frac{2500}{500} = 5$$

There are three types of lever, all of which have a fulcrum, load and effort (see figure 9.5).

Try the following exercises

1   Make a list of as many examples of levers as you can. Start with those in your school workshops.
2   Classify your first list into first, second and third class levers.

2   Pulleys

A pulley is a rotating wheel with a grooved rim. It is also a first class lever. Pulleys have a number of uses.

1   They can move objects by changing the direction in which the effort acts.
2   They can be used to give a mechanical advantage to make lifting a load easier. For example, figure 9.6(d) shows a block and tackle used to lift heavy loads. One pulley is fixed to an overhead structure; the lower pulley moves up and down with the load. In this case the mechanical advantage is 2. This means that it is twice as easy to lift the load as it would be without the pulley, but you have to pull the rope twice the distance that the rock moves off the ground.

Try the following exercises

1   Make a list of as many kinds of pulley as you can.
2   Take two or three of these. Make notes and sketches to show precisely how they work.

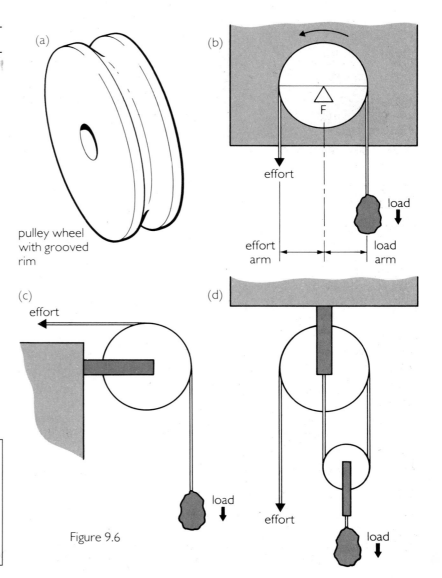

Figure 9.6

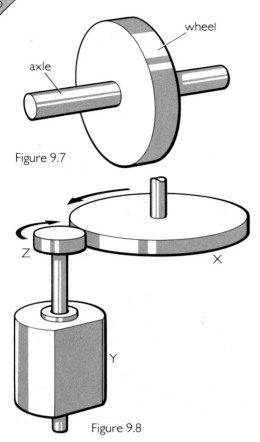

Figure 9.7

Figure 9.8

3 Wheel and axle

The wheel and axle is also a type of rotating lever. It gives a rolling action which makes it easier to move loads. The mechanical advantage depends on the ratio between the wheel radius and the axle radius. The smaller the wheel compared with the axle, the lower the mechanical advantage. The mechanical advantage can also be varied in ways other than changing this ratio.

In figure 9.8 wheel X touches wheel Z moving on a shaft. The shaft is driven round by motor Y. As Z touches X, X is driven round in the opposite direction. As the two wheels which touch have different radii, a mechanical advantage is gained. As wheel X is larger it travels at fewer revolutions per minute than Z, and gives a more powerful turning action.

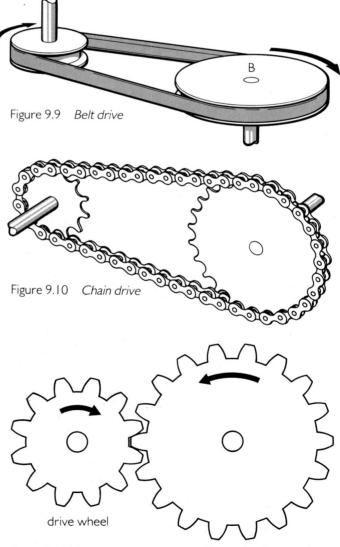

Figure 9.9   *Belt drive*

Figure 9.10   *Chain drive*

Figure 9.11

drive wheel

driven wheel

Belt and chain drive

In figure 9.9 a belt joins up the pulley on the motor shaft with pulley wheel B. In this case the larger wheel is driven by the smaller one, giving a similar mechanical advantage and speed difference. This is called a **belt drive**. Where a lot of power has to be transmitted, such as on a bicycle, a belt might slip. To prevent this you can use wheels with teeth (gear wheels) together with a chain. This does not slip – it is called a **chain drive**, and is shown in figure 9.10.

Gear drive

You can also transmit this movement by using gear wheels which touch each other directly, like in figure 9.11. Each tooth of the **drive wheel** acts as a lever forcing the other wheel to turn. Once again, mechanical advantage and speed difference can be gained by using wheels of different sizes.

The drive wheel turns the driven wheel in the reverse direction. However, if you use an **idler gear**, as shown in figure 9.12, the drive and driven wheels will turn in the same direction.

Rack and pinion

You can also use gears to convert rotary (round and round) motions into linear (straight line) motion, and vice versa. You can do this with a **rack and pinion**, as is shown in figure 9.13.

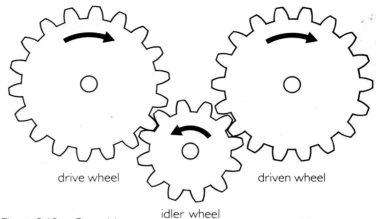

drive wheel

driven wheel

idler wheel

Figure 9.12 *Gear drives*

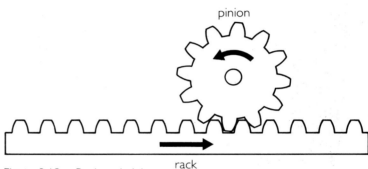

pinion

rack

Figure 9.13 *Rack and pinion*

Try the following exercises

1 Find and study as many examples as you can of these mechanisms:
   a belt drive; **b** chain drive; **c** gear drive and **d** rack and pinion. Start by looking in the school workshops.

2 Take one example of each and make notes and sketches to show exactly what they do and how they work.

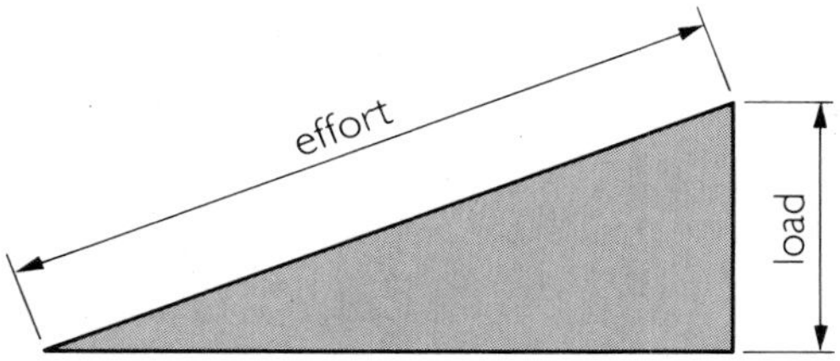

Figure 9.14

effort

load

4   Inclined plane

This is another way of getting a load to move by more than the effort you put in, that is to gain a mechanical advantage. Consider the load being raised from A to B in figure 9.15. It is easier to push it up the slope than to lift it directly. The slope is longer than the height you need to lift the load, and the effort distance is longer than the load distance, thus giving a mechanical advantage. Wedges, axes and chisel blades are all examples of the use of the inclined plane.

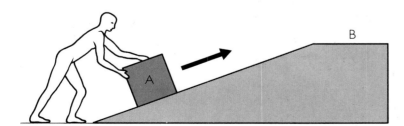

B

Figure 9.15

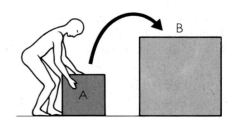

B

Figure 9.16

5 The screw

A screw is simply an inclined plane wrapped around a cylinder. When a screw is turned it moves. It converts rotary (round and round) motion into linear (straight line) motion. You can use it like this to move objects, e.g. tightening a G-clamp, or to fasten things together.

Try the following exercises

1 Find and study as many examples as you can of the inclined plane and screw mechanisms. Start by looking in the school workshops.

2 Take three differing examples and make notes and sketches to show exactly what they do and how they work.

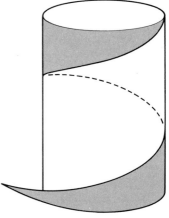

Figure 9.17

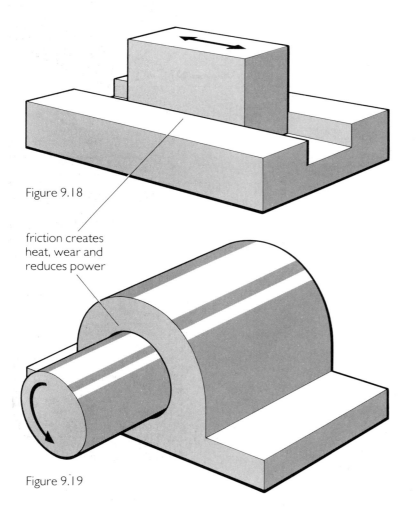

Figure 9.18

friction creates heat, wear and reduces power

Figure 9.19

How are these mechanisms affected by friction?

These mechanisms can be combined to form many different kinds of movement and machine. This movement is always accompanied by friction. Friction *resists the movement of one surface over another*. It is increased as:

1 the surfaces become rougher;
2 the pressure between the surfaces increases;
3 less friction-resistant materials are used.

Friction has a number of effects:

1 it produces heat;
2 it causes parts to wear out;
3 it reduces a machine's power.

Figure 9.20

vice jaws hold material with the aid of friction

material

How to reduce friction

Sometimes, you want a lot of friction. Bicycle or car brakes would not work without friction; nor would a vice hold an object whilst you were cutting it!

However, when you need smooth movement, you must reduce friction. You can do this by:

1 using low friction materials such as brass, bronze, nylon or white metal;
2 separating surfaces with a lubricant such as oil or grease;
3 ensuring that surfaces are as smooth as possible;
4 using moving bearings like a roller bearing.

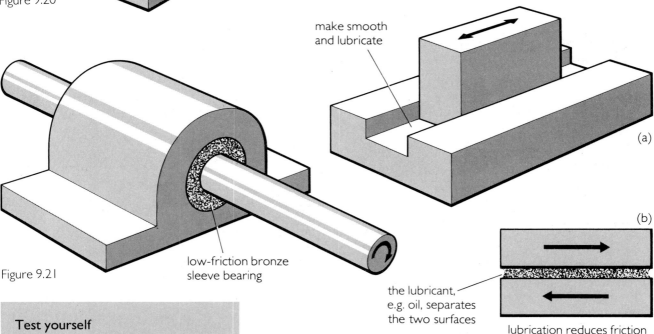

make smooth and lubricate

(a)

(b)

Figure 9.21

low-friction bronze sleeve bearing

the lubricant, e.g. oil, separates the two surfaces

lubrication reduces friction

Figure 9.22

Test yourself

1 Describe the five basic mechanisms and an example of each in use.
2 What is friction? How can it be reduced?

Try the following exercises

1 List as many examples as you can of wanted and unwanted friction.
2 Study three different ways of lubricating moving parts. Make notes and sketches to show the effects of the lubricant.
3 Study and sketch two kinds of moving bearing.

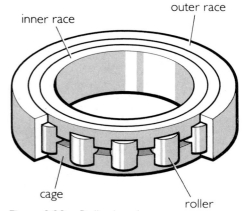

inner race

outer race

cage

roller

Figure 9.23   Roller bearing

10
THE EFFECTS OF
DESIGNING AND
MAKING

CONTENTS

10.1   INTRODUCTION

You have learned from this book that people design and make things for two reasons. Firstly, people have *needs to satisfy*. Secondly, people are *creative* and are able to design objects and systems to satisfy these needs. Much of this book has been about *how* to design successfully. But how far are people actually successful in designing? How do we judge this? Just how much benefit does this important activity bring and what are the prices that have to be paid for those benefits?

When you have studied this chapter you should be able to:

1   begin to see your own designing and making as part of a wider activity;
2   see that designing and making often has effects which we cannot foresee;
3   think more clearly about the future as something which people shape.

You can use the chapter in *two* ways:

1   Study it closely as a unit — it will help you to understand some of the consequences of design.
2   Use it as a starting point for more detailed investigations or discussions about certain topics.

The mini is one of the most popular cars ever made. The Sinclair C5 however (opposite), was a commercial failure.

This chapter is intended to make you think about your own designing; about why you do it and where it will lead to. It is also concerned with the way designing can affect the society you live in and your future. You cannot predict the future, but you can look at present trends to give you some clues as to what is likely to happen. Often, you cannot see the consequences of designing until you have used the products and systems for some time.

10.2 THE UNFORESEEN CONSEQUENCES OF DESIGNING

When you design things you are trying to satisfy a need that you have identified. You do this by designing products or systems which function in particular ways. But, because you cannot predict the future with any certainty, sometimes your products or systems fail. (How many products or systems that have failed can you list?) On other occasions they function in ways which you did not foresee. I doubt if the designer of the Bic pen foresaw its use as a pea shooter! These *unforeseen consequences* of designing are always there, and they are sometimes tremendously important or dangerous. Here are some examples.

This block of flats was destroyed by a gas explosion.

1 Coffee table

A pupil feels that she needs a coffee table at home to solve a problem. The problem involves eating and drinking in front of the television without a flat surface to rest cups and plates on. She designs the table, makes it and takes it home. Soon it is being used. It makes eating and drinking whilst watching television much more comfortable.

However, the pupil's younger brother is just beginning to climb. One day, while no one is watching, the young boy climbs onto the coffee table, reaches up to a higher shelf and knocks down a valuable ornament. The ornament is smashed. This would not have happened if the coffee table had been designed to resist climbing, or had not been designed at all. It is a consequence which it would have been difficult to foresee.

> **Try the following exercise**
>
> Name as many things as you can which you know have had unforeseen consequences. Separate 'bad' consequences from 'good' consequences.

2 Telephone

In 1861 a school teacher in Germany, invented a way of making sounds travel from one place to another. He knew that mechanical vibration could be changed into electrical signals. After a lot of tinkering about he produced a device which transmitted sound pulses via an electric current to a receiver. The receiver then reproduced the original sound. He demonstrated the telephone to a learned society, but was not taken very seriously. At that time the telephone was not seen to be of any real consequence.

Some time later the idea was developed by A.G. Bell in the USA. The design and development of the telephone has had tremendous consequences for people. It has made communications quicker, easier and cheaper between, for example:

1   friends living far away from each other;
2   different parts of towns, countries and the World;
3   parts of businesses and other organisations.

Today, anyone in the UK with enough coins can telephone virtually anywhere in the World. What was once an idea for transmitting sounds has made our planet seem a much smaller place. We have push-button dialling, cordless telephones, paging of people with bleepers in their pockets, car phones and so on.

A car telephone is useful for people in business.

3 Cars

The motor car was introduced at the beginning of this century. It was intended to make personal transport easier. How many other consequences of the car can you list?

The motor car has certainly improved mobility, for those lucky enough to own one. For those who do not have a car it has reduced mobility. How? Because the bus and train services they rely on have declined as the car has taken a lot of their business away.

61·64 TIMETABLE

NO. 81 CANCELLED
NO. 64 RESTRICTED

Try the following exercise

Find out about the latest developments in one of the technologies listed below. Prepare a short talk for the rest of your class which outlines: 1 the scope of the development; 2 the intentions of designers and 3 any possible unforeseen consequences.

Technologies: picture telephones or videophones; personal home computers; cable television; wrist-watch telephones; robots in the home.

The problems and benefits of cars

Car ownership has changed towns and cities beyond recognition. Roads take up a lot of land. With cars, people can live, in the suburbs and the country further away from work. This has led to many town centres becoming run down.

Cars have created congestion, noise, air and water pollution. They use up vast quantities of our resources, such as oil, plastics and steel. They are the third main cause of death and are also a focus for robbery.

Cars have also greatly increased personal freedom to travel, to shop in large out-of-town supermarkets and to take holidays. Car industries bolster the economies of many modern states. They give employment and contribute to government taxation.

It would have been very difficult to foresee all of these consequences at the beginning of this century. The car is a clear example of how our designing can have extremely far-reaching consequences.

Did this town centre decline because of cars?

A typical London scene!

Cars enable many people to live far away from their workplace.

In your own designing you need to try to judge the consequences of existing things and to predict the consequences of the things you propose to make.

Try the following exercise

Discuss in groups the benefits and harmful consequences of the following:

1	Soft-drink cans	6	Plastic packaging
2	Knock-down furniture	7	Television
3	Walking sticks	8	Central heating
4	Wheelchairs	9	Motorways
5	Throw-away tools	10	High-rise flats

10.3 THE COSTS OF DESIGNING

You can fulfil many of your needs through designing, but the benefits you gain often have costs to go with them. What, then, are the costs of designing and making? This section looks at this question under two headings: personal costs and social costs.

What are the personal costs of designing

1 Money

The most obvious cost is the money that you or your school has to spend on buying materials, components and tools. You can keep costs down in a number of ways, for example:

1 use second-hand or recycled materials or components wherever possible;
2 design your objects to be made from the minimum amount of material, or from low-cost materials;
3 shop around and buy from the cheapest source you can find.

2 Time

Another cost is the time that it takes you to design and make anything. Often you will not take this into account. When you are at school it may not seem to matter . . . but if you spend too much time on a project you may not have enough time left to do other necessary work. To avoid this you should keep records of the amount of time that you spend on each part of the project.

In business, people's time is often costed by the hour. Obviously, the more time spent on a job, the more expensive the end product will be.

3 Energy

If your projects need a power supply for them to work this will lead to a long-term cost. You may have to use mains electric current, which is usually paid for by householders four times a year, or you may have to keep on buying batteries to power your design with.

4 Repairs

The costs of repairing or maintaining equipment should not be overlooked. Some factory-made objects are designed to wear out after a certain time, so that people will buy new ones. This is called **planned obsolescence**. Although it keeps factory workers in jobs it means that the customer has to keep on buying things over and over again. How many things can you think of that you use that have planned obsolescence?

Try the following exercises

1   Choose a project that you have completed and try to work out its costs. Use a chart like that shown below to help in your calculations.

2   Discuss the following statement with other people in your class:
'The cost of any product that you make is the other product that you might have made.'

name of part	sizes	number of pieces	cost	price

time taken	stage 1	stage 2	stage 3	etc
energy running costs				

What are the social costs of designing?

1   Resources

A few hundred years ago large areas of this country were covered by hardwood forests. Over the centuries these have been chopped down for timber, charcoal and to provide land for farming. British hardwoods are now much more expensive than they were just a few decades ago. Hardwood trees can be planted, but they take many years to grow. Softwood trees grow much more quickly, so a lot of the hilly parts of the country have recently had softwood forests planted on them.

Softwood trees grow relatively quickly and have replaced many hardwood forests.

Forests must be replaced

Using wood for making things with can cost society dearly if the trees are not replanted as quickly as they are cut down. In the UK softwoods are replanted in this way. However, in some South American, African and Asian countries huge hardwood forests, like the Amazon jungle, are being bulldozed and not replaced. In the long run this kind of resource will disappear if it is not looked after more carefully.

Other resources such as coal, metals and oil (from which most plastics are made) cannot be renewed. Eventually their supplies *will run out*. Then you will have to design things using alternative resources, or do without these products altogether. How do you think your life would be altered if there were no more oil for fuel and plastics?

Recycling

Recycling of waste materials is part of the answer to this problem. Recycling means taking waste products and turning them into useful products again. Chipboard and newspaper are two examples of recycled materials. In the USA 60% of all car bodies are recycled, but this still uses up fuel to smelt them down.

Should we recycle more materials?

Pollution comes from power stations designed to produce electricity.

2   Environment

We shape our environment through designing. Ever since people have lived in groups, they have changed their surroundings. Early farmers chopped down forests, later farmers built walls to enclose their fields. Our homes and roads are constantly changing the countryside. Factories and motorways make huge changes to the environment.

The motor car has affected our environment far more than your products will. However, you should still consider the effects your projects will have. A go-kart, for example, may be fun, but it will create air and noise pollution wherever it is used.

Conservation groups

Organisations like Friends of the Earth and Greenpeace have grown up recently to organise a reaction to the pollution and breakdown of our environment which is caused by some of people's activities.

3   Alternative technology

Pressure groups try to show people just how dangerous designing and making can be. Other people have tried alternative ways of making things, and they criticise all sorts of the things that most people make and buy.

You have already seen that the motor car has undesirable consequences. Alternative technologists would say that different forms of transport should be used instead. They would look for forms of transport which would do less damage to people and the environment. Here are some examples.

1   Use **buses** because they carry more people than cars and on the whole cause less traffic congestion and air pollution.
2   Use **electric trains** because they can carry even more people and create less pollution.
3   Use **electric cars** because they create less air pollution.
4   Use **bicycles** because they cause no air pollution, are cheap to run and help to keep you healthy.

Bicycles are a common form of transport in China.

Try the following exercises

1   Think about each of the alternatives to cars listed above. Why do you think that they have so far failed to catch on? Discuss this in class.
2   Think up other alternative forms of transport which would be less harmful than cars.

Alternative energy

Finding alternatives to what most people design can be a very profitable exercise, providing that you know all the relevant facts. Countries which have a lot of sunshine can get energy quite cheaply from the Sun if they use good enough solar cells or collectors. It is also possible to use the energy of the wind and the sea. Each of these energy sources causes far less pollution than oil or coal, and will not run out. Also, a lot of the energy people use can be saved by careful design. The photograph opposite shows a house which has been designed to use as little energy as possible.

An energy-saving house in Milton Keynes. Note the solar panels on the roof.

Try the following exercise

Find a product in your school or home which causes pollution, damage or which needs energy to run. Think up alternative ways of designing and making this product to reduce its harmful or costly effects.

---

4 Accidents

Have you ever noticed that just before Christmas dangerous toys get mentioned a lot on television and in the newspapers? You hear some terrible tales of electrical toys which can electrocute children, cuddly toys which hide sharp metal points, plastic toys which shatter, leaving sharp edges, and so on. Did you know that over one million people are killed or injured every year by cars around the world: by cars that other people have designed!

One of the most difficult social costs of designing to accept is the cost of the accidents it sometimes leads to. Section 5.7 drew your attention to designing for safety. Re-read it now and see how your attitudes to this very important aspect of designing have changed.

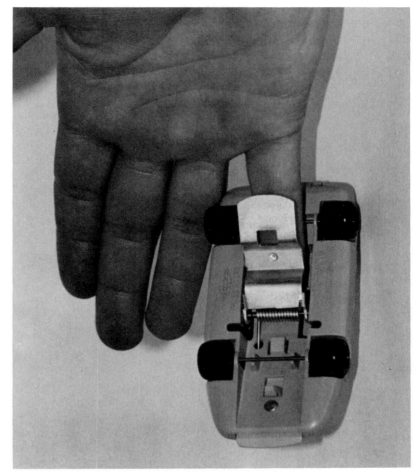

This toy is clearly dangerous for children to play with.

5 Getting the balance right

The importance to people of designing has been stressed throughout this book. It has enabled us to make great material progress during the centuries, as we have worked to satisfy our needs. However, it has had its costs. The personal costs are fairly obvious, and you usually have to pay for them with money. The social costs are less obvious but still very important. It is essential to get the balance between the benefits and the costs of designing right. In your designing you should constantly ask yourself what the costs and unintended consequences might be. Also, when you look at products designed by others, think carefully before you buy them.

Designing is an important human activity. It is also a dangerous one if carried out irresponsibly. This chapter has tried to make you think about *your responsibilities* as a designer. You should always consider them, so that your designing is directed towards improving, not destroying, the quality of life. Good luck!

Figure 10.1   *Getting the balance right*

11
UNDERSTANDING
MATERIALS

CONTENTS

11.1 INTRODUCTION

You will have found in your designing that you have to make use of many different materials. But just what are materials? The world around us is made up of substances like air, water, soil, sand and plants. Some of these are useful to us, others are not. Sometimes substances are of no use to us in one form, but are very useful in another. Rock in a hillside is of little use, but when it is quarried and shaped it is transformed into a very useful material . . . stone. This chapter helps you to think and learn about which materials are of use to you, and how the materials that you choose can be worked to help you in specific projects.

When you have studied this chapter you should be able to:

1 understand the main characteristics of materials;
2 judge the characteristics of the materials you may need to use;
3 make sensible choices between materials.

You can use the chapter in *three* ways:

1 Study one section at a time to learn the basic ideas.
2 Return to relevant sections whenever you need information in designing and making.
3 Return to relevant sections whenever you need information about making things with specific materials.

People who are not involved in the design business often take materials for granted. You, however, will be concerned with materials in all of your designing. This is a reference chapter. You should refer to it whenever you need information about materials during your CDT course.

Which material should you choose?

Whatever you are designing, be it a dress, a chair, a model bridge or a piece of jewellery, you need to understand what materials can and cannot do. You also need to recognise that there are many, many materials that you can choose from. Here are just a few:

Ceramics (clay)	Leather	Plastics
Concrete	Metal	Rubber
Fabrics	Paper	Stone
Glass	Plaster of Paris	Wood

In this chapter you will look mainly at metals, plastics and wood, but you should be aware of the huge range of other materials that are available to you and how you can work and use them.

11.2 HOW TO CHOOSE MATERIALS

Everyone knows a little about materials, about the ways they feel and look, for example. But this commonsense knowledge is not enough if you are to be a successful designer and maker. Your knowledge needs to be systematic. This section shows you how to think about materials in your designing.

How can you choose suitable materials?

The choice open to you may sometimes be very easy. If you only have access to balsa wood for making models at home, then you will use balsa wood! If you have a choice between plywood and tin plate for a child's toy, you will probably choose plywood because it is less dangerous.

Guidelines

But often choices are not so easy. In most cases there is no single correct answer. You need guidelines to help in your decision-making. Here are four basic questions to ask yourself when you have to choose materials:

1 What materials are *available*?
2 What will their *cost* be?
3 Which materials will best suit the way you plan to *use the item*?
4 Which materials will best suit the way you plan to *make the item*?

1 Availability

You can find out about available materials from home, school or local suppliers simply by asking. You may also be able to buy materials from a mail order firm, and then you can use the catalogue to check on availability. You can also use the *Yellow Pages* telephone directory to search for local suppliers. Materials can be bought in various forms, shapes and sizes: this will be dealt with later in the chapter.

2 Cost

When working out the costs of materials, take into account the costs of buying, delivery and any likely wastage. If you were running your own business, you would also cost your labour.

Questions **3** and **4** are more complicated to answer. Before you can start you need to know about materials, or at least know where to look for information about them. With this information you are able to make sensible comparisons and choices. The rest of this chapter will give you the information you need to make informed decisions about materials.

How can you compare materials?

When you are comparing two or more things you must measure them in the same way. If, for example, you are comparing the lengths of two streets, it would be difficult if you measured one in metres and the other in feet. Then you would have to convert one of these measurements into the other form, which would take time. If you had the lengths of both streets in metres, comparing them would be easy. When comparing materials, you need similar standard ways of measuring them. There is a group of measures readily available for you to use.

Characteristics
In this book they are called **characteristics**, and you can use the term with any material that you have to deal with. Remember, however, that other people may use the word **properties** or **qualities** to mean the same thing. You can look at materials under three types of characteristics: **aesthetic**, **mechanical** and **others**.

"TWELVE PACES"

"SIXTEEN PACES"

1   Aesthetic characteristics

Aesthetic characteristics are linked to the way we feel (our emotions), and our sense of what is beautiful. They therefore depend heavily on individual opinion, and they cannot be measured in the same way as other characteristics.

Colour

Light travels in different wavelengths. Colour is the way things appear different to us because they have differing abilities to absorb or reflect light of different wavelengths. The **hue** is the actual colour of a surface. The **tone** is how dark or light the colour is.

Feel

When you touch any object you get a feeling. We sometimes call the object **tactile**. Objects can feel hard, soft, rough, smooth, furry and so on.

Opacity

When we cannot see through a material it is **opaque**. When we can see through it clearly, it is **transparent**. In between these extremes, a **translucent** material will let light pass through but we cannot see through it.

Smell

Smell is not always of interest because many of the materials we use do not smell for long when the object is finished. Some woods, however, such as Spanish Cedar, are used to line boxes because of their pleasant smell.

Texture

Texture is the surface structure of the material. It can vary from rough to smooth, with many conditions in between. You can change the natural texture of a material by the way you work it.

2   Mechanical characteristics

Mechanical characteristics are the way materials perform, and many of them are directly measurable and comparable.

Density

Density gives an idea of how closely packed the atoms (and cells) in a material are; it is linked to weight through volume.

Ductility

Ductility is the ability to be stretched into a longer, thinner shape without breaking.

Durability

Durability is the ability to last, often in difficult conditions. It includes resistance to decay and corrosion.

Hardness

Hardness is the ability to stand up to wear and cutting.

Malleability

Malleability is the ability to stretch in all directions without returning to the original shape or breaking. Malleable materials can be pushed, hammered, pressed and rolled into many different shapes. Putty is a malleable material.

Stability

Stability is the ability to stay the same shape and size even under great pressure.

Strength

Strength is how well a material can stand up to a steady load without breaking.

Tensile strength is how strong the material is in tension, i.e. when it is being stretched or pulled apart.

Compressive strength is how strong the material is when it is being compressed or squashed.

Shear strength is how strong the material is when it is being pushed in opposite ways.

Bending strength is the resistance of a material to loads which cause bending to occur.

Toughness

Toughness is the ability to stand up to sudden impacts. Materials which are not tough are **brittle** and tend to shatter easily, like glass.

Mechanical characteristics are affected by the way materials are joined together in structures (see chapter 8).

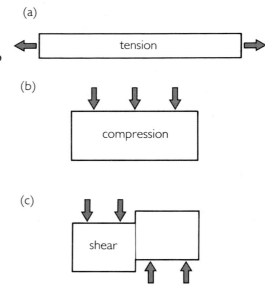

Figure 11.1 The four types of strength

3 Other characteristics

Chemical

You may have to consider the ability of a material to stand up to chemical breakdown, for instance if you were making a container for a corrosive chemical. Most materials break down in some way under chemical attack. This **corrosion** usually involves solution of the material surface in some form of solvent, together with oxidation, i.e. combination of the material with oxygen. For example, rust is oxidised iron.

Electrical

Some materials can hold up the flow of electricity. They are used to **insulate**. Other materials conduct electricity well. Both characteristics can be used in design.

Thermal (heat)

At certain temperatures metals melt, thermoplastics soften, thermosetting plastics set and woods burn. Some materials conduct heat well; others act as heat insulators. You can use these characteristics as long as the materials are in the correct temperature range.

Cars eventually corrode as iron oxidises to rust.

11.3 UNDERSTANDING METALS

Nearly a quarter of the Earth's crust is metal. Metals have been in use for a few thousand years. Those which occur in a ready-to-use form such as gold and iron were probably used first. Then people learned how to smelt metals from rock which contained them in small quantities. These rocks are called *metal ores*. During the industrial revolution of the last 200 years metals have helped to transform people's ways of life. What are the characteristics which make metals so useful and how do metals come to possess them?

Silver is used for its aesthetic qualities.

What are the characteristics of metals?

Different types of metal have very different characteristics, but within each type of metal we can be fairly sure that they will behave the same from piece to piece. Unlike wood, metals are very **consistent**: if you take a piece of high carbon steel you can be sure that it will behave the same as another piece of the same size.

1   Aesthetic characteristics

Metals come in a variety of colours. Grey is usual in ferrous metals, but non-ferrous metals can be silver, gold, reddish-brown or yellowish-brown. Metals can be highly-polished and lustrous. This lets them reflect light. They are always totally opaque. They feel hard and cool, and are often used for this 'clinical' characteristic. The texture of polished metal is very smooth and featureless. Metals do not generally have a distinctive smell in the finished state.

2   Mechanical characteristics

Metals are much denser, heavier, harder, stronger and tougher than plastics or wood, although there is a big difference between, say, aluminium and steel. In a way they are highly durable, but at the surface they are prone to breakdown. This takes the form of corrosion or oxidisation. Most metals are ductile and malleable. At room temperature they are stable, but as the temperature increases they expand and eventually melt. Although metals do not have a clear directional structure like wood does, they are not perfectly uniform. They do have a distinctive grain structure. Some metals like zinc have grains which can be seen by the naked eye. However, for hand- and machine-working metals are treated as uniform, unlike wood.

3   Other characteristics

Some metals like zinc are resistant to chemical attack. Most, however, are attacked by a variety of chemicals. This leads to corrosion. Metals are very good conductors of heat and electricity and are not, therefore, useful as insulators.

Why do metals have these characteristics?

This question can be answered by looking at the structure of metals.

Metals are smelted out of ores at high temperatures. At these temperatures they are molten (or liquid), unstable and their atoms are in a disordered state. As the metal cools, its atoms lose energy. Their movement slows down until they eventually freeze into a stable solid state. (If the atoms are excited again, by heat or electricity, they become good conductors of heat or electricity.)

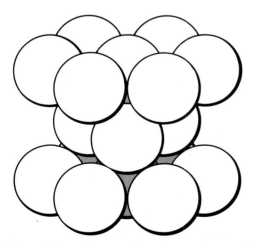

Figure 11.2   *Close packing of atoms in a metal*

The Golden Gate Bridge in San Francisco is a metal structure.

Close-packing of atoms

At freezing temperature, the atoms pack together very tightly. They form into compact three-dimensional structures and the atoms are strongly bonded together by interatomic forces. This tight packing causes metals to be strong, dense, hard, heavy and opaque. The metal does not freeze all at once: it begins to freeze separately in many areas. At the centre of each area is a nucleus where freezing starts (see figure 11.3). It can be a dust particle or a group of solidified atoms. Each area grows by linking to more and more atoms in an outward movement (figure 11.4). Eventually these areas grow and meet each other. When they meet and finally freeze, they are called **grains** or **crystals**. They meet at grain boundaries. At these boundaries, the grains are joined together by strong interatomic bonds (figure 11.5).

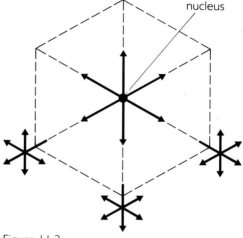

Figure 11.3

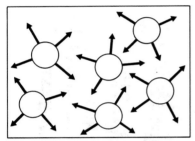

Figure 11.4   *Growing grains*

Figure 11.5   *Grains solidified*

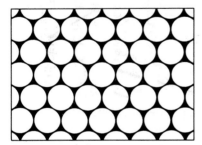

Figure 11.6   *Closely-packed atoms*

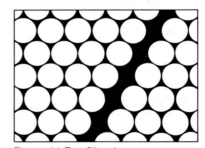

Figure 11.7   *Slip plane*

Not all of the atoms pack together so closely. Within each grain there are areas where atoms do not quite meet. This produces a **weakness** or **dislocation**. If the metal is put under enough pressure, say by hammering, it will slip at these points of weakness. These slips allow you to work metal: without them metal would be extremely difficult to manipulate (figures 11.6 and 11.7).

Alloys are mixtures of metals. They are generally much stronger than pure metals because the mixture of atoms distorts the atomic structure and reduces the chance of slip.

At another level the characteristics of metals are caused by grain size. Slip between atoms is difficult to transmit from one crystal to another. The crystal boundaries act as barriers. It follows that if crystals are smaller there will be more grain boundaries and slip movement will be reduced. So it is harder to work a metal with small grains than a metal with large grains.

Can you change grain sizes?

Yes you can, and doing so is of great importance. You can change grain size in a metal by **heat treatment**. Heating metal causes grains to grow. This process is called **annealing**.

When a metal is worked, say by bending, drawing or hammering, the grains tend to break up into smaller grains. What effect do you think this will have on the metal? It is accompanied by the tangling up of slip planes as they get pushed into each other inside the crystal. The metal becomes hard and brittle; it loses ductility and malleability. It becomes **work hardened**.

Finished objects often benefit from being work hardened. However, it can make further work on the metal very difficult. In this case the metal can be annealed (softened) for further working.

When metal is worked hot, say in forging, work hardening is prevented: the high temperature keeps making the grains re-form.

This blacksmith is work hardening molten iron.

Corrosion

When metals are in use, they are subject to **corrosion**. The surfaces are destroyed by chemical attack. In some cases the metal combines with a gas to form a surface film. This is a particular problem in polluted atmospheres. When moisture is present, even in the small quantities in the air, another kind of corrosion takes place. This **electrochemical** corrosion is the most common. An electric current flows and breaks up the atomic structure of the corroding surface. Corrosion can be reduced by design and surface protection.

You can see how the characteristics of metals are caused by atomic and grain structures. The next two pages give examples of metals, and summarise their characteristics.

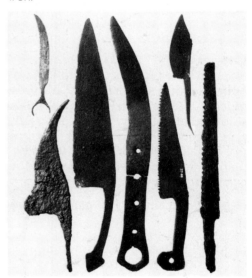

These ancient knives are *corroded*.

Aluminium is used to make many cooking utensils.

1   Non-ferrous metals

Aluminium

Aluminium is a white metal with a bluish tinge. It is very light, ductile, soft and malleable. Its surface quickly covers with an oxide film which resists further corrosion: this film can be deepened and dyed by anodising. It is resistant to most chemicals except hydrochloric acid and strong alkalis. Because it is soft, it is often alloyed. Duralumin contains 4% copper, 1% manganese and 95% aluminium: it is light, ductile, malleable, has good working properties and machines well.

Uses: aircraft; coach and boat bodies; window frames; pans; packaging (foil).

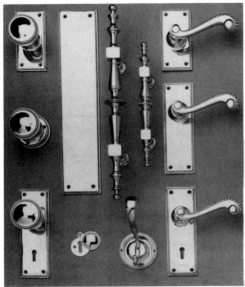

Brass is used to make attractive door 'furniture'.

Brass

Brass is a yellow alloy of copper and zinc (65% to 35% is a common mixture ratio). It is harder than copper. It casts, machines, solders and conducts heat and electricity well. Although its surface easily tarnishes it is resistant to corrosion.

Uses: valves; pipe connections; castings; ornaments.

Bronze

Bronze is an alloy of copper and tin which is used particularly for casting. There are various kinds of bronze, e.g. gun metal and phosphor bronze. They are harder and tougher than brass or copper, resistant to corrosion and generally machine and cast well.

Uses: sculpture; valves; pumps; bearings; gears; instrument parts.

Copper

Copper is heavy, ductile and fairly strong. It can be pressed or beaten into shape readily, although it work hardens quickly and needs frequent annealing. Copper can also be soldered effectively. When exposed to air, the surface turns green (through oxidisation). The green covering then prevents further corrosion. It can be polished to a brilliant lustre. Heat and electrical conducting properties are excellent.

Uses: electrical wire; pipes; roof coverings; gaskets.

Lead

Lead is the heaviest common metal. It is soft, bluish grey and once its surface has oxidised it is highly resistant to chemical corrosion. Because it is soft and ductile it is very easy to work, but it will not keep its shape under pressure. It is poisonous and contact with the skin should be avoided.

Uses: batteries; radiation shields; solder; roof coverings; printing alloys.

Silver

Silver is the whitest of all metals and is precious. Because it is very ductile and malleable it can be formed into very intricate shapes. When being formed in this way it work hardens. Parts can be joined effectively with silver solder. It is resistant to corrosion from most chemicals, but not from nitric acid. It takes a very high polish but tends to tarnish in the air. Its electrical and heat conducting characteristics are excellent. Usually it is alloyed with a little copper to give sterling silver.

Uses: jewellery; ornaments; instruments; relays.

These copper vessels are from Egypt, about 2300 BC.

Silver is used in these ornaments.

2 Ferrous metals

Cast iron

Cast iron is a very hard, strong but brittle combination of iron and 2–6% carbon. It has good compressive strength and does not need oil lubrication. As its name suggests, it is readily cast into almost any shape. It is cheap and machines well, except for white cast iron which is extremely difficult to work.

Uses: castings for machinery; engines and tools.

Wrought iron

Wrought iron consists almost entirely of iron with some silicates. Very little of it is produced today. It is fibrous, tough and ductile, and can withstand sudden impact. It is highly resistant to corrosion, can be worked both hot and cold and machines easily.

Uses: haulage gear and lifting tackle; decorative gates; railings and outdoor furniture.

Steel

Steel is an alloy of iron and carbon, and comes in various grades.

Dead mild steel, with only up to 0.1% carbon, is very soft and ductile.

Mild steel is the most popular of the carbon steels (0.1–0.3% carbon with 99.9–99.7% iron). Although it cannot be hardened throughout, it can be case hardened. It is tough, has high tensile strength and works, machines and welds easily. It rusts when exposed to air.

High carbon steel, with 0.6–1.4% carbon, is very hard and tough, but not very malleable. It can be hardened.

Uses: Dead mild steel is used for rivets and wire.
Mild steel is used for general construction, girders, nuts and bolts.
High carbon steel is used for tools such as hammers and files.

Stainless steel

Stainless steel is an alloy of iron and chromium. Other metals such as nickel are sometimes added. It is tough and highly resistant to rusting and corrosion, due to the non-porous surface of chromium oxide which forms on the outside.

Uses: kitchen sinks; pipes; car exhausts; aircraft.

Wrought iron railings are common in older towns.

Molten steel strip is used to make girders for building construction.

In what forms is metal available?

Some of the main forms in which you can buy metals are shown here.

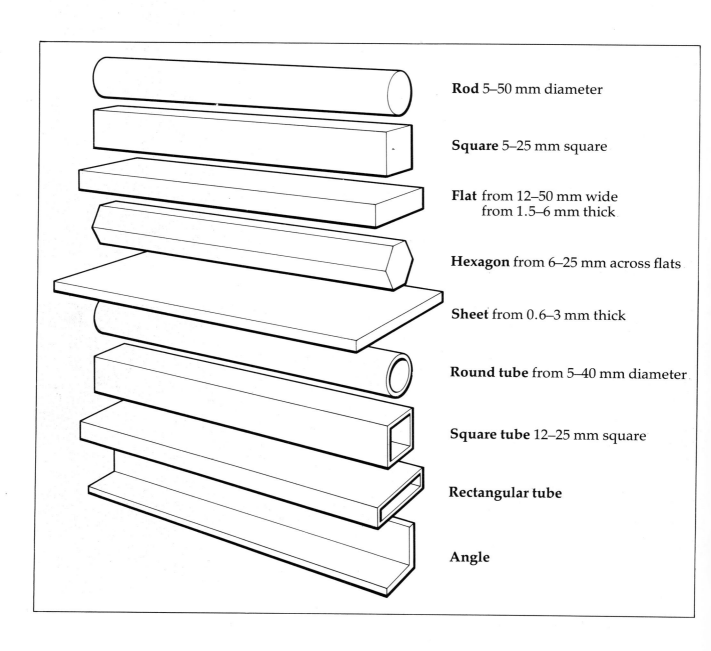

Rod 5–50 mm diameter

Square 5–25 mm square

Flat from 12–50 mm wide
from 1.5–6 mm thick

Hexagon from 6–25 mm across flats

Sheet from 0.6–3 mm thick

Round tube from 5–40 mm diameter

Square tube 12–25 mm square

Rectangular tube

Angle

11.4 UNDERSTANDING PLASTICS

Plastics are very new materials; few of them have been in use for more than 50 years. Yet, already they have become enormously important to us. In some areas they have overtaken metals and woods; mainly because they are cheap to form and mould.

There are many different kinds of plastic. What are their main characteristics and just how do plastics come to possess them?

What are the characteristics of plastics?

Plastics are synthetic materials, and so, to a large extent, can be given whatever characteristics their manufacturers want. They are all made from oil and so have some common characteristics.

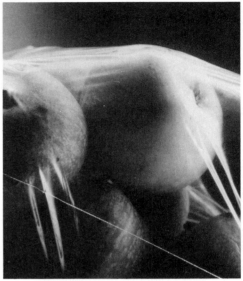

These apples are protected by a plastic wrapping.

1 Aesthetic characteristics

Plastics have uniform characteristics. This means that they are the same all over. (This, however, is not so when they are combined with other materials; see page 172.) Plastics vary from transparent to totally opaque. They are usually very smooth, but they can be moulded to a rough texture. They are easy to clean and are 'clinical', but are not as cold to the touch as metals. Because they can be pigmented during manufacture, they can be produced in a wide range of colours. It is also easy to produce exact copies of patterns on the surfaces of some plastics: for example, a lot of furniture is covered with a plastic laminate which has an imitation wood grain on its surface.

Lots of kitchen equipment is made from plastic.

Until recently plastics were used to imitate materials in all sorts of ways. Some of the results were not much liked, and plastics got a reputation for being cheap substitutes for 'real' materials. Now plastics are seen as pleasing materials in their own right.

2   Mechanical characteristics

Plastic materials are very consistent. One piece of 'nylon 6' will have very similar characteristics to another piece. However, each of the many different kinds of plastic has different characteristics. Some plastics, such as polythene, have different **grades** which each have slightly different characteristics. Low-density polythene is quite different from high-density polythene.

Common characteristics
Plastics are usually non-directional and are consistent all over. They are not as dense as metals, but are denser than wood. Their durability varies: in sunlight some weaken and turn yellow; others last well. They resist vibration and shock very well.

An important characteristic is their reaction to heat. Some plastics change when heated: they can be softened and formed or moulded. These are the **thermoplastics**. On the other hand, **thermosetting** plastics do not soften when heated. All plastics become brittle at low temperatures.

3   Other characteristics

Plastics do not conduct electricity well: they are good insulators. Most are fairly resistant to chemical attack and corrosion. Chemists are creating plastics to meet even more of the needs of designers than they can today.

Why do plastics have these characteristics?

Plastics are made chemically, from the raw materials coal and oil. To understand the way they behave you have to look at their atomic structure.

Plastics are all formed from a backbone of carbon atoms, together with atoms of other elements. These atoms are linked to each other in long chain molecules, or **polymers**. Atoms within a chain are strongly bonded to each other. However, they are not as tightly packed together as metal atoms, and plastics are therefore not as dense as metals are.

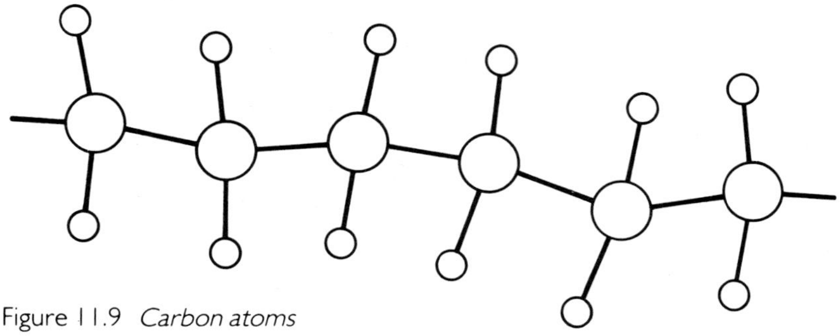

Figure 11.9   *Carbon atoms*

How are the molecules joined together?

Many characteristics of plastics are the result of the way in which the molecules are joined to each other. This varies from very rigid joining which cannot be broken down without destroying the plastic, to very loose joining which gives rubbery characteristics.

Elastomers

The rubbery plastics, known as **elastomers**, have long chain molecules which are mixed together in a loose and random way. Usually materials made like this can be stretched and will return to their original shape, e.g. rubber.

Crystalline structures

When molecules are more closely linked they form a **crystalline** structure. It produces **thermoplastics**. The long chain molecules are partly lined up and are joined by weak van der Waals forces. Usually, the crystalline areas are interspersed with amorphous areas. These thermoplastics are more rigid than elastomers. However, when heated, the weak forces break temporarily, and the plastic goes soft. The molecules move apart. When cooled they return to their original positions. In this way, thermoplastics can be formed or moulded by a variety of methods. They can be heated until they are soft, then formed or moulded and cooled to become rigid once more.

Some plastics have molecules which are connected to each other by strong bonds between atoms. This is called **cross-linking** and the resulting plastics are **thermosetting**. They are generally hard and rigid. The interatomic bonding will not loosen under heat, unlike the weak forces above. Therefore, thermosetting plastics cannot be softened again once they have been made.

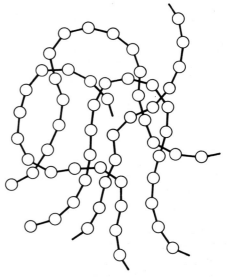

Figure 11.10 *Polymers*

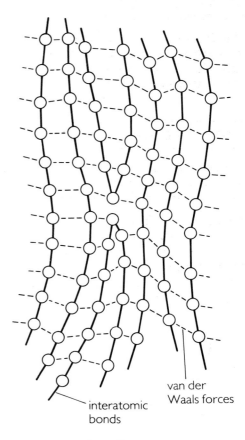

interatomic bonds

van der Waals forces

Figure 11.11 *Crystalline structure*

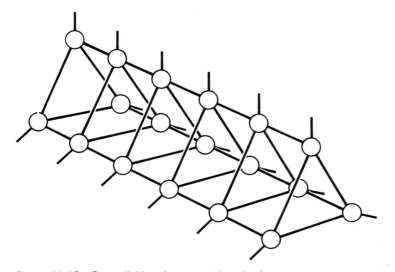

Figure 11.12 *Cross-linking thermosetting plastic*

Can plastics be modified in any other ways?

Yes, they can. Here are some examples of modified plastics.

1 Foams

Some plastics can be expanded into a lightweight foam. This is done by injecting gas into the plastic to form cells, e.g. polystyrene.

2 Fillers

Fillers can be added to plastic. They are cheap and are used to create bulk. Fillers cause a plastic to become opaque.

3 Plasticiser

If a plastic is too rigid, plasticiser can be added to weaken the van der Waals forces. Although this makes plastics more flexible, it usually weakens them as well.

4 Reinforcement

Reinforcing plastics with glass fibre and, to a lesser extent, carbon fibre is very common. Glass can be used to reinforce nylon, polyester, epoxy and other plastics. These plastics are hard and rigid but they lack tensile strength and toughness. Glass fibre has very high tensile strength. When they are combined the resulting material is tough, strong *and* rigid. Polyester resin is the plastic which is combined with glass to give 'glass reinforced plastic' (grp). The glass is obtainable in a variety of forms. Some of these are shown opposite.

You can see that the characteristics of plastics are caused by:

a atomic and molecular structures and
b the use of additives.

The next section gives some examples of plastics, and summarises their characteristics.

Glass fibre is used to reinforce some plastics.

This monument is made from glass reinforced plastic.

1   Thermosetting plastics

Epoxy

Epoxy resins are expensive, but are strong and have good electrical characteristics. They stick well to metals and non-metals alike, are hard and are resistant to heat up to 250°C. They are highly resistant to common solvents, oils and chemicals.

Uses: adhesives for ceramics, glass, metals and some plastics; encapsulation of electronic devices; surface coatings.

Epoxy resins are strong adhesives. Use them with care.

Polyester

Polyesters are hard and stiff but very brittle. They can be made stronger and more resilient by laminating with materials like glass fibre. (Glass reinforced plastic is the most common kind.) The resins have good heat, electrical and chemical resistance and high adhesion. They can also be brightly coloured.

Uses: (Alone) casting; encapsulating objects for display. (With reinforcement) boats; chairs; car bodies; models; outdoor furniture; roofing panels; decorative panels.

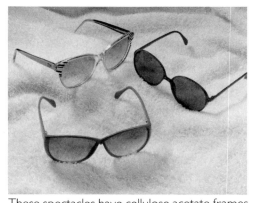
These spectacles have cellulose acetate frames.

2   Thermoplastics

Acrylic

Acrylic is fairly strong, hard and stiff. It tends to be brittle, but not as brittle as glass. It is very weatherproof, has good resistance to acids and common solvents and is a good electrical insulator. It is easily cleaned and is safe to use with food. It is easily worked by hand and machine and it takes a high polish. It is also more clear to see through than glass.

Uses: light and lamp units; skylights; illuminated signs; baths; jewellery; lids for electrical goods.

Cellulose acetate

Cellulose acetate is a transparent amber-coloured material with high clarity. It is hard, tough and stiff and can be made flexible. It is easily machined and is non-flammable. Although it absorbs moisture, it is quite resistant to oil and chemicals.

Uses: photographic films; handles; containers; lids; spectacle frames.

Nylon

Nylon is a very useful engineering material. It is tough, rigid, hard and resistant to creep and fatigue. It is resistant to oil, solvents and chemicals, but not to strong mineral acids. It is self-lubricating and machines easily and accurately. Unless mechanical methods such as screws or rivets are used, it is difficult to join. There are many different types, e.g. nylon 6.

Uses: gears; bearings; equipment parts; casings for power tools; fittings for curtains and doors; hinges.

Polypropylene

Polypropylene is fairly rigid, tough and lightweight. It floats in water and is resistant to many chemicals. It can also be sterilised. Being resistant to fatigue, it can be flexed along a line without fracturing. This makes it particularly useful for hinges. It can be joined by welding.

Uses: hinges; seats; crates; chemical pipes; rope; battery cases; syringes; containers.

Polystyrene containers.

Polystyrene

Polystyrene is light, hard and stiff, but fairly brittle. However, it can be toughened. It can be moulded into intricate shapes, comes in a variety of colours and has good dimensional stability. Because of its hard surface and good water resistance, it is safe to use with food.

Uses: cups; plates; food containers; cabinets; toys; model kits; linings for refrigerators.

Polystyrene foam

Polystyrene foam is very light and buoyant, but because of its foam structure it crushes easily. Despite being prone to burning easily, it is a good insulator against heat and sound.

Uses: tiles; model-making; packaging.

Polythene building blocks for children.

Polythene

Polythene is the most common of plastics. It comes in different densities: high-density polythene is fairly hard and stiff. It can be sterilised and has good electrical and chemical resistance. Some grades are fairly tough. It has very low water absorption and feels waxy to the touch.

Uses: release-agent film; bottles; crates; bowls; toys; buckets; pipes; machine parts.

Polythene drinks bottles.

Polyvinyl chloride – PVC

PVC is tough, hard and stiff, but when mixed with a plasticiser it becomes flexible. It has good resistance to chemicals, electricity and weather. It comes in a wide variety of colours, and can be welded or joined with adhesive.

Uses: outdoor pipes and gutterings; containers; roofing sheets; fabrics; chocolate-box trays.

In what forms are plastics available?

Plastics are available in a wider variety of forms than metal or wood. Not all types of plastic are available in every form. Look at a catalogue for more details. Here are some of the forms available.

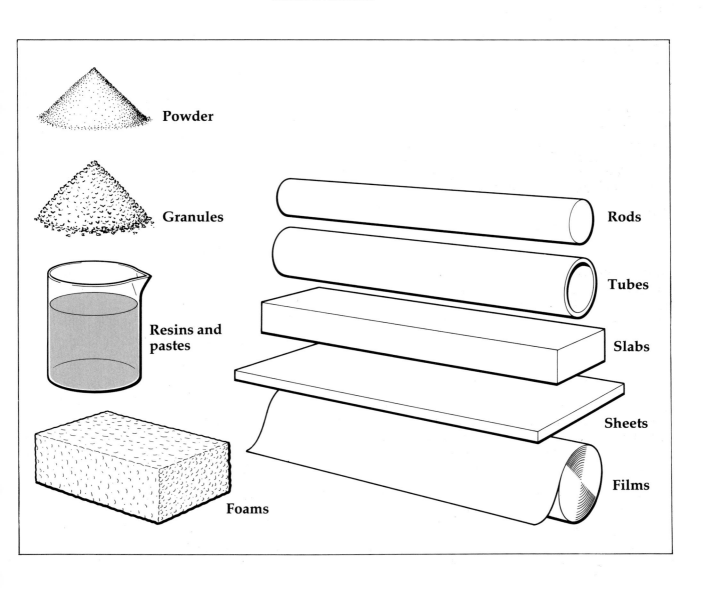

Powder

Granules

Resins and pastes

Foams

Rods

Tubes

Slabs

Sheets

Films

11.5 UNDERSTANDING WOODS

Wood is one of the most ancient of our materials. It was used alongside stone and animal skins when our ancestors lived in caves. During the industrial revolution of the last 200 years it has been overtaken in many ways by metals and, more lately, by plastics. But, as scientists learn more about the nature of materials they are realising that wood can be very efficient if used and modified intelligently.

What are the characteristics of wood?

1 Aesthetic characteristics

Wood is an opaque material whose surface can sometimes be lustrous. Depending on which side of a board you touch, it has a variety of textures which can usually be made quite smooth if desired. It is warm and inviting to the touch, and some woods have a pleasant smell. There are many colours, ranging from white, through creams, yellows and browns, to deep purple, green and very dark brown. It is common to find a few different colours on a single piece; some boards have different coloured stripes. The most complex features are the grain and the figure. These can be seen as patterns on the surface. But they run right through the wood, and change as they do so. If you cut into a board, no matter how little, you will find a slightly different pattern underneath.

All this adds up to a great deal of variety and beauty: this is one of the main attractions of wood as a material for designing.

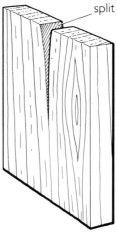

Figure 11.13

2 Mechanical characteristics

It is very important to remember that the characteristics vary in wood. They vary from tree to tree, and one part of a piece of wood may be quite different from another part.

Density varies from seasoned balsa wood with a density of only 60 kg per cubic metre, to oak with a density of 750 kg.

Wood is a directional material. Not only does the grain run parallel to the direction of the growth of the tree trunk, so do most of wood's working characteristics. For example, wood will split *along* the grain, but not *across* it. It will shrink or

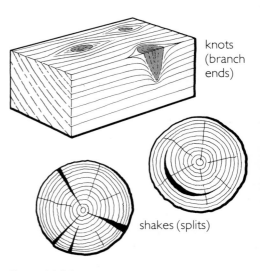

Figure 11.14

expand, often by as much as 10%, across the grain, but hardly at all along the grain. Its toughness, stiffness, bending strength and resistance to shear stress are greatest across the grain. On the other hand, the tensile strength is highest along the grain. All of these characteristics are likely to vary as defects such as shakes, splits and knots appear in the wood. It is always best to choose pieces without these defects if you can.

3   Other characteristics

Wood does not conduct heat and electricity very well, and is therefore a useful insulator. Although some woods are resistant to attack by insects and fungus, most are not.

Fungi usually attack wood in warm, wet, still areas. Wet rot is the most common form of decay, and it makes the wood soft and spongy. Dry rot thrives in similar conditions, and is very difficult to cure. It also makes the wood disintegrate.

Insects bore into the wood and cause it to break up. Their attack can usually be prevented by applying a surface finish to the wood. You should always coat wood in preservative before making it into anything, as this will help to prevent decay and rot.

Why does wood have these characteristics?

This question can be answered by looking at the structure of wood. Most of the wood used for construction comes from the tree trunk. The trunk grows outwards by adding a new layer of wood around its girth every year. This gives rise to **growth rings**. If you remove the bark and the sapwood on the outside of the trunk you are left with useful wood, called the **heartwood**.

The heartwood is then normally cut up into useful sizes. There are two main methods of doing this, which provide boards of different characteristics.

The growth rings are a major cause of **figure** in wood: the swirling pattern that you see on the surface of most pieces of wood. The drawing opposite shows them as a series of light and dark bands on the board. If the log is cylindrical, and the boards are cut at exact right angles to the growth rings, the boards would look like figure 11.17(a). Some actually do. But if the log is converted in a different way, a different figure is produced. One example is shown in figure 11.17(b).

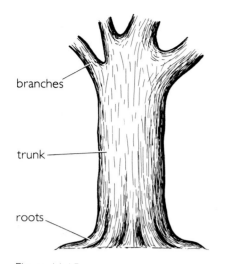

branches

trunk

roots

Figure 11.15

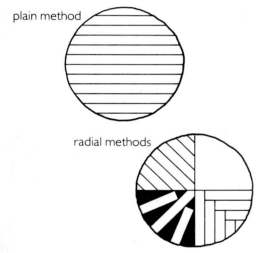

plain method

radial methods

Figure 11.16 *Ways of cutting heartwood into boards*

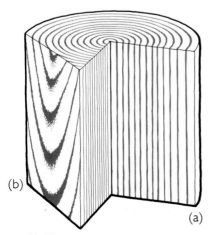

(b)

(a)

Figure 11.17

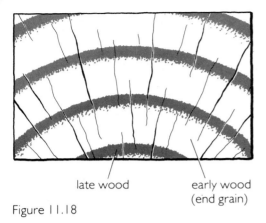

late wood   early wood
                 (end grain)

Figure 11.18

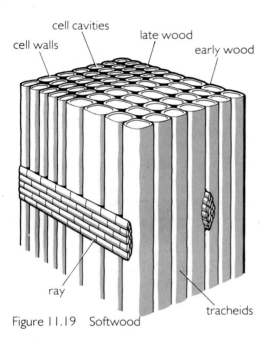

cell cavities
cell walls   late wood
                  early wood

ray

Figure 11.19   Softwood

tracheids

Why is wood like it is?

If you magnified a piece of wood about ten times, you would see that the growth rings consist of a dark band and a light band. The dark band is wood which has grown slowly in late summer. It is dense. The light band is wood which has grown quickly in spring and early summer. It is not as dense. Usually, the light band is thicker than the dark band.

If the wood is magnified further, say by 200 times, this layering becomes much clearer. Firstly, you can see that the wood is made up from bundles of hollow tubes (or cells). The cells run parallel to the length of the log and they give rise to the grain of the wood.

Hardwoods and softwoods

Depending on the type of cell, you can differentiate between softwoods and hardwoods. Softwoods have just one main type of cell running in this direction, called **tracheids**. Hardwoods have two, known as **fibres** and **pores**. The fibres and tracheids give the wood much of its mechanical strength. Fibres are smaller and have thicker walls than tracheids. This makes hardwoods harder, stronger, denser and less likely to split than softwoods. The cellular structure gives wood its warm feeling and distinctive texture. It also gives rise to wood's directionality, and the fact that the cell walls crush easily across the grain. Although wood is weaker in this direction it can be nailed and screwed because of the cellular structure.

Figure 11.20

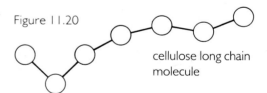

cellulose long chain
molecule

How does wood move?

Perhaps wood's most important characteristic is its tendency to expand and shrink. To understand why this happens we have to examine wood even more closely.

Cell walls are made up of 60% cellulose. The long chain cellulose molecules lie in lines parallel to the length of the cell. They give the cell walls their density, strength and rigidity. During cell growth, glucose molecules combine to create the cellulose. In this process water is given off and trapped between the cellulose molecules inside the cell wall. It is called **bound water**. There is another kind of water, known as **free water**. This lies in the cell cavities and is a remnant of sap.

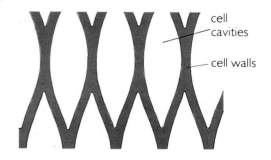

cell
cavities

cell walls

Figure 11.21

Seasoning

When boards are sawn from a log, they are usually dried out or **seasoned** in special kilns. The 'free' water evaporates without trouble. But when this has gone, and the wood has dried to about 30% moisture content, the bound water dries off. When it leaves the cell wall structure the cell wall shrinks. If wood dried to below 30% moisture content absorbs water the cell walls will swell. If the cell walls shrink or swell, so does the rest of the wood. As a result the wood can drastically change shape or even split.

A log may split around its circumference as the shrinking cell walls also force the growth rings to shrink (figure 11.22). If the log has already been cut, the boards can shrink and distort, again as the growth rings shrink (figure 11.23).

This movement cannot be prevented in natural wood except by using expensive air conditioning. Paint and varnish help but can only delay the movement. It is vital to allow for this movement when you are designing with natural wood.

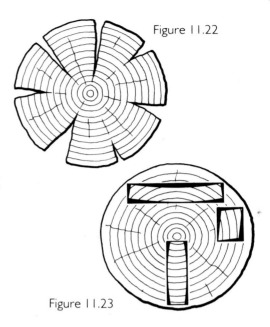

Figure 11.22

Figure 11.23

How can wood's strength and movement problems be overcome?

Logs can be sliced or peeled into very thin sheets called **veneers**. Veneers with interesting figures are often used to cover dull, cheap wood, or man-made boards.

Man-made boards

These have two main characteristics:

1 they are available in large sheets;
2 they do not shrink, expand or warp under reasonable conditions.

Some types of man-made board are described here.

Plywood

Plywood is made from layers of veneer glued on top of one another. The grain of each layer is at right angles to the one below to resist movement and improve strength. There are different grades, from 'water and boil proof' to 'interior use only'. Standard sheet sizes are 2440 by 1220 mm, or 1525 by 1525 mm. Thicknesses range from 1.5 mm to 25 mm.

Figure 11.24

Blockboard

Blockboard is made from a sandwich of thin plywood and strips of softwood. It is expensive but strong and stable. Standard sheet size is 2440 by 1220 mm. The most common thickness is 18 mm.

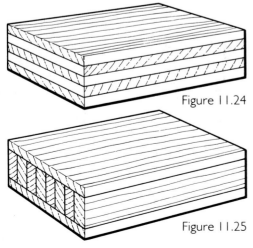
Figure 11.25

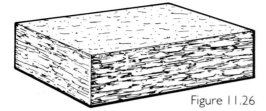

Chipboard

Chipboard consists of ground-up particles of wood glued together and pressed into sheets. When dry it is stable, but breaks down very easily when wet. Although not as strong as plywood and blockboard, it is popular because it is cheap. The standard sheet size is 2440 by 1220 mm. Chipboard is available covered with a veneer of wood or plastic in a variety of sizes.

Figure 11.26

Hardboard

Hardboard is compressed wood fibres and glue in thin sheet form. It is normally used to cover a frame cheaply. Standard size is 2440 by 1220 mm, with a thickness of 3 mm.

You can see that the characteristics of wood are due to its structure and growth. The next two pages give some examples of hardwoods and softwoods.

Figure 11.27

1 Hardwoods

Ash

Ash is a yellowish-white wood which turns brown on exposure to the air. It is dense and close grained and polishes well. It is strong, hard and stiff, and its long, straight trunk makes it very elastic and resistant to shock. One of its main drawbacks is its poor resistance to weather. Some varieties are tough and need very sharp tools.

Uses: tool handles; garden and sports equipment, e.g. hockey sticks and tennis rackets; wooden wheels.

Beech

Beech is white to pinkish-brown, often showing small marks in the grain. It is fine grained, strong and tough and stands up to shock very well. Although it is hard and difficult to work (tools must be very sharp), it smooths and polishes well. It lacks durability outdoors, and tends to warp and twist with changes in moisture.

Uses: tool handles; veneer and plywood; aircraft; furniture; benches; floors; toys.

Elm

Elm is a light reddish-brown wood with an attractive figure. It is tough, elastic and hard and fairly easy to work. Because of its often twisted grain it does not split readily, but it does tend to warp unless carefully seasoned.

Uses: furniture; flooring; chairs; stools; outdoor furniture; fences; boat structures; coffins; wheel hubs.

An elm rocking chair.

Oak (European)

European oak varies from light to dark brown, and often shows strong figuring. It has a coarse, open grain and a firm texture. Although it can be very hard, it works well with sharp tools and takes a good finish. It is very strong, tough and durable and it shrinks very little. The presence of tannic acid causes steel and other metals such as lead to corrode quickly, so it should not be used with steel screws, hinges and other fittings. Being rather expensive it is not used as much as it was in the past.

Uses: flooring; high-quality furniture; boat building; dock equipment; gate posts; veneers; railway wagons; lorry frames; window sills.

Sycamore

Sycamore is a white to yellow colour. It has a close, fine texture and works very well with sharp tools. It has a lustrous surface and takes a fine, delicate polish. It is tough, strong and resistant to splitting, but it tends to possess wavy grain and knots and is not very good for bending. It lacks natural durability. It is excellent for turnery.

Uses: veneer; flooring; furniture; bobbins; rollers.

Wooden railway sleepers (left) are now being replaced by concrete (right)

2   Softwoods

Redwood (Scot's Pine)

Scot's Pine has a light reddish-brown colour with prominent growth-ring figuring. Most boards are straight grained, but occasionally a wavy grain is found. It is fairly strong, slightly harder than many softwoods and it works well by hand and machine. Knots can be troublesome. It takes nails and screws easily.

Uses: heavy building, e.g. roof trusses; chemical vats; tanks; gates; interior furniture; plywood.

Sitka Spruce (Whitewood)

Sitka Spruce is a pale reddish-brown wood. Having a straight grain, it works easily, taking nails and screws readily, and it paints, varnishes and glues well. Knots can be a problem. It is cheap and in good supply.

Uses: inside joinery and furniture; turnery; house building; lorry frames; railway sleepers; telegraph poles; pit props. It is the most used softwood in the UK.

Whitewood is used to build house frames.

Douglas Fir

Douglas Fir varies in colour from almost white to pale yellowish-brown and has a natural lustre. It is fairly soft, resists splitting and works well with hand and machine tools. It takes nails, glues, paints and varnishes well. Knots cause some working problems.

Uses: joinery; carpentry; boxes; cheap furniture.

Western Red Cedar

Red Cedar is a reddish-brown colour and is not resinous. It is weak, light, straight grained, coarse in texture and shows a prominent growth-ring figure. Although brittle and with a tendency to split on the end grain, it works easily and does not blunt tools. Knots can be a problem. It nails, screws, stains and paints well. Because of its natural oil content, it is durable outdoors.

Uses: interior joinery; exterior cladding and weather-boarding; kitchen and bathroom panelling.

In what forms is wood available?

Planks are the largest forms. They are over 40 mm thick.

Boards are thinner than 40 mm and wider than 75 mm.

Strips are narrower than 75 mm.

Squares are square sections of various sizes.

Veneers are thin slices of wood, often used to decorate other wood.

Wood sizes vary from dealer to dealer: for more information look at a dealer's catalogue. It is very important to remember that only rough wood will be of the exact size you order.

OTHER MATERIALS

So far, we have looked mainly at metals, plastics and woods. Your examination may also concentrate on these materials. However, there are many other important materials you may use to achieve the results you need.

Ceramic

Ceramic, or pottery, is made from clay. Clay is dug from the ground, and treated until it is 'plastic'. In this plastic state, it can be formed into many shapes by coiling, joining slabs, and throwing on a potter's wheel. When the finished form has dried, it is fired in a kiln to make it hard. It can then be covered with glaze and re-fired to give a durable and decorative surface.

Concrete

Concrete is a mixture of cement, water and aggregate. When water and cement are mixed, they harden chemically. The aggregate (usually a mixture of sand and gravel) is trapped by the hardening cement to create a dense, hard substance. Concrete can be coloured by putting dyes into the original mix. It can be cast into various forms using moulds.

Enamels

Metals can be decorated by covering with enamels. Enamel is ground glass which can be melted at high temperatures to fuse onto the metal surface. The finish can be transparent or opaque. You can use many techniques to obtain different patterns.

Leather

Leather is a tough natural product, derived from animal skins. It can be used to cover furniture, make clothes and produce decorative or sculptural objects. Although it needs specialised tools, these are not expensive and you can learn the skills fairly quickly.

You may wish to use other materials such as fabric, plaster of Paris, stone and glass. To get information about these, see your teacher and use the library.

Ceramic storage jars.

An enamelled brooch.

A leatherwork bag.

11.6 MATERIALS' CHARACTERISTICS CHART

Materials' characteristics chart	Colour	Opacity	Tensile strength (1000 psi)	Density (specific gravity)	Hardness: Brinell/Rockwell	Electrical resistivity	Durability: sunlight	Durability: corrosion	Durability: decay	Melting point/ softening point (°C)
Aluminium	Blue-white	Opaque	20	2.7	38	Low		Good (surface oxidises)		660
Brass	Yellow	Opaque	40	8.5	82	Low		Good		985
Bronze	Bronze	Opaque	60	8.8	70	Low		Good		1870
Copper	Red-brown	Opaque	32	8.92	45	Very low		Good (surface oxidises)		1100
Lead	Dark grey	Opaque	3	11.34	6	Low		Good		320
Silver (sterling)	Silver-white	Opaque	40	10.4	59	Very low		Good		960
Iron (cast)	Grey	Opaque	25	7.15	170	Low		Good		1100
Iron (wrought)	Dark grey	Opaque	48	7.87	100	Low		Good		1500
Steel (mild)	Grey	Opaque	65	7.86	188	Low		Rusts		1400
Steel (stainless)	Silver-grey	Opaque	100–200	7.93	200	Low		Very good		1400
Epoxy	Varied	Transparent to opaque	8	1.2	M100	High	Turns yellow	Unaffected by most chemicals		
Polyester	Varied	Transparent to opaque	6	1.4	M90	High	Good if stabilised	Affected by strong alkalis		
Acrylic (PMMA)	Varied	Transparent to translucent	7	1.2	M100	High	Good	Affected by strong acids		110
Cellulose acetate	Amber	Transparent to translucent	5	1.3	M90	High	Stable	Resistant to many oils and acids		125
Nylon 6	Varied	Translucent to opaque	11.7	1.13	R112	High	Affected by Sun	Affected by strong acids		220

Materials' characteristics chart	Colour	Opacity	Tensile strength (1000 psi)	Density (specific gravity)	Hardness: Brinell/Rockwell	Electrical resistivity	Durability: sunlight	Durability: corrosion	Durability: decay	Melting point/ softening point (°C)
Polypropylene	Varied	Translucent	5	0.9	R90	High	Good	Affected by strong acids		100
Polystyrene (high density)	Varied	Transparent to translucent	5–8	1.1	R70	High	Weakens and yellows	Affected by strong acids		85
Polythene (low density)	Varied	Translucent	2.5	0.92	Shore D40	High	Weakens	Affected by strong acids		80
Polythene (high density)	Varied	Translucent to opaque	4	0.95	R50	High	Weakens	Affected by strong acids		120
PVC (rigid)	Varied	Transparent to opaque	8–9	1.35	R60	High	Weakens	Affected by alkalis		70
Ash	Light brown	Opaque	15	0.63		High			Perish-able	
Beech	Pinkish-brown to white	Opaque	13	0.65		High			Perish-able	
Elm	Brown	Opaque	13	0.56		High			Non-durable	
Oak	Cream-brown	Opaque	16	0.77		High			Durable	
Sycamore	White	Opaque	13	0.59		High			Perish-able	
Douglas Fir	Red-brown	Opaque	8	0.56		Very high			Fairly durable	
Redwood	Cream-pale brown	Opaque	8	0.42		Very high			Non-durable	
Sitka Spruce	Pale cream	Opaque	7	0.45		Very high			Non-durable	
Western Red Cedar	Dark red-brown	Opaque	7	0.36		Very high			Durable	

12
A CDT PROJECT

Surviving in the great outdoors

More and more people are taking part in outdoor leisure activities such as hiking, climbing, skiing and mountaineering. Mountain accidents have increased as these sports have become more popular. The photo shows you what can happen if you go out into the 'great outdoors' unprepared. Many of these accidents could be avoided. What follows is a look at how one group of pupils tackled a real CDT problem connected with outdoor survival. This project was undertaken by pupils in an inner city comprehensive school where outdoor pursuits are popular, and was sparked off by a talk given in a school assembly.

How did the project begin?

At the start of a new school year, the fourth year pupils were given a talk about the **Duke of Edinburgh Award Scheme**. The Awards are intended to encourage young people to take part in a wide range of challenging activities. The pupils were captivated by the exciting slide show. Many liked the idea of going on an expedition as part of the scheme. Some of them approached a teacher they knew to be a keen mountaineer with the idea of setting up an Award Scheme in their school.

Equipment

To safely take part in a Duke of Edinburgh Award Scheme expedition you have to wear and carry certain items of equipment. This CDT project was developed with those items of equipment in mind.

| make the problem clear | think up ideas | develop solutions | make or model the solution(s) | see if the solution solves the problem |

Making the problem clear

A school journey

"This term we are going to look at a very different type of CDT project," said the teacher. "For your Friday morning lesson please bring to school a pair of boots or strong shoes, plenty of warm clothing, and a snack to eat during mid morning."

Why? Because the pupils were going off for the morning into the Peak District. Equipped with waterproofs, clipboards, pen and paper, the fourth year CDT group headed off into the Derbyshire Peak District in the school mini bus. It was not until the journey was underway that the pupils were told the purpose of the trip. They were given the following hand out:

> **4th YEAR GROUP: A CDT PROJECT**
>
> **– SURVIVAL –**
>
> During this morning's trip into an area of the Peak District look around you. Look at the nice things; the beautiful things, the dangerous things. Below are a number of questions. Think about them carefully and then try to answer them honestly in your notebook.
>
> **a** Identify the potential dangers which exist in this area.
> **b** Could you survive here in harsh conditions? How?
> **c** What materials could you use which are found around you to make your situation more comfortable?
> **d** What could you carry with you that would guarantee your survival?
>
> In other words:
> Could you survive on an expedition if you were separated from your friends and lost in the wilds of the Peak District?

Their observations

The fourth year pupils still did not know what the connection was with their CDT lessons and the trip into the Peak District. They were finding out the potential dangers which exist in this normally beautiful and peaceful environment. With help from their teacher the pupils were able to record their feelings and what they observed during the morning trip. Two of the group took cameras with them, and they used a small portable tape recorder to record conversations.

Where are we :- Peak District
Landscape : Gritstone, peat
                moorland streams
                deep valleys
Weather :- Mist, low cloud,
                snow, rain, wind
Natural Resources :- crags
                caves, stone walls
Natural Hazards :- cliffs,
                sharp crags, severe
                weather
What we need to survive
                First Aid
                        ↓
                        survival

A selection of one pupil's photographs taken on the school journey.

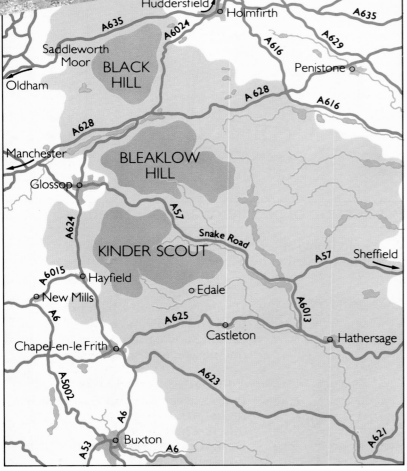

Back at school

Having seen at first hand the potential dangers of areas like the Peak District, the group returned to the classroom. The teacher now explained the connection between the trip and their CDT lessons. He outlined the project to them.

What was the project brief?

You are involved in the Duke of Edinburgh Award Scheme. You are going on an expedition into unfamiliar countryside with three school friends. The hike will take you across Bleaklow and Kinderscout in the Peak District. The weather forecast for the trip is good but with the possibility of rain showers. The time of year is April.

Imagine that on the first day of the expedition you become separated from your friends. You are lost with little chance of rescue because of a bad change in the weather. Your only chance of survival in this harsh environment is to rely on the equipment you have with you in your rucksack.

Getting started

The pupils could now see why the project had started with the trip into the Peak District. From their findings they should now have a better understanding and appreciation of the type of environment in which they needed to survive.

Each pupil now had to identify the various needs for survival. The group then split into pairs. Each pair had to select one main area for developing into a project.

Ask someone who knows

To help the pupils get more information for their various projects, the CDT teacher had invited the team leader of a local **Mountain Rescue Team** to give a talk to the group. She told them about the hazards and dangers to be found in open country, and how to avoid getting into difficulty. This would prevent the need for help from a Mountain Rescue Team. The pupils asked the speaker a number of interesting and searching questions which they had prepared.

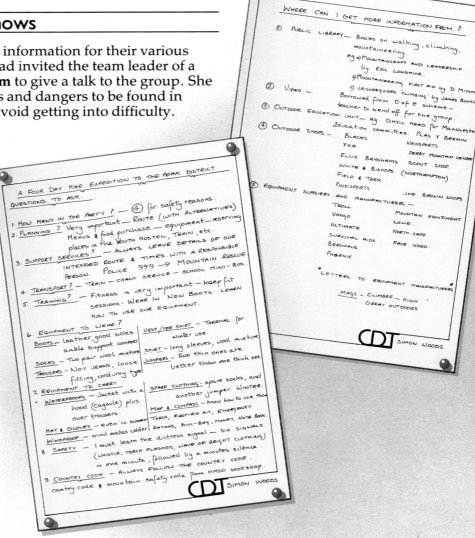

A FOUR DAY HIKE EXPEDITION TO THE PEAK DISTRICT

QUESTIONS TO ASK.

1. HOW MANY IN THE PARTY? — ④ for safety reasons.
2. PLANNING? Very important — ROUTE (WITH ALTERNATIVES) Menus & food purchase — equipment — reserving places in the YOUTH HOSTEL, TRAIN, etc.
3. SUPPORT SERVICES? — ALWAYS LEAVE DETAILS OF OUR INTENDED ROUTE & TIMES. WITH A RESPONSIBLE PERSON. POLICE 999 → MOUNTAIN RESCUE
4. TRANSPORT? — TRAIN — COACH SERVICE — SCHOOL MINI-BUS.
5. TRAINING? — Fitness is very important — keep fit sessions. WEAR IN NEW BOOTS. LEARN HOW TO USE OUR EQUIPMENT.

6. EQUIPMENT TO WEAR?
BOOTS — leather, good soles ankle support comfort
SOCKS — Two pair wool mixture
TROUSERS — NOT JEANS, loose fitting, corduroy type
VEST/TEE SHIRT — THERMAL for winter use.
SHIRT — long sleeves, wool mixture
JUMPERS — Two thin ones are better than one thick one

7. EQUIPMENT TO CARRY
— WATERPROOFS — Jacket with a hood (cagoule) plus over trousers.
HAT & GLOVES — even in summer
WINDPROOF — Wind makes colder
SPARE CLOTHING — spare socks, and another jumper. WINTER.
MAP & COMPASS — know how to use them
TORCH, FIRST-AID KIT, EMERGENCY RATIONS, BIVI-BAG, MONEY. NOTE BOOK.

8. SAFETY — I must learn the distress signal — SIX SIGNALS (WHISTLE, TORCH FLASHES, WAVE OF BRIGHT CLOTHING) in one minute, followed by a minutes silence.
9. COUNTRY CODE — ALWAYS FOLLOW THE COUNTRY CODE. country code & mountain safety code from HMSO bookshop.

CDT   SIMON WOODS

WHERE CAN I GET MORE INFORMATION FROM?
① PUBLIC LIBRARY — Books on walking, climbing, mountaineering.
eg a) MOUNTAINCRAFT AND LEADERSHIP by ERIC LONGMUIR.
b) MOUNTAINEERING FIRST AID by D. MITCHELL
c) LEISUREGUIDES 'CLIMBING' by JAMES BUNTING
② VIDEO — Borrowed from D of E scheme — teacher to send off for the group.
③ OUTDOOR EDUCATION UNIT — eg. GHYLL HEAD for Manchester Education committee. PLAS Y BRENIN
④ OUTDOOR SHOPS — BLACKS   NEVISPORTS
YHA   DERBY MOUNTAIN CENTRE
ELLIS BRIGHAMS   SCOUT SHOP.
WHITE & BISHOPS (NORTHAMPTON).
FIELD & TREK
PINDISPORTS   JOE BROWN SHOPS
⑤ EQUIPMENT SUPPLIERS AND MANUFACTURERS —
TROLL
VANGO   MOUNTAIN EQUIPMENT
ULTIMATE   LOWE.
SURVIVAL AIDS   NORTH CAPE
BERGHAUS   FACE NORD.
PHOENIX

* LETTERS TO EQUIPMENT MANUFACTURERS *
MAGS — CLIMBER — HIGH.
GREAT OUTDOORS

CDT   SIMON WOODS

A selection of problems are identified

With help from the teacher, four problem areas were identified for further development.

1 Nourishment
Design a package which provides food and drink and a means of cooking and eating it. It should last one person for three days.

2 Signalling and location
In poor weather conditions and at night, attracting the attention of others who can help is difficult. Design an electronic device which can be used to call for help.

3 First aid

Because of the remote and hazardous nature of the countryside in which hikes normally take place, it is wise to carry a number of pieces of first aid equipment. Design a package which will hold a number of basic first aid items which would be useful on an expedition.

4 Shelter

Devise a system which will provide adequate shelter and isolate you from the wind, rain and cold. It should also attract other people's attention to help them find you.

Two of the pupils, Simon and Joanne, were interested in designing some form of survival shelter.

Finding ideas

Simon and Joanne's project

Simon and Joanne decided that it would be helpful to investigate their project in more detail, so they arranged with Simon's older brother to go back to the Peak District one weekend. They looked to see if they could make a shelter from rocks and boulders. Could they use bracken and trees in a forest? What colours would stand out best if you were trying to attract attention?

Investigating materials

Back at school Simon and Joanne wrote letters to firms who manufacture materials which could be used for their project. Simon investigated tent fabrics in great detail, while Joanne read through books and magazines for ideas.

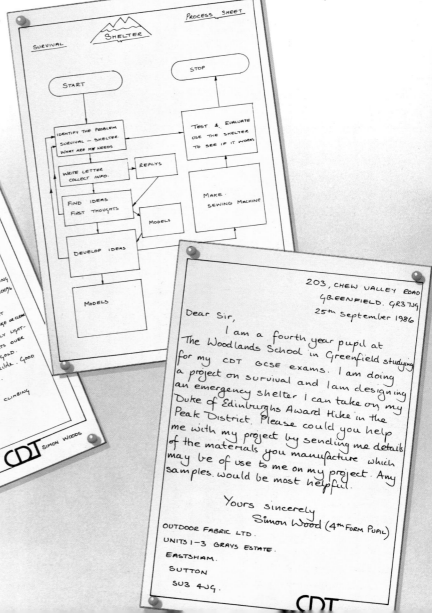

Developing solutions

Once the problem was clear, they drew some design ideas for the shelter. Using sheets of polythene and some string, they constructed a few full-size models in the workshop.

Simon and Joanne used an 'Action man' as a scaled model to work out ideas and to build models around. They also identified four important factors which would affect their design ideas.

1 Shape and size
How easy was it to get in and out and move about in? What about air circulation? How easy was it to put up?

2 Colour
Should this be bright or reflective?

3 Weight
Is the shelter light enough to carry around?

4 Safety
How quickly could you get in and out? Could you cook and eat in it?

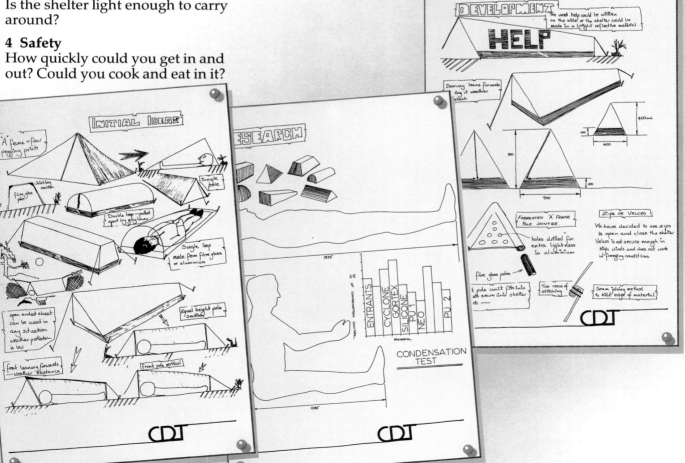

Making the final design

Simon and Joanne had looked at many ideas for their shelter design. They decided that it must be as lightweight as possible so that it could always be carried. A lot of care went into the detail of the shelter as they developed their final idea. The Outdoor Pursuits department was asked for its comments.

The materials

After discussion with the CDT teacher, Simon and Joanne decided upon their final design. Plans for making the shelter were drawn up. From this they worked out how much fabric and other materials they need to buy. They bought a lightweight orange-coloured fabric at reasonable cost.

They needed three poles to hold the shelter up. They were made from fibre glass rod given to them by a local manufacturer. The joints were made from aluminium. With help from the Home Economics department, and after practising beforehand on scrap material, the shelter was sewn together. They attached lines and 'D' rings to peg the shelter down.

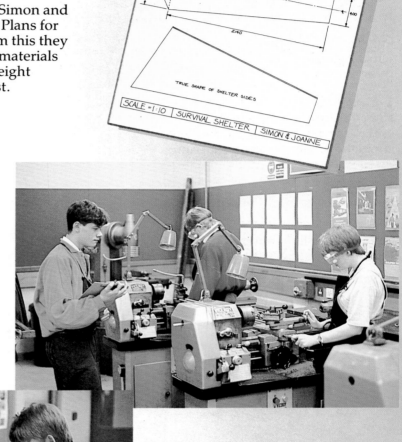

WORKING DRAWING

SCALE = 1:10 | SURVIVAL SHELTER | SIMON & JOANNE

TRUE SHAPE OF SHELTER SIDES

Testing the design

Will it work?

They put up the finished shelter on the school playing field to check that it worked. Simon and Joanne were pleased with their work. All they had to do now was to try it out!

At the start of the project the CDT teacher had told the group that all of the finished designs would be tested. This was to see if their ideas answered the problem that each pair had set themselves. They were to be tested on a weekend camping trip. Those who had designed a survival shelter had to spend the night in it. Those who had designed and made a cooking unit had to prepare a meal on it, and so on. From this experience, the pupils could write an **evaluation report**.

On the first night Simon put their shelter to the test. The following night it rained and the tent was found to leak. A tube of seam sealer soon solved that problem. During the daytime they carried out other tests. They wrote the test report during the next week at school.

EVALUATION REPORT

Size:- We both found the size of the shelter to be just right. Simon is taller than me but found it comfortable. There is room to put a few items of equipment down the sides. An internal pocket would be a good idea to store a few bits. Comfy.

Shape:- The front of the shelter leans forwards. This stops rain going in the door of the shelter when it is open. OK to get in and out of.

Erection: Easy to put up. More peg holes would be a good idea down the long sides.

Stability: Seems quite good although it was not too windy when we tested it.

Colour:- Great - you can see it for miles when it is clear.

Weight: Just under 1 kilogram. This includes the fabric, poles, 'A' piece and 6 pegs. With a lighter weight fabric we could get the weight down some more.

Waterproof: One or two of the seams leaked but we solved that with some seam sealer I think we used too larger needle.

CDT   SIMON WOODS
      JOANNE NAYLOR.

Improvements: more pegging down points on the ground sheet - perhaps 2.

:- Pockets on the inside.

:- a hook to hang a light on.

:- two guys at the back instead.

Simon Woods
Joanne Naylor

CDT   SIMON WOODS
      JOANNE NAYLOR

INDEX